WHERE HOPE GOES

Tim Cameron Long

www.timcameronlong.com

for Mia and Nell

find your own truth

A thick fog hangs amongst the branches of the open woodland, blurring its edges as a solemn silence holds in the shallow early morning light. Cobwebs cover low lying plants like doilies, their nets revealed sketched in glistening water droplets. Down in the dirt under a canopy of grasses, each tall blade adorned with jewels, a solitary ant heads home. Stopping occasionally to inspect obstacles in its path, he leaves the cover of the grass, heading up the compact earth to the entrance of the nest. As he skirts around a mottled stone, a slight bird with blue glossy feathers lands lightly in the dust. Cocking his head and looking down with a glassy eye, he plucks up the sorry ant in his beak and wheels away into the mist. Acrobatically he darts left and right through young saplings amongst the scrub, rising in an arc over dense brambles that give way to a meadow peppered with tall upright stems. Landing on one at speed, he grasps its top as it sways wildly before coming to rest like the pendulum of a clock's final breath.

esperanza = hope (v)
a passion for what is possible

Did I ever tell you about the tyre races we used to have
in Borde? Well basically they were about the most fun
thing you could do as a kid living in a place where
people made their own houses and the roofs leaked
when it rained and nobody had any money. Not that it
mattered in the end anyway. Before each race I was sure
I would win but then my Ma did call me Esperanza so
maybe hope is just who I am.

So I'm stood in a line with Sol and Diego up where
the path widened out just past Jana's place where she
was always sat out front smoking. Sol looks nervous as
usual but Diego's all cocky looking and catches my eye
before drawing a finger across his throat and even
though I am really trying hard to focus I can't help but
laugh. As usual we got the tyres from the bit of
wasteland just past the last houses where a whole load of
crap was dumped and we weren't supposed to go but
always did anyway. I'm stood there trying not to look at
Diego and instead keeping my eyes on Nef's door which

2

is up on the right. And just so you don't think I'm totally loco that's how we started the race. We'd wait until she waddled inside and the second you saw her coming out was the signal to go. Just to fill you in Nef was this lady with wild hair a ton of wrinkles and big hands that were pretty steady considering she must have been at least ninety or something. Her house was next to the abandoned one with the fallen in roof where apparently before we came a woman who lived there went crazy and killed her husband and three kids with a knife and the place was so full of blood no one wanted to live there again. Nef kept chickens in there and sold them out front and most of the kids called them huevos de sangre - blood eggs.

Hey isn't that your mum? Diego says pointing ahead so Sol looks just as Nef appears in the doorway. Sol totally falls for it but the second I see her I'm off slapping the top of my tyre to get the speed up. I hear Sol shout something behind but I'm too concentrated on keeping up with Diego to hear what it is. We rush past the turning to Diego's house the tyres jumping over the lip in the path which makes mine wobble so much I think for a moment it's going to go. I might be small for a thirteen year old girl but I've always been a fast runner but those races weren't as simple as that. You had to keep the tyre steady while avoiding people going about their business who were mostly not so impressed with you ruining their nice little walk with a nearly out of control tyre coming straight at them. Anyway we reached the bit where the houses turned two stories and hit the straight but it was busier there because of the stalls selling cooking oil and CDs and hanging down strips of sweets and all that. I was neck and neck with Diego and pretty determined not to let him get ahead.

I know Snakes Corner's coming up so I guide my tyre over to the right a bit only just missing this woman I don't know who shouts something pretty rude at me which when you think about it is not great adult behaviour. Snakes Corner wasn't really a corner more of a wide area where the alleys met with the central tap in the middle poking out of a whole load of trampled mud that even the baking sun couldn't dry out. People were always crowded around with their buckets and containers and little kids would make mud cakes like we used to.

By this point we're running at full speed and I glance over to see Diego going left around the tap as he always does even though it's busier there and some older kids Mateo and Nicolas are shouting at him from their favourite place on the wall. I get my head down and swerve past this sad looking dog with disgusting looking sores on its back leg which is pretty disturbing being an animal lover. It might have been the longer way around to the right but it was smoother and mostly less people were hanging out there. I glide past the tap and turn left seeing the final straight up ahead and above it is the washing hung to dry between the houses that I always imagined were colourful flags and that people were hanging out the upstairs windows cheering us on.

I'm feeling all angry with myself because I can see Diego already hitting the straight and I'm dreading his smug face if he wins again. So I slam down on the warm rubber a bit more than I should and for a second it wobbles but holds thank sweet Jesus. The path was smooth and flat as it headed to the square and you could get up some real speed and plenty of times someone snatched victory at the last minute which was pretty exciting. The finish line was scratched in the dirt between two concrete posts with wires sticking out the top where people piled rubbish. I have a quick look up and see I've gained a little on Diego but there's no way I'm catching him before the finish.

Suddenly when he's only a few metres from the line little two year old Luana comes storming out of their doorway! Paola had her when she was only fourteen. Yeah I know young right? Everyone was pretty freaked out especially as she wouldn't say who the dad was which got all sorts of rumours flying around as you can imagine. I mean that's like me popping one out next year which has to be about the scariest thing I can imagine especially considering all that's gone on.

Anyway I'm rambling. So Luana my personal hero strolls out giggling away chasing some imaginary god knows what when she gets right in front of Diego's speeding tyre. Fair play to him he swerves pretty quick so he doesn't run down a toddler and get grounded for the rest of his life. But he loses control and his tyre swerves off towards the houses and straight down some steps and disappears into a doorway. Luana thinks Diego falling in the dust is about the funniest thing she's ever seen and just points at him and laughs some more. I'm so distracted I nearly fall myself but I hold on and cruise over the finish line for a famous victory. In my head when I think about it I imagine one of those crazy football commentators going wild and everyone cheering and dancing with delight. I have a pretty active imagination like that.

When I go back to find Diego he's stood with his head bowed getting this massive telling off from Old Man Brando who is red in the face and waving his finger about. Turns out he'd been having a snooze in his bed and sat up to take a sip of water when the tyre comes crashing in knocking it from his hand and making a massive dent in the back wall. Diego's Pa made him do chores for Old Man Brando for a month after that which Diego was pretty pissed off about considering he mostly made him wash his underwear which is so gross I don't even want to think about it.

Come to think of it around then must be when I found the hole in the wall. Pretty much everything changed after that.

Before I tell you about that you need to know why everyone called our little tumbled down home Borde. The whole place was built right next to the very high wall around the hotel which we all knew was there to keep us out but made me more determined to know what it was like on the other side. It's fair to say I was pretty obsessed with the place back then.

I found it on the day of the big strike across the city. Ma didn't strike though. She said she was lucky to have her job in the laundry and without that we couldn't survive repairing clothes all day.

They put this big stage on the football pitch by the wall and people took turns to talk into the microphone that kept breaking so no one could hear what they were saying and it was so boring me and Diego thought we'd die. Sancho once told me people had tried to build on the pitch but each time Las Aguilas just came and cleared them out. Las Aguilas were kind of like the police for Borde. You didn't mess with them because they had guns and well were just scary as. Ma didn't like them but Sancho said he'd rather them than the police. If you were short of money or needed help you could go to them and they'd help you out at a price. I asked Sancho once where they got the name from and apparently before we arrived this guy called Matias was in charge who kept a massive eagle in this rusty old cage which sounds cruel to me. Have you seen how big those birds are? But he was pretty horrible to everyone from what I hear stealing money and beating people up that sort of thing. Apparently he would get the eagle out and have it sit on his arm. What a total show off. The story goes that Matias gave Mauricio's daughter a beating when she was only fifteen because she wouldn't go with him. She had a real mouth on her and put up a good

fight but she was in a bad way after and never got her
sight back in that left eye. Angry as hell Mauricio
stormed up to have it out with Matias but he wasn't
home so when Matias and his gang got back they found
the eagle hanging from its broken neck which was
pretty mean because it's not like the bird did much
wrong. That led to the famous eight day war where
loads of people got shot and died including Matias.
After that Mauricio's gang were in charge and everyone
called them the Eagles from then on.

Anyway where was I?...Really you gotta stop me if I
go off on one. Ma always says if there was a competition
for talking I'd be world champion but then she's the
quiet thinking type isn't she. I must be more like my Pa
I guess....so yeah the strike day. Later when they were
done talking and everyone had gone we had a massive
game of football it must have been thirty aside and I was
on Diego's team as normal. He was named after the best
footballer ever but everyone said he was going to be
better because he always nutmegged all the dads and
they'd shake their heads and smile or get embarrassed or
angry. It was windy and the dust was getting in our eyes
and then Maria's dad cleared the ball and it went flying
into the thick bushes next to the wall. Everyone was
looking for it but couldn't find it and they were all
arguing about where they thought the ball went so
being the smallest I went in.

Inside the branches are all close together and it's
really hard to see anything so I crawl through to the

back. I don't see the ball at first but then I spot it near the wall deep in the branches. Outside they're all like

Espe can you see it?

More to the right Espe.

Keep looking chica.

I keep quiet because I want to come out with the ball and see the surprise on their faces. When I finally reach it I'm standing right by the wall and I wouldn't have noticed it if it hadn't been so dark in there but a stream of light comes right through it and I can see the dust drifting like snowflakes. The hole is about the size of my fist and I put my eye up to it and look through.

It's so beautiful. Everything is so perfect and clean and so green. More green than I'd ever seen in my life. There are plants all trimmed making pretty shadows on the smoothest looking grass and a polished stone path that leads to a massive swimming pool with a big waterfall dropping into it. I didn't get how there was no dust or rubbish lying around and so much space with nothing in it but plants. I want to stay there and watch forever but Diego's shouting my name and saying he's coming in so I tell him I'm coming and take the ball out promising myself I'll come back the second I get a chance.

The second I wake up the next day it's all I can think about. I'm so desperate to go and look through again I'm about ready to explode. I didn't need an alarm clock back then because my bed was right next to Ma's and when she got up at five all the springs creaked. She gets up and puts the kettle on the stove and I lie in bed for a few more minutes daydreaming about walking across that perfect grass in bare feet. I always loved that feeling when I was awake in bed and knew I could stay there for a little longer the air smelling of frying food and smoke and the clicking of the sewing machine. It was quieter at that time and you could hear the water starting to boil which was totally different from during the day when there was never a quiet moment. The people in the house behind us were always shouting and sometimes I'd hear a lady singing happy songs that made me smile. A few times in the middle of the night I even heard people having sex which was pretty gross. Ma never said anything about it even though she must have heard it too. It makes me laugh the way adults are scared of talking about sex to kids going all red and not knowing what to say. Because Ma loves Jesus she thinks no one should have sex before being married and back then I told her I didn't want to have sex or be married which she looked pretty pleased about.

So anyway the whistle of the kettle ruins my daydream and I jump up put on my clothes and go make the tea. I turn off the gas quickly because Ma was always worried about it running out. Some people in Borde just cooked and did everything on an open fire but we couldn't because all the clothes would smell and then we'd have no money. Ma worried a lot about money back then because we didn't have much and because of the price rises. Diego told me lots of the hotel workers weren't happy because their pay hadn't changed but everything we wanted to buy was going up every week. Ma had this rusty tin with this funny man and woman dancing on it that she put a little money in each week for when the gas ran out.

As I pour water into the cups and add two spoons of sugar for Ma and one for me I'm already planning my escape to the wall. Ma leaves for work at six twenty so I figure I'll get my chores done as quickly as possible and then head up there. She didn't start til seven but she always said getting there early made a good impression which made the boss like her more even though he was a complete arsehole and was always shouting at everyone and sacked ma's friend Gina because she was late for work. It wasn't even her fault her brother got

11

badly injured in a moped crash but he went and sacked her anyway. Basically everyone at the laundry was really scared of him. But Ma said with things the way they were in the country she was one of the lucky ones because she had a job and she didn't want to mess that up.

When Ma is gone I do the sewing she left me trying not to rush. When I was little I made loads of mistakes but I got better. Back then I thought sewing was boring and pointless but turns out it is a pretty handy skill to have so what do you know I don't have all the answers. With the sewing done I walk to the tap and fill the plastic water tank and carry it back on the little trolley with wheels. The whole time I'm totally off the planet wishing I was on the other side of the wall. Once I've wiped down the stove and made the beds and taken the cushions outside to beat out the dust I grab the clothes Ma asked me to deliver to Andre and Berto and bolt out the house.

I'm striding past the bar in a I'm trying not to run but walking really isn't cutting it kind of way when I see Alicia and she's like

Hi Espe where you going?

Alicia was the same age as me and all sad looking which was no real surprise seeing as her little two year old brother Christopher had just died. Ma told me I shouldn't talk to her because her brother died of TB and she said if I caught it she couldn't afford the hospital bills. Everyone was really scared of TB which was pretty stupid looking back on it. But a few people died including Sara who was my friend and she slowly got sicker and sicker and Ma didn't let me see her near the end so I didn't get to say goodbye. Ma said they'd gone to heaven and were with Jesus but I don't get how that's supposed to make anyone feel any better.

I tell her I'm just heading to drop off some clothes and ask if she wants to come before thinking about it and then realising my mistake straight away. She looks so happy I could hardly say oh actually forget that could I.

I ask her how she's doing which is clearly the last question she wants to answer right now but for some reason the one we always ask people like it makes us feel better or something.

Ok.

She says doing that thing where people don't look at you. I ask her if she's going to Rosa's party to move on from the awkward topic of her whole world falling apart.

She says her Ma won't let her go because......and then trails off and looks at her shoes which have a big hole on each big toe. Yeah I know great work Espe let's see if we can make her feel any worse shall we? In desperation I tell her all about the other side of the wall the pool the garden the beautiful people the whole lot. I tell her when she's older one of those good looking guys from America would come to Borde and see her and fall in love at first sight and she'd go and live in a big house with a garden and all the food she could ever want. She laughs and pushes her messy hair out of her eyes and I think what a cute nose she has all covered in those dark freckles. I keep telling her about her new life so by the time we get to Andre and Berto's house we're laughing all over the place.

Berto is standing outside smoking but sees us and backs into the doorway acting all funny. Alicia stops a bit away from the house so I wait by her and being the idiot I am I just don't get what's going on. I shout to Berto that I have their clothes and he tells me to just leave them outside then disappears inside when usually he'd invite me in and Andre would give me some pistachios and some fizzy orange. Then I finally get it. I'm slow like that sometimes. Alicia is looking back at her shoes again and I'm feeling bad for making her feel shit twice in one day so I put the bag outside and touch her arm and say

Come on let's go.

She flinches but looks at me straight with those stormy eyes. I decide right then I'll show her even though I'd promised myself the night before it would be my secret. I lead her through a maze of little alleyways and cut throughs.

Is it always like that?

I ask not knowing what else to say. Most of the time she says and tells me I'm the first person to talk to her in ages. And then she goes hiding behind her hair again. I mean what do you say to that. I felt so bad for her.

Just then we pass a sad looking boy a couple of years older than us with a big bruise on his cheek. I won't repeat what his mum says when she sees us looking. I just want to take him with us on our misfits of Borde day out but we hurry off because she has a look in her eye that scares the hell out of me.

When we finally get to the bushes I look around but no one is about so I pull Alicia by the hand into the opening and we crawl through. Alicia gives me this look like I'm off my head but she follows me anyway. Eventually we get to the wall all dusty and scratched and it's not there. We're stood in the little clearing I was in yesterday but there's no hole just a towering wall and Alicia is looking at me waiting for the big reveal. I'm thinking yep I have finally stopped being able to separate fact from fiction when suddenly I realise we're a bit too far up. We squeeze along the wall a bit and come out in another little clearing and this time there it is.

I let her go first because she needs something good in her life more than I do. She's taller than me and doesn't have to stand on tiptoes so she just walks right up and stands calmly with her face to the wall. For what feels like forever she just stands there without moving whilst I'm jiggling from foot to foot like I need a pee or something. In the end I can't take it any more and I touch her shoulder and say

What do you think?

She pulls herself away and there's tears rolling down

her cheeks which I wasn't expecting and she says it's the most beautiful thing she's ever seen and then just throws her arms around me and hugs me whilst sobbing uncontrollably. I try to hug her for as long as possible to show I care but I also badly want a look myself. She pulls herself together and we awkwardly swap places and she brings over a big stone when she sees me on tiptoes which was nice of her.

The second time isn't any less amazing especially as right in front of me two little birds are pecking at the grass then flying up to this bush covered in these huge pink flowers and then flying back down again. They look so blissed out under the shade of the trees in their little peaceful garden I half expected a unicorn to come strolling out from behind a bush and give me a wink.

We take turns looking for god knows how long until my head starts to hurt and we crawl out blinking into the daylight feeling half happy and half sad. We walk aimlessly in a daze for a while not saying much until we come to the north tap. There were six taps in Borde but I didn't often come to this one. David's mum is finishing filling a barrel when we get there and she takes one look at Alicia and tuts before turning to go and I think here we go again. I'm so mad I shout at her

What's your problem?

She turns and fixes me a mean look and says

Everyone has to use this tap you know.

The red mist comes down and I feel like I want to go over and punch her stupid face but I don't... instead I say

She's a person with feelings too you thick bitch!

Which I must admit wasn't my finest hour but I wasn't exactly in total control and anyway sometimes you have to tell people when they're being out of order don't you think?

When Alicia is done staring at me like I just fell out the sky we put our mouths under the tap and drink big gulps of water and wash the sweat off our faces. A lonely looking dog finishes drinking out of a puddle and looks up at us with sad eyes hoping for a stroke. As you might have guessed I love dogs so I rub his nose and chin and he leans against my legs in that way they do. Some people got really annoyed with all the dogs in Borde because they'd steal food and had diseases and Ma told me I shouldn't touch them but when I wasn't with Ma I'd stroke them anyway. I know it sounds weird but I've always talked to dogs and I'm sure they understand what I'm saying I think they just don't know how to talk back. Did I just say that out loud? If you didn't think I've lost it already that should be the clincher.

Just then I have an idea. I grab Alicia's hand and lead her to this place at the north edge Diego showed me a few months back. It was a big solid concrete building that used to be an office or something with a flat roof where they started to build another floor but didn't finish. At some point it got abandoned and became part of Borde and Diego showed me that if you go to one corner you can use this window ledge to pull yourself up onto the roof. Alicia isn't so sure but I show her how and she makes it up to the roof with a push. There's rusty wires sticking up out the concrete and it's hot because there's no shade but the view makes up for it. It feels good being up there seeing the amazement on her face as we sit on the edge and look over the whole of Borde. I point out the square where the tree sticks out above the roofs and Alicia says it all looks like a patchwork blanket her Ma has and I see what she means with all the different coloured roofs jumbled one on top of the other. From up there we can see the wall towering over our little home and going on forever in the distance. I don't think I realised how huge it was until I was up there looking down.

I'm going to go in there one day.

I say pointing to the tops of the hotel buildings that look like some kind of futuristic spaceship next to Borde.

I've got to get used to it anyway for when I go to America.

I tell her all matter of fact because back then I thought I had it all worked out which is looking pretty funny sitting here talking to you after all that's gone on.

So I tell her about my Pa and how he left when I was young and went to America and left me and Ma and how I'm not angry because I know he loves me and wants me to go live with him because he put it all in the letter.

Even now Ma doesn't know that I've read the letters

which is ridiculous of me I know but I can't quite bring myself to admit it. One day when I was little when she'd gone to work and I was bored I found them in this secret compartment of the jewellery box she kept under her bed right at the back in her brown leather suitcase. The box was really pretty with ribbons and flowers and small white birds on it. Inside it had two pairs of earrings one with gold crosses the others blue shiny stones that sparkled in the sun. There were all sorts of photos in the box of people I don't know but I recognised the ones of Pa and Abuelita and Carlos. There was one photo of the three of us. Pa is holding me when I was two or something and I'm leaning back looking up at him and Ma is laughing looking at Pa. We all look so happy. I still have it and keep it with the letter.

In the box there were a few other things like a beer matt with Le Rojo written on it and a gold button but I didn't find the letters at first. It was only because I hear this big bang in the next room that makes me jump and I drop the box on Ma's good shoes. I run into the next room all worried Ma's back early but it's just a chicken that's jumped in through the open window and knocked over our plastic tray. When I get back to the box everything's fallen out and the underside of the lid has come away. I'm thinking oh no Ma's going to kill me but when I look closer it has a secret door and under it are the letters. It was pretty clever really you didn't see it at first but if you put your nail in the thin line at the edge you could pop it open.

I find two envelopes. The paper's gone yellow and smells a bit of cinnamon. One has *Christina* in messy handwriting on the front and is empty. I've always wanted to ask her what her letter said but never quite had the courage. The other one had my name on it. I've read it so many times I know it by heart which I figured is the best way to never lose it. It goes like this:

Dearest Espe

I don't know when you will receive this or how old you will be but I wanted to explain to you why I'm not there to see you grow up. I'm now going to live in America where I hope you will visit me one day. I'll send money back to Ma so you can take a plane and visit me. I feel so sad to leave you and also sorry I haven't been the greatest of fathers. It is really hard to explain why but I want you to know that I love you very much and it breaks my heart to leave you.

In the last few months I've made a lot of stupid mistakes and now I have no choice but to leave. Your Ma will probably say lots of bad things about me and she has every right to be angry. I have been a terrible husband and somehow I couldn't quite make it right. I will one day though once I have a good job and life in America I'll come back and find you and make everything right.

Until then be good for your mother and know that I love you no matter what.

Papa

It's not true what he says about Ma saying bad things about him. I've stopped now but when I was little I would ask her about him and she would just go quiet and get this look on her face like she wasn't here any more. Most of the time she'd say

Ask me another time sweetie.

And once when I was supposed to be asleep I heard her telling Lucille about him. Actually she said nice things about him and cried so much I wanted to get out of bed and hug her but I couldn't otherwise they'd know I was listening.

When I tell Alicia I'm leaving she goes all quiet and it's like I can feel the sadness just tumbling right out of her. She says she'll miss me which to be honest takes me by surprise considering we weren't exactly long time amigas. It did get me thinking about leaving Ma and Rosa and Diego and everyone which I must admit I hadn't really thought about until then. So I tell her I'll be back lots to visit and try to make us both feel better.

We stay up on the roof for a while until it gets too hot. Alicia gets her foot stuck trying to climb down and I start to giggle because she looks so funny. She freaks out at first but then starts to laugh too. We lose it laughing until we're both crying and every time we think we've stopped we burst into giggles again which is a welcome relief from all that heavy sad stuff. When we finally get back I say I better get home as Ma will be back soon and Alicia hooks her hair behind her ears and takes my hand and says

Thank you that's the best day I've had for a long time.

I'm thinking wow if hanging out with me is the most fun you've had in a while then things must have been pretty rough. But I don't say that obviously. I just hug her because in truth what do you say to that.

We hung out a fair bit over the next few weeks doing silly stuff like our paperclip orphanage. Ok yeah I know hear me out! You couldn't get much for free in Borde but we always found paperclips and we were bored most days so me and Alicia started an orphanage for lost paperclips. We had this thing where we'd walk the streets with our eyes fixed on the floor looking for them. It became a bit of an obsession.

This one day me and Diego go along with his Pa to this place where you get your driving paperwork. It's packed outside and people are pushing to get inside and I look down and they're everywhere. Diego comes back to find me on my hands and knees filling my pockets and fixes me a look I probably deserve. When I explain about the orphanage he tells me I have to be the craziest person he's ever met. I found my favourite ever on the floor of the market just outside this stall that sold lamps and kettles and toasters that sort of thing. It's just sitting there by a bike wheel shining up at me. A gold paperclip. I'm so scared I'll drop it I hold it tightly in my hand all the way home. Together me and Alicia were going to save all the poor abandoned paperclips in the world and give them a home. We kept them all clipped to one of my magazines.

Every now and then Diego would bring me back these magazines he'd find lying around the hotel. I loved them. I had this one with a beautiful woman in a bright orange bikini on the cover and she had this perfect white skin smooth like milk. Her tummy was flat and muscly and she was smiling with these dazzling white teeth. Back then I worried that I wouldn't be beautiful enough to go to America even though once when we were sat by the stream Sol said I was the most beautiful girl he'd ever seen but it's kind of hard to know if you're beautiful isn't it.

You know even now if I see a paperclip I can't help but pick it up and it always make me think of Alicia and Borde and that gets me wondering about a whole lot of stuff I'm never going to know the answer to.

From: Andrew Clayton

To: All staff

Subject: Annual Review

 Dear employee,

Firstly, I would like to wish you and your family a very happy Christmas and hope that you all enjoy the festivities. It certainly has been a terrific year at Ampulex that has seen us go from strength to strength, something that has only been made possible through your dedication and hard work. At the start of the year, we knew this would be a special twelve months for the Ampulex family with the opening of offices in India, Argentina and the United Arab Emirates. As the year draws to a close, we now have 54,000 staff worldwide. We've come a long way from our 12 employees who started the company 18 years ago! We may have grown but our values haven't changed; we have always sought to provide a range of world class services to the public and private sector. As you will know public sector contractors are now our core business, a market that grew by 17% globally last year. There have been so many highlights from the last year that it is impossible for me to summarise them all, but here are some of the headlines:

In March we began operating our first two prisons in Canada. This will grow with a further two next year in Australia. As well as operating five adult prisons in the UK, we now run 14 worldwide. It was also a fantastic year for our Healthcare team, winning a ten-year contract to supply a range of medical services in Argentina. This in addition to taking on a record number of NHS contracts. This is just the beginning of our considerable plans for development in Latin America over the next few years.

We were proud to begin work this year on providing a communications network for Skyweb, a joint satellite missile program between the USA and UK. Alongside this, we are now supporting the MOD at its Defence Academy with the training of key personnel. Education now represents 19% of our work, providing training to schools and education specialists in the UK. We have secured further contracts to build schools in Australia and hope to do the same in Latin America. We continue to provide children's services to local authorities in the UK and this will expand again next year. Our Transport team has secured a large contract to provide transportation solutions and planning in UAE, the largest that Ampulex has ever undertaken. These are just some of the many success stories this year, sorry if I didn't mention yours!

We have also welcomed Clare Rutchinson as our new Business Development Director, we are delighted to have her as a new member of the board. She comes with a wealth of experience that will help push us forward in the years to come.

Next year promises to be another fantastic year for the company. For now enjoy the break, have a wonderful festive period with your family and thank you again for all your hard work this year.

Yours sincerely

Andrew Clayton

Chief Executive

A water droplet cut a haphazard path down the window of the taxi, magnifying London's lights as it went. It had been raining heavily for hours and the Christmas shoppers scuttled from one brightly lit shop to another in saturated footwear. Alex was feeling surprisingly awake but behind a caffeine glaze lay a deep rooted exhaustion that came from a day's travel. He tried to find a comfortable position but his body longed to be on its feet breathing some fresh air.

He pulled the coin from his jacket pocket and ran his finger along its fine edge, calming himself. Squinting he held it close to his face, tipping it towards the window. The mellow light glistened off George's impressive moustache. Often he'd wondered what the king was thinking as he gazed to the left, lips pursed as if he might be about to whistle. It was an image so familiar, he could have sketched it from memory. Gently, he traced his finger over the lettering that curved around its edge GEORGIVIS V DEI VA:BRITT:OMNII:REX FID:DEF:IND:IMP.

'George V by the Grace of God, King of all the British territories, Defender of the Faith, Emperor of India.' he whispered to himself, clutching the coin tightly in his right fist as the driver eyed him suspiciously in the rearview mirror.

On the whole the trip to Laos had been a success, the contract was signed, Alex having smoothed over any lingering concerns amongst the six members of the all male panel (all smiles and overly long handshakes).

Clayton would be satisfied with the outcome. Alex considered calling him to let him know but decided it could wait.

At last they pulled up in his quiet street, an orange glow reflecting off the wet tarmac. The driver brought his luggage into the lobby and bid him goodnight with a stiff nod and averted eyes. A deep ache had set about Alex's body, creeping into his bones and leaving his skin painful to touch. Stepping into the lift his reflection in the mirror shocked him. Despite the skin treatments and fortnightly hair appointments, the young man he believed himself to be was slipping from his grasp like sand. The cold light of the lift brought out a yellowish, translucent quality to his skin that appeared to be stretched over a more sinister blue. Around his pale eyes this blue was most pronounced, as if it were collecting in the well of his eye sockets. He needed to rest more he told himself, to sleep more than a couple of hours here and there.

In the empty hallway that led to his flat, the light just past No.24 was still flickering sporadically. Twice in the last month, he'd called the management company to complain. The second time, Steven, their customer manager, had assured him they had changed the bulb and that they were terribly sorry for the inconvenience and that they would have someone look into it right away.

Pushing the door to his flat closed, Alex sighed with relief as he stood motionless in the silent hall. He'd learned to manage the chaos of his trips abroad, but his flat, all clean lines and smooth surfaces, soothed him. The living area was large and open plan, sparsely furnished, with a balcony overlooking the street. In the summer his parents had been in town and they'd eaten lunch out there; his mother, sunglasses propped on her head making a face at the supermarket Brie. Dad, legs crossed, his considerable frame hidden behind The Telegraph that billowed like a sail.

Alex slumped into the chair in the hall, removed his shoes and then, as he always did, pulled off his right sock, flossing it between each toe, before repeating with the left. He took the socks to the utility room and dropped them in the laundry before padding methodically back to the hall to put away the shoes. Carefully, he pulled open the maple cupboard that stretched across the hall wall, placed his shoes in a gap to the right and stood for a moment. He considered two pairs on the second shelf down that had been troubling him. Despite holding them to the light he just couldn't decide which was darker; just when he seemed to have settled on one he would look again and swap them around. It bothered him. Otherwise it was perfect; a sliding scale of colour, from light to dark starting with his white golf shoes (that he'd only used once) all the way to a black pair of Tricker's that he decided were a shade blacker than the pair next to them. Pressing fingers to his temple, he closed the doors, promising himself to revisit it in the morning, before taking off his jacket and hanging it.

Drifting into the kitchen, he removed a bottle of sparkling water from the fridge. Looking like it had been installed last week, it hummed rhythmically making light work of chilling the three bottles of Peroni, a six-pack of water and the eye mask for his migraines.

He wondered if he would be permitted to sleep. It had become a common problem, the jet lag, the time difference, he always seemed just a shade too tired to sleep. Pulling out his phone he checked for new messages he knew full well weren't there. He tried watching tv for a while but everyone irritated him. Eventually he turned in, unable to put it off any longer. He lay there for hours before sleep finally slipped in unnoticed once he'd abandoned all hope.

Alex's alarm woke him at five thirty as it did every morning. He'd bought the alarm clock on a trip to Kyoto a couple of years back. It boasted an unnecessary number of wake options and connected to his phone so he could download more. He'd settled on 'Waterfall' - the sound of running water (after trying 'Tropical Chorus' and 'Buddhist Temple'). He silenced the alarm the minute he woke and, as always, swung out of the right side of the bed. On the bedside table was a small tabletop brushed metal fridge that he kept a couple of bottles of water in. He couldn't bear water that had been sat on the side all night.

Standing naked by the bed, he drank a full bottle,

before placing it in the bin he kept inside the cupboard. As he did every morning he stopped by the full-length mirror and studied himself. He checked if his teeth were white enough, whether he needed to make his waxing appointment any earlier, were there more wrinkles around his eyes? Last week he'd found a grey hair, that had troubled him. Alex thought maybe the daily gym work was starting to have the desired effect as he pirouetted, chest puffed out like a pigeon. Working through a daily checklist of self-maintenance, he endeavoured to beat back the unrelenting landslide of ageing.

He stepped into the shower, the water at forty-one degrees Celsius, so it burned ever so slightly. Habitually he washed his hair first, then body, then face. Once done he took a neatly folded towel (a clean one every day) and dried his feet thoroughly then systematically worked his way up his body making sure every part of him was completely dry. Only when he was satisfied there wasn't a suggestion of damp did he return to the bedroom.

Glancing at the clock with irritation he saw it was five forty-nine. His allotted time to return to his bedroom to begin dressing was five forty-five. He chastised himself for daydreaming in the shower. Quickly he dressed and headed to the kitchen.

It wasn't yet light outside and a fine drizzle worked its way into every surface of the deserted street. Sipping his coffee he looked through the day's appointments.

Alex wasn't much of a breakfast person; sometimes he might eat a pastry mid-morning but more often than not he ate nothing until lunch.

At six fifteen precisely, he stood with his shoes and coat on by the door. It was quiet except for the low hum of the building.

It was still dark when he arrived twenty minutes later at the office. Alex stepped across the spacious lobby and took the lift up to the third floor. His office was furnished with a large white desk, a mid-century style sofa and a coat stand. Hanging his coat he sat at his desk and made a start.

Just before half-past eight his assistant Olivia, only twenty, her hair always in complicated plaits, knocked on the door.

'Morning Alex, just a reminder that your first meeting is with Catherine Walker at nine-thirty. Coffee?'

'No, and yes I'm well aware.' Alex replied coldly without looking up from his screen.

'Well good morning to you too Olivia and just how are you today?' Olivia replied to herself with a smirk before pulling the door closed behind her. Skinny and pale-skinned, you'd be forgiven for thinking Olivia was at Ampulex on work experience. She'd been working for him for just over a year now and was the best assistant he'd ever had. She didn't take his moods personally, getting to the point quickly, gently teasing him like an older brother. As an only child, Alex was pretty inexperienced at this kind of banter but he was pleased he hadn't upset her yet like the last two.

When he returned to his desk after his meeting, he found an email from Clayton asking him to pop in. His office door was ajar as Alex knocked and entered finding his boss waving him in whilst wrapping up a phone call. Alex drifted over to the window and watched a modest tourist boat amble through the caramel waters of the Thames, under a concrete sky.

'Sorry about that Alex, how are you? I wasn't expecting you in today. All well in Laos?' Clayton asked, gesturing for Alex to take one of the chairs at his meeting table.

'Good thanks, all signed and delivered. How was the cycling thing?'

'Exhausting but brilliant.' Andrew enthused, his eyes lighting up. 'Pretty tough on the third day, my thighs are bloody killing me. Amelia always says she thinks I love that bike more than her! It is a beauty, should be for the price mind.'

Alex had no interest in cycling and couldn't understand why anyone would want to put themselves through a torturous weekend of riding up hills.

'So you wanted to see me?' Alex prompted, keen to get on with his work.

'Yes, I've been talking to Ben Williams from the Australia team and they'd like someone to front up some training for negotiators out there in October. You'll be there for 11 days in total. I'll send all the details to Olivia.'

Clayton pushed a hand through his flop of sandy hair and studied him carefully. 'That ok with you Alex? You seem a little preoccupied.'

'I'm fine,' Alex said, trying to make himself seem brighter, 'just not been sleeping too well, just the jet lag I should think.'

'Well don't forget to take some time off whenever you need it.'

'Of course, thanks Andrew.' Alex said getting to his feet and heading for the door.

That evening it was gone eight by the time the taxi dropped Alex at the top of Exmouth Market, under the arcing bare bulbs strung between brick buildings. It was the Friday before Christmas and the restaurants and bars were bustling with friends enjoying drinks, before dispersing around the country to see their families. Those outside walked briskly, keen to escape the biting cold, a metallic smell mixing with the scent of cooking food. He watched a young couple in animated conversation over a glass of wine, sat in the window of a bar he passed. Lingering a little too long, he scuttled away as she caught his eye through the glass. Of late this secret voyeurism had become something of an obsession for Alex. Regularly, he would take long meandering routes home so he could sneak a glimpse into people's lives through illuminated windows. An elderly woman sipping tea in a high-back chair, a couple snuggled on the sofa lit up by tv, a serious looking man playing the flute. Alex compulsively stalled in the shadowy darkness. He loved winter for it, the early dark evenings his perfect cover.

Sliding his ringing phone out of his pocket, he studied the screen before accepting the call.

'Darling, it's me.'

'Hi mother.' Alex barely had time to say before she continued.

'What time will we see you on Sunday? It's just we have the annual Christmas Eve drinks at the Richards' at twelve and then your father is playing Bridge straight after. I keep telling him it's only a game and he needs to think about his heart but he won't listen to me of course. Only last week the specialist said he needs to avoid stress as much as possible.....Alexander are you still there?'

'Yes mummy.'

'It's just it went very quiet there, a conversation takes two you know,' she replied sounding cross.

'I have a few things to tie up here.' Alex lied, sidestepping a cyclist, 'I'll be with you late afternoon.'

'Yes well, your father and I look forward to seeing you, drive carefully darling.'

With that she was gone. Habitually he opened one of his dating apps and swiped lazily before losing the will. Tugging his coat around his neck, he pushed on back to his flat, deciding it would be too depressing to sit alone amongst the crowds.

On Christmas Eve the imposing sky hung like a grey sheet above the slip of land, as Alex headed down the A12 towards his parent's home in the Suffolk countryside. It wasn't even four o clock but what little light had yawned across the day was already ebbing away. The carcasses of wild Britain laid to rest where they fell, a crash barrier for a headstone. Alex found the land's uniform quality comforting. He passed dull fields and new build housing estates, three story brick family homes popped out of a mould with names like Meadowside, all with delightful views of the dual carriageway.

Soon he cut off onto the small winding roads that led him into Suffolk, the landscape of his youth. Without fail Alex always had the same feeling coming back here. As he approached the village of Lavenham loneliness crept under his skin, a melancholy that left him weak. Inevitably he would be frustrated by his inability to shake off his thirteen-year-old self, under house arrest on the edge of a village with an average age of sixty plus. His friends from school were always a drive away, leaving Alex to make his own entertainment in the interminable summer holidays.

His mother, for her part, was constantly encouraging him to take up some activity or other.

'How about chess dear? There's a Tuesday morning club in the village hall.' she would suggest pushing an arm through the sleeve of her coat on the way to flower arranging at the church. She'd stopped taking him to her women's meetings and afternoon teas, embarrassed by his sullen face.

Of course these days, she spoke of nothing but her only son.

'Alex is in Dubai this week, some big contract, he's doing awfully well, there's even talk of another promotion.'

Despite being surrounded by some beautiful countryside Alex was never a big one for the outdoors, he didn't much like getting dirty and preferred to spend the long hot summer days inside reading or doing school work. With his father fled to London at first light, he had the imposing six bedroom house to himself. Alex liked to creep silently around the house in socks, trying not to make a sound, stepping around the many creaking floorboards. Scattered with lamps that were never turned off, sloping wooden floors and an enormous stone fireplace in the lounge, the house was several hundreds of years old. Ever the perfectionist, his mother kept it immaculate, everything in its carefully considered place. She once fired their cleaner, Sophie, a bubbly woman in her thirties who a fourteen-year-old Alex had unspeakably shameful thoughts about, for putting a bronze statuette of two horses back in the wrong place. With flushed red cheeks and blond curls tucked behind her ears, Sophie had done her best not to show her despair when her employer explained non-committally that it just wasn't working out. Alex had been so angry with her at Sophie's departure that he'd begun stealing his mother's possessions and throwing them away in a bin at the edge of the village. He would hold his breath as he heard her shout down the hall to his father.

'Henry, have you seen the Jade necklace you bought me in Berlin? I can't for the life of me find it.'

Pulling through the stone pillars onto the gravel drive, Alex thought about his parents coming to view this house for the first time and was struck by its classic beauty. White fronted with four pale olive window frames either side of the heavy wooden front door. Two large chimneys stood symmetrically either side of the slate roof, mature holm oak and ash providing the backdrop to a beautifully maintained garden that even now in the depths of winter was impressive. The elegant windows glowed invitingly and white lights twinkled in the shaped yew tree to the right of the house.

'Hello darling, happy Christmas.' His mother said,

kissing him on both cheeks as he stepped onto the stone floor of the hall. Dressed in a long flowery dress as if it were summer, gold earrings and plenty of make up, you'd be forgiven for thinking she was on her way out if it weren't for the pinny tied around her waist. Alex followed her into the warm kitchen, where she returned to chopping some parsnips.

'How was the journey down? Beautiful new car.'

'Good thanks.' Alex muttered helping himself to some sparkling water from the fridge.

'I've been trying to get your father to get rid of that horrid old Jag but he won't have it. I swear he loves that car more than me.' she laughed, dropping some fresh rosemary into a baking tray.

'You look tired Alex.' she stated, stopping what she was doing and studying him carefully.

'I've not been sleeping, that's all.' he replied, turning away to avoid her eyes.

'Have you tried sleeping tablets? Beatrice put me on to them, never slept so well, I'll give you some to take back.'

Alex sat at the long wooden table half-heartedly picking through the paper. The room was decorated with branches of holly and ivy, all part of his mother's annual decorating of the house that she took incredibly seriously. From the Christmas day table centre piece to the handmade tags on her precision wrapped presents, nothing went unconsidered.

'Been a busy month Ma, I've hardly had time to stop,

we're expanding a lot in Asia and Latin America.'

'Well don't forget to have fun now will you, you're not getting any younger and you can't go on living alone forever.' she pointed out, turning her back to him and disappearing into the fridge.

This was a well visited conversation between them that Alex knew was coming like clockwork. She would work her way around to asking if he'd been seeing anyone lately and would dig for breadcrumbs of information that Alex would reluctantly give up. Inevitably there would be a jokey comment, that they both knew was nothing of the sort, about how a mother can't wait forever for her child's wedding day.

'I did like that Emily, very sweet girl, shame you couldn't have held on to her.' she added, looking down her beak-like nose and ignoring his exaggerated sigh.

Alex wholeheartedly regretted the one time he'd brought Emily to lunch. His mother had made a huge effort, fresh bunches of flowers everywhere, three courses, on full charm offensive, which Alex had found excruciating. In the car on the way home, Emily had told him she thought his parents were both very sweet but they were both relieved when it was over.

In truth, she'd known almost instantly that she wasn't looking at her future daughter-in-law, the daughter she had always been desperate for. Mothers have an instinct for that sort of thing.

'What time's daddy back?' Alex asked in an unsubtle attempt to move the conversation on.

Ignoring him she soldiered on. 'Seriously Alex I'm sixty-five this year and the only one of my group who's not a grandmother, even Ilsa's Casper has managed to get married and have one, and he's an alcoholic for goodness sake.'

'Terribly sorry ma, I'll marry the next girl I meet, I wouldn't want you to be the embarrassment of your sewing circle.' Alex snapped, attempting to read (for the third time) the first line of an article under the title: Britain's great lost gardens.

'No need to be like that darling.' she said, bruised and leaving Alex feeling guilty.

Just before seven, his father, red cheeks, a full head of wild white hair, clattered through the door, holding a golfing umbrella in one hand and a barber jacket in the other. A delicious smell of lamb and rosemary had begun to fill the kitchen.

'Hello Alex….Cynthia darling.' he said, striding in to meet them, wardrobe shoulders and broad hairy neck stooping through the kitchen door. Despite his years, he was strong and active, the kind of man who point blank refuses to accept he's getting older.

'You won then dear.' Cynthia said, wiping her hands on a tea towel and stepping over to accept his kiss.

'Wiped the floor with them,' he beamed proudly, 'couldn't seem to put a foot wrong.'

Alex, who had no interest in Bridge whatsoever, nodded dutifully listening to his father ramble on about this hand and that. Henry had removed a bottle of white from the fridge and was pouring them all a glass to add to the few he'd clearly already had at the club. Both Alex and his mother had played this game for years, perfect in their roles as the impressed audience. Dropping in a cursory, 'really?' Or, 'crikey, you didn't,' for good measure. All of this was done without a second thought, both of them infinitely grateful not to have to deal with a dour figure crashing about angrily after a loss.

They sat in their museum of a dining room for dinner, all dark wood and polished silver. Cynthia had laid the table with a crisp white tablecloth and the good cutlery. A large tree dominated the corner, sparkling with glass baubles and intricate wooden decorations.

'Lovely lamb dear, beautifully cooked as always.' Henry commented, dabbing his chin with a napkin.

They'd always been a quiet family; conversations centred around practical matters or retelling of stories Alex had heard from his father's withering repertoire. They asked him about work, about his new car, about the flat. He asked about the house, what was happening in the village, how their week in Italy had been. They were film sets of conversations, comfortably scripted. It was safe ground that was the very grain of their family, all crust and no filling. As a result there were no dramas, no arguments, just a comfortable silence that had left Alex often in search of solitude. The consequence being three individuals who for all their close unbroken family ties, barely knew each other or themselves for that matter.

'There's been quite a fuss in the village over the plans to build a horrid housing estate off Wren Lane. Twenty houses not in keeping with the village at all.' Henry offered, as the conversation ran dry.

'Ghastly looking things.' Cynthia added, passing Alex the gravy.

'Well we'll see about that, we won't be ignored that easy here I can tell you. Just because this bloody government lets every Tom, Dick and Mohammed in. Why should we have our village ruined?'

That wasn't the first time Alex had heard that line and he was pretty sure it wouldn't be the last.

'I mean London might be swimming in them but we don't want them out here.' Henry lectured shoving another roast potato in his mouth. 'Those at Downing Street can't seem to manage the economy, the pound's on the slide again, we need to look after ourselves. Everyone talking about another economic crash around the corner. Look at those idiots in Europe, debt up to their eyeballs and not a job in sight.'

After dessert, Alex and Cynthia cleared away the bowls whilst his father made an important phone call.

'We've cleared some bits out of the attic,' she said folding the table cloth. 'I left a box of your things in your room; be a darling and go through them would you? Take what you want, the rest I'll send to the charity shop.'

Nodding silently Alex headed for the stairs, pausing at the door of the lounge to take in the catalogue

43

Christmas scene. An inviting fire crackled contently under an imposing marble mantle packed with cards. Alex had always been amazed at the number of Christmas cards they received - hundreds of them. He'd had a fair few from work of course, that always left him feeling guilty that he'd somehow forgotten again this year. In the opposite corner, another enormous tree touched the ceiling as if on tiptoes. A few of the decorations he recognised from childhood: a wooden soldier, an antique tear-shaped glass crystal but most were new. To Alex, this was just the Christmas scene he'd known all his life but to an outsider, the room would have looked like a scene from a children's book. All it needed was stockings strung above the fire and a robin perched on a snow covered branch outside the window.

It felt strange entering his old room. The same blue curtains and single bed made ready for his stay; his stone chess set sat patiently on top of the oak chest of draws. On the wall above the bed you could just make out rectangular shadows, where his posters had been; a red Ferrari, a NASA space shuttle later replaced by Cindy Crawford in a swimsuit.

On the ageing beige carpet lay the box, 'Alex' penned neatly in black marker on the side. He pulled out his old microscope that sat on top, quickly returning it when he saw how dusty it was; Alex couldn't bare dirt. A frame lay face down beside it. Turning it over his seven-year-old self beamed back, Grandpa's thick arm around his shoulder, shirt rolled up to his elbow. Alex remembered the picture being taken one autumn when his father had helped Grandpa chop down a cherry tree that was getting too close to the house. His mother had taken the picture, soft afternoon light catching their faces, the fallen tree in the background. Alex blew the dust from the frame, set it on the chest of drawers and sat lightly on the bed.

Gently, he took the coin from his pocket and flipped it over, giving it a quick polish on his trousers. He'd spent most of his early years with him, his parents too busy with work. He hadn't known much about his grandmother, only that she'd died before he was born but he did recall the one time Grandpa talked about her.

Alex had been beating him at draughts as usual, Grandpa perched on the edge of his high-backed armchair, glasses on the end of his nose. Alex remembered waiting impatiently for him to make his next move. It must have been winter because the fire was lit and he recalled studying the pictures on the mantelpiece to kill time. In the middle, in an oval frame was a black and white picture of Iris, a grainy sea behind her, smiling eyes twinkling at the camera.

'That was taken on our first ever holiday.' his Grandpa said, following Alex's stare. 'We were only twenty, four nights at The Empire Bed and Breakfast in Bournemouth.'

'What was she like?' Alex asked.

'She was a wonderful woman, always laughing and seeing the funny side...you'd have liked her Alex.'

He'd looked so sad saying that, Alex hadn't dared ask about her again. Sometimes though, when Grandpa was in the greenhouse seeing to his tomato plants, Alex would sneak into the main bedroom and gently lift the lid on the silver make-up box that sat like a memorial on the dresser. Amongst the tab of matches with a flamingo on the front and the various items of jewellery was a miniature brass bound bible, no taller than Alex's thumb, a small polished clasp holding the bulging pages together. The words on the thin paper were barely legible and between guilty glances through the net curtains, he would try to read the tiny words that drifted in and out of focus like last night's dream.

Most Thursdays straight from school Alex and his Grandpa would drive the twenty minutes or so through narrow country lanes to visit Françoise. She lived at Cedar Manor, at the end of a long drive banked by swelling rhododendrons. The visit was the highlight of Alex's week. He loved that house; it seemed endless, every door leading to another bizarre room filled with strange plants, exotic paintings and stuffed animals in glass cases. He longed to explore the place alone but Grandpa made clear he wasn't to wander off and he was to ask Françoise before touching anything.

Françoise, slim and always balanced on a walking stick (its silver handle in the shape of a toucan's head) waved away his politeness.

'Don't be such a killjoy Stanley.' she lectured. 'You touch whatever you like Alex dear.'

She had no time for fussiness and spoke with a directness Alex hadn't experienced elsewhere. Alex completely adored her. Right from their first meeting when he was just past his fifth birthday, she'd spoken to him differently from the way other adults did. Gone were the stupid baby voices of his mother's friends, stooping in their flowery dresses: 'Well aren't you a big boy now.'

Instead, she shook his hand and spoke to him in French before returning to English asking him if he liked rocks and fossils. Not waiting for a reply she'd led him down two wood panelled corridors and into a room with floor to ceiling shelves on all sides, except the wall which held a tall window, looking out onto an immaculately kept walled garden. For the best part of fifteen minutes, ignoring his Grandpa completely, she talked him through all the different specimens carefully catalogued and labelled on the well lit shelves. Alex was captivated; there was something in the way she spoke that demanded attention. But at the same time she was attentive, brushing an eyelash from his cheek as she answered his many questions.

Françoise's late husband Alfred had been Stanley's first boss at the Ministry and even after he left to take a senior government position they remained friends. His Grandpa had been a regular visitor to the house for over forty years. He'd brought a bottle of whiskey to celebrate with Alfred after the birth of Beatrice and watched her flourish into an inquisitive girl with hair that wouldn't be tamed and a pensive frown. He'd walked with Alfred, under singed October leaves, through the woodland that flanked the west of the house, the day Beatrice complained of feeling poorly. At first it seemed nothing out of the ordinary, but three days later she couldn't move her arms and legs and the family doctor was called. Her limbs were draped in hot packs of wool to prevent the spasms. But tragically a few days later, on a cold clear night, the moon casting long shadows across the lawns, Beatrice began to struggle to breathe and later died in her mother's arms.

Being a biologist Françoise had only one approach to channel the grief that engulfed her. She met with every leading mind on the Polio epidemic, travelling all over the world and investing a fair amount of her personal fortune to find a cure.

Alfred, a shadow of his former self following Beatrice's death, regularly complained to Stanley that he never saw his wife. Françoise, sensing they were getting somewhere, spent more and more time in the United States. That's where she was when Alfred was found in a field a mile from their home. It wasn't until years later that Françoise told him it hadn't been a heart attack; he'd taken his own life.

In that dark time, Stanley didn't visit Cedar Manor for many years. Françoise was living in the States and was working for Jonas Salk, a medical researcher who was developing a vaccine that would ultimately end the epidemic. Years later Jonas and Françoise married and returned to England but things didn't work out and he scuttled back to better climates.

Stanley had been stationed for 17 months in Lyon during the war, as a result most conversations at the house were in French. On his early visits Alex, shut out of their conversation, busying himself exploring but as time passed he realised he understood more and more. Later he recognised that this was the birth of his love for languages. By the time he was seven, he joined in their chats with ease, much to Françoise's satisfaction.

Françoise was quite the storyteller. Amongst her circles, it was quite common to enter a room to find a large group in absorbed silence as she recalled a dramatic trip down the Pailian River close to the Vietnam border.

For Alex these stories created a rich, exotic world in his imagination that he longed to see with his own eyes. Inspired by her, he set on a future where he travelled the world helping sick children just as she had done.

One wet afternoon, he admitted his plans to her as they listened to the rain's cheer on the circular glass atrium of her laboratory. Built in the 1950s, the high ceilinged lab was all polished wood doors, glass and brass fixings. Alex revelled in the labelled jars, glass cabinets filled with animal skeletons and glass beakers. As he inspected her considerable butterfly collection all neatly categorised, each delicate specimen perfect under the spotless glass, he asked, 'how did you know you wanted to be a biologist?'

'I didn't,' she replied, not averting her gaze from a large blue butterfly with shimmery metallic colouring.

'That's the Blue Morpho,' she said, her nose nearly touching the glass, 'they're quite territorial you know, people don't tend to think that of butterflies. When you study the wings under a microscope you can see they're on many layers, looking a bit like a Christmas tree in structure. Light reflects off the different layers giving us these wonderful colours at different angles.'

'But you've been on so many adventures around the world helping people and finding things, did you always want to do that?' Alex asked, tipping his head to the side to observe the varied colours in the Morpho's wings.

'It's hard to remember what one always wanted to do Alex, so much time passes and the world is always changing. We must change to keep up with it. What's more you're too young to be worrying about things like the future; it's a fruitless occupation anyway.'

'I want to be like you when I'm older.' Alex mumbled averting his eyes.

Such simple, childish words made Françoise turn and stare at the boy she had become so fond of.

'Tu ne veux pas etre comme moi.'

She replied, turning to look out the window.

'Why not? You've been all around the world on amazing adventures and you've helped all those children. That's what I want to do, go to places and help sick children.'

She smiled approaching him, pushing a slender hand through his hair. 'You go and do that Alex, don't let anyone tell you otherwise.'

He could have only visited Cedar House a handful of times after that before everything changed.

He'd known something was wrong as soon as he'd seen his mother stood stiffly at the school gate, navy scarf wrapped around her shoulders. Grandpa always picked him up, in his tweed jacket, waving the minute he saw him at the door. His mother didn't come to meet him halfway across the playground like Grandpa did, taking his bag from him and passing him a biscuit with a wink. Instead, she stood there ignoring the other parents.

Only once they were in the car did she turn in her seat and say, 'I'm afraid Grandpa's in hospital, he's very poorly, we're going straight to see him now.'

With that she turned around and started the engine, driving away in silence.

Alex didn't see his grandfather again. By the time they reached the hospital he was already dead. It was the only time in his life he'd seen his father cry, his face in his hands, shaking without a sound, in a beige hospital side room that smelt of bleach.

For quite some time he just couldn't understand it, one minute he'd been there, the next he was gone. It was like he'd been kidnapped or gone on a long holiday.

Life for Alex changed quickly after that; his mother announced he would be going to a new school at the start of term and would be staying there during term time.

'That'll be fun won't it?' she'd assured him, folding some clothes and laying them on his bed.

Alex had been petrified the first day, arriving with a zip up leather bag and a pale face, as the last leaves made their descent. In an unusual show of solidarity both his mother and father had driven him there, radio news replacing the million questions he had wanted to ask. They left him with Mr Chapple, his form tutor and History teacher, an awkward man with thick glasses and crooked nose who lent heavily on the phrase 'between you, me and the gate-post'. The children called him Sparrow due to his passion for birds. Many a lesson would be successfully stalled when a hand was raised and some boy would politely ask, 'Excuse me sir, I saw a strange bird out the window just now with yellow feathers, do you know the name of it?'

Alex's father clapped him on the back and his mother dropped to one knee to give him a peck on the cheek before they turned and walked away, leaving him to live with a bunch of strangers at the age of eight.

Like anything new, the first part was the hardest. The crippling loneliness wasn't helped by the unchecked cruelty of just shy of four hundred boys left to establish their own pecking order. So sure there were beatings and humiliation (not least the time he was locked outside naked in December for forty minutes by Lawrence William and his following) but also there were many hours of fun. Sneaking into the dark attic above the dorms, shitting himself after Matthew had told the story of the dead ex-pupil who still roams there, or the hours spent writing messages in the coded language he had invented with Jeremy and Max. His interest in languages grew. They came easily to him; he studied French, German, Russian and Latin. They were like a puzzle that he delighted in unpicking. Mrs Deliere, Head of Languages and no stranger to a custard donut, adored him, regularly pulling him to the front so he could share his latest achievement.

'Perhaps Martin if you worked as hard as Alex you would know more than the first line....Alex if you would come to the front and recite it please.' forcing Alex to stand, red-faced and reel off the Lord's Prayer in German. Of course, he took beatings for making everyone else feel stupid, such is the natural order of things.

One thing they all learnt quickly enough was that weakness was punished without mercy. Alex soon set into a survival pattern of non-committal aloofness.

He'd seen what had happened to those that cried or screamed and shouted. For eight years this was Alex's home. A Tudor castle of young boys, Pavlovian in their suppression of emotion.

Months after his Grandfather's death, when he was

home for the holidays, his father had called him into his study (a room he was normally forbidden from entering) and explained that Grandpa had left him something in his will. He knew the room well; like any child forbidden something he had waited until his parents were out. Too afraid to touch anything in case he should be discovered, he'd tiptoe about wondering what was in the safe or staring at the large painting of an impressive ship on the wall behind the desk, sails like plates of armour, cutting magnificently through the rough sea. Alex had stood to attention by his father's grand desk, holding back his rising guilt, as his father shuffled some papers looking for it.

Eventually, he'd placed the coin in Alex's palm. It was the only thing of his Grandpa's he'd wanted, and now it was his.

Only twice, at school, did he speak about Grandpa. Once when he showed Jeremy the coin, which he kept wrapped in a sock at the bottom of the drawer, terrified it would be stolen. He'd explained it was from his Grandpa but had hastily put it back when Seb and Harry had entered the dorm. The second time was under the shade of a sprawling oak, at the edge of the cricket pitch. The air was filled with the scent of cut grass, as Alex and Jeremy sat for hours escaping the heat. Only Jeremy protected Alex from the bottom of the batting order and their pristine cricket whites weren't in danger of any grass stains. They knew, as well as everyone else, that an end to play would be called before the action reached them.

They'd become friends after Alex found him curled in a ball at the top of the Biology stairs. Beyond the second floor laboratories, the stairs continued up to a locked door that was no longer in use. No one went up there except boys like Jeremy trying to disappear. Smaller than most in their year, Jeremy's mop of curly hair (that in later life his husband Dan admitted was the main reason he started dating him) was a cause of many beatings. But on the day they met it was his refusal to enter into what he'd labelled 'the blasphemy of biting' that had got him the beating. Jeremy felt with quite some passion that a boiled sweet should be sucked down to the very last. This in itself was no big deal but Jeremy's mistake was admitting his passion out loud. Three of them had pinned him down around the back of the squash courts, as Lawrence, with a devilish grin, had retrieved a pack of peppermints from his pocket.

Uninterested in the game that trickled on in the summer sun, they debated their favourite war planes. Alex was adamant that the F-15 Eagle was unbeatable. Jeremy couldn't see past the Spitfire; it won the Battle of Britain after all. As the argument ran out of steam, a light breeze pushed through the trees that cast a camouflage of shade on the neat grass. Alex broke the silence, tugging at a blade of grass and saying, 'My Grandpa was a secret agent in the war.'

'Really?'

'Yeah, he worked at the Ministry of Information, this

top secret place where they held all the secrets about the Nazis.'

Actually, Alex didn't know what his Grandpa had done there and at that age wasn't really sure what the place was all about, but never let doubt get in the way of a good story.

'Wow, did he crack Nazi codes and listen in to Hitler's secret tapes?' Jeremy asked, getting to his knees enthusiastically.

'Not only that but he met Churchill who gave him a special mission he wasn't allowed to tell anyone about.' Alex added, growing into his exaggerated truths.

'He showed me a picture of the top secret building in London once where he worked. It looked a bit like a giant grey robot.'

In truth, the Ministry had been visited by Churchill once and his Grandpa had shaken the big man's hand. But the place was legendary to Alex because it featured in the story of the coin. Some children had their favourite book they would want every night before bed until their parents were sick of the sight of it. For Alex, it was the story of the coin.

His Grandfather never disappointed, lowering his voice (as if others might overhear) as he pulled up a chair...

'Well, I remember it'd been a particularly cold January and the office was freezing. Eileen, Albert and I were sat at our desks in coats for the most part.'

Usually by this point, Alex had climbed onto his lap

or pulled his duvet up to his chin.

'That morning Albert had just made some tea and Eileen was telling us about her parents memorial to her brother they were installing at their home. Poor Eileen got thinner and thinner at that time, the loss of Lawrence was a terrible blow. Little did we know in a few years she'd be gone herself. Anyway, she got rather upset and stepped out for a few minutes. She'd been gone for rather a while and Albert and I were starting to get a touch worried. Albert was always better with these sort of things than I was so he said he'd go and see if he could find her and check she was alright. So there I was sat alone in our office, up on the eighth floor sipping a cup of tea and stamping my feet to keep warm, when I heard a tap on the window. At first, I assumed it was a pigeon flown into the window by mistake but then I heard it again; a clear knock on the glass. Shocked, I span around and I was sure I saw some movement out there. Well as you can imagine I went to investigate what it was. I opened the window but was afraid to lean out and look, I've never been much of a one for heights. Eventually, I thought 'come on Stanley', what if there was someone out there, he could fall to his death. So I leaned out and looked along the ledge but couldn't see anything or anyone out there. Puzzled, I leaned back in and closed the window.'

At this bit he would lower his voice mysteriously.

'I was about to return to my desk when I noticed the window on the other side of the office was wide open. A terribly chilly wind was blowing through it. I knew for a fact that the window hadn't been open just a moment earlier.

Just then, Eileen and Albert came strolling back into the office. I must have looked somewhat panicked because Eileen said to me, 'whatever is the matter Stanley and why on earth is the window open?'

I laughed then because I thought they must have been playing a trick on me but they just looked at me blankly. I explained about hearing the knock and looking out. 'Just opened on its own you say?' Albert asked, looking at me like I'd gone mad. I tried to explain but the more I said, the more ridiculous it sounded.'

This was Alex's favourite bit coming up.

'I went over to the window to close it and there, sat right in the middle of the ledge, as if it was supposed to be found, was a shiny one penny piece. I picked it up and slipped it in my pocket without mentioning it to the others, I felt foolish enough as it was. I know it sounds silly but to this day it felt like someone had left it there for me to find. I've kept it ever since.'

At this point he always pulled the coin from his pocket with a flourish, like a magician, and handed it to Alex.

'The most puzzling thing is this coin is one of only a few ever made. I had no idea at the time but years later an old friend of mine, a bit of a coin boffin, told me. He saw it on my desk and could barely contain his excitement - worth a fair few bob as well. He did his damnedest to get me to sell it but I'd grown rather attached to it. Then just a few years ago a few of us from the Ministry went back to Senate House for a reunion. We had a tour of the building, lovely day out it was. They've got a small museum of sorts in there that tells you all about the building's history. Turns out that when they laid the foundation stone there was a grand ceremony: the King and Queen, prime minister etc. Anyway, under the foundation stone the King laid a time capsule of sorts containing a newspaper of the day, a printed program of the event, that sort of thing. I was so shocked I had to read it three times but right there in black and white it said one of the items included was a 1933 One....Penny....piece.'

Doing his best to impersonate his grandfather he started to tell the story to Jeremy. It didn't feel right and he felt a horrible pain pierce through his sternum. Feeling dizzy he stopped, tried to start again, but grief washed over him. Unable to look at Jeremy he buried his head between his knees and tried to swallow the tears.

His mother calling upstairs brought him back from his memory. Rising to his feet he hastily pushed the items back in the box and without a backward glance stepped out the room, meeting his mother on the stairs.

'Anything you want from that lot darling?' she asked, studying him carefully.

'No, chuck the lot.' Alex replied pushing past her.

On Christmas morning after a lavish breakfast (homemade drop scones, summer fruits, yogurt, coffee) as was tradition, they took a walk in the village. The air was damp but the rain held off as they clumped down the main street with its sandy coloured, wonky wooden beamed houses that looked like something straight out of Dickens. It was not hard to see why it was popular with tourists in the summer, stumbling off the coach into a Tudor theme park. They passed the grand church with its intricate windows and imposing tower, all of which reminded Alex exactly why he had bolted to London the minute he was eighteen.

As they passed houses that faced onto the street Alex dawdled for as long as he dared. In the first he saw an elderly man hunched in front of the tv; there was no sign of Christmas. Further down the main street, he glimpsed a large family around the tree - three or four children in pyjamas ripping paper from presents. At another, the curtains were drawn downstairs but he spied a boy of six or seven leaning on the windowsill looking down on the street. The boy fixed him an angry stare so Alex quickly moved on.

As they crossed the road they met a slight man, briskly walking, stooped forward as if pulled by an invisible lead.

'Merry Christmas Terry!' his father shouted as they approached.

He stopped on the spot and turned to meet them.

'And to you, sorry, in my own world there. Ah, Alex how lovely to see you.'

He had a limp handshake and sad looking glossy eyes.

'Just down for a couple of days over Christmas, so busy jetting off around the world with work he hardly has time to see us these days.' Cynthia interjected, taking command of the conversation as she was so accustomed to doing.

'Very good, keeping you busy are they?' he replied, turning to Alex.

'How's Tom?' asked Alex.

He hadn't spoken to his childhood friend for close to ten years. In their teens they'd spent time together, largely because there was no one else their age within walking distance. Tom, a cheeky figure, with thin wired glasses and a mess of blond hair, was always getting into trouble. By contrast Alex was painfully shy at that age, following his lead, smoking cigarettes he offered him, looking together at magazines stolen from Tom's older brother.

One long summer, at the height of their friendship they'd lived in each other's pockets, mostly at Tom's cluttered house. Both Tom's parents were at work, so they were left to entertain themselves for days on end. Tom had bought a radio transmitter from one of his brother's friends and they spent hours escaping the sunshine, playing songs and talking to their imagined audience. Tom would be hunched at the pine desk in his room in shorts and a Liverpool shirt, adjusting settings, whilst Alex selected the next song. They named it Radio Stratosphere, taking turns to DJ. Tom did a sports show that mostly involved him talking about how brilliant Liverpool were, whilst Alex lay on his bed reading comics. Later, Alex would take over for his regular space show, a particular obsession at the time. Only after weeks had gone by did they discover that the transmitter had seen better days. Tom, deciding to test its range, had taken his small portable radio out into the garden only to discover the signal dropped out just past the pond.

They didn't see each other again after that for several years; summer came to an end and Tom went to a different school. But on a visit home from university Alex popped into the pub for a pint with his father and there he was. At first, he hadn't recognised him, he'd filled out and was a foot taller. They'd spoken politely for a few minutes and that was the last he'd seen of him.

'He's good thanks son, Tom's in Spain at the

moment, got a job for an insurance company. Although he's worried about his job with all the trouble out there.'

'Alex here has just got the most beautiful new Mercedes, you should see it.' Cynthia interrupted.

After a few more minutes of small talk they went their separate ways, Alex thinking about his friends from school and university; where had they all gone? He thought how he really must contact some of them but time had passed and lots of them had busy family lives. He wondered how much they'd have in common now anyway.

Alex and his father returned to the house, leaving Cynthia at the church. When she returned they gathered in the lounge and Alex distributed the gifts. As ever he was surprised by the number of presents under his parent's tree, considering there were only three of them.

He couldn't help thinking about the family he'd caught sight of earlier (people squeezed into every chair, wrapping covering the floor) and wondering what it was like to have a big family. Having never had a sibling to share Christmas with, Alex had no frame of reference. But he liked the romantic idea of lots of people around, a clutter of voices over the rip of paper, the chuckles and gasps of appreciation. In his imagination that crowded room felt complete instead of the long silences filled only by his father's choral choir music, sporadically interrupted by his mother's hyperbolic exclamations at each gift, balanced by his father's flat-lined responses.

Like most years of late Alex struggled to know what to buy his parents. After all, what do you get people who have everything? In the end, he'd settled on a range of premium golfing accessories for his father that a work colleague had kindly talked him through. His mother was easier, expensive designer earrings and accessories always did the trick. Unsure quite how much was enough and keen to avoid his mother's disapproval, Alex always bought more than necessary.

Once the gifts were all open, Cynthia excused herself to check on lunch, his father hauled himself up to pour them all a drink. Alex was left to gaze out the back windows at the blackbirds, puffed up against the cold, dashing down to the bird feeders, then back into the silhouetted skeletons of a long forgotten summer.

Around three they sat for lunch in the dining room, only filling one end of the antique, dark wood table. On the thick, white table cloth, two impressive silver candlesticks, six candles flickering in each, took centre stage surrounded by sprigs of holly and delicate silver decorations. His mother arranged dish after dish, carefully placing them so that the colours complimented each other, and never allowed Alex and Henry to help. Only when she had stood back to survey the whole scene (steaming turkey surrounded by enough food to feed a family of fifteen) did she nod her head slightly and call them in.

Knowing the degree of effort involved and never

forgetting her wrath the year they plonked themselves down without a word, Alex and his father drowned her in praise. Circling the table they commented on every detail.

'Look at those delightfully tiny glass baubles.'

'My goodness, what an incredible spread.'

Alex took some pictures on his phone that would be seen by no one, before Cynthia urged them to sit and eat. Under the gaze of the imposing gold framed portrait of Henry's great grandfather (military medals proudly pinned to his chest) they tucked in, murmuring noises of appreciation.

Later when they retired to the lounge to watch a film, Alex was so full he felt a little sick. He knew he shouldn't have had Christmas pudding and his mother's homemade truffles but he hadn't wanted to upset her. He felt like he would never need to eat again and chastised himself for turning something so pleasurable into discomfort. Sitting gently next to him, glancing over to smile and roll her eyes at Henry's snores, his mother felt the satisfaction of a job well done. They saw out the rest of the day like that, drink in hand, lit by the warm glow of the tree, turning away offers of sugar dusted almonds and Medjool dates.

The following morning the garden sparkled with frost under a pale sky, a tinge of woodsmoke lingered in the sharp air. Alex gathered himself to make the drive back to London, his mother hugged him tightly at the front door and pushed a small bottle into his hand.

'So lovely to see you darling, don't leave it so long next time. Here, give these a try.'

His father, rosy cheeked, shook his hand firmly. In the car Alex sat in silence for a moment letting it defrost, the coin cool in his hand, before dropping it back in his pocket and driving away.

I've told you about Rosa before right? My kind of grandma but not. For her 70th birthday we had this big party. Ma says we can have the morning off sewing to get ready so we hang the decorations we'd made all around the old tree in the square and people bring tables and chairs out to put all around. Sancho has some coloured lights we hang from the branches and Diego gives us this amazing shiny Happy Birthday banner he got from somewhere in the hotel. Everyone brings a little food until we have a feast laid out and me and Ma make lemonade from lemons and sugar which is surprisingly easy actually. We borrow the CD player from the bar and Jana gives us some CDs. I'm super excited and the square looks so pretty and everyone who loves Rosa is there.

So off I go to get Rosa nervous as hell my hands will shake or I won't be able to look her in the eye or generally give away what's going on. We told her Ma was cooking her some dinner at our place. I lie about needing to buy some matches from the shop on the corner of the square otherwise she's going to ask why we're going the long way round. Rosa is wearing her lacy dress that she kept from when she was young and she takes my arm as we walk because of her bad hip and the whole time I'm trying to stop myself smiling. When we finally come round the corner everyone jumps up and cheers and shouts

Feliz cumpleaños!!! which gives me this shiver down my spine do you ever get that?

Rosa's so surprised she just stands really still and grips my arm hard and then everyone runs up to hug her and she has tears of joy in her eyes which if we're honest is what we all hope for from a surprise isn't it? I love parties but surprise ones are the best. It's the look on their faces I love.

We have the best night. It seems like all of El Borde is there dancing and singing and raising their glasses to Rosa. I'd never seen Rosa dance before either even though she told me she used to dance all the time when she was younger.

Later me and Diego climb the tree and look down on everyone and see Ma sitting with Rosa listening to one of her stories. Rosa was rich once and had a big house and a good looking husband and people who made her food and everything. But then the Communists came. I don't know if you have those where you're from but anyway they stole it all and killed her husband who she had this black and white picture of in a silver frame in her room. In Borde lots of people called her La Reina because she still had some stuff from her old life around like the big vase with the pineapple on it and the old chair she sat in with the legs with lions carved in them.

So Diego pulls a can of beer from his pocket and opens it like that was the most normal thing ever. I don't really want to drink any but he always teases me for being younger so I gulp some down. It's pretty disgusting and makes my nose hurt but I pretend to like it.

Shaking his head Diego points down at Gismar his older brother who's showing off to three younger girls how he could balance a chair on one finger and they're all flirting with him really badly like total idiots. Of Diego's three brothers Gismar is the oldest then Victor who got himself a job at a pizza place and finally Nibaldo who was always in some trouble. His ma Carla worked all day at the hotel cleaning rooms and his pa Oscar drove a taxi in the city. Oscar wasn't at the party because he always worked late but I could see Carla over at the bar getting drunk as usual.

Diego starts telling me this long story about this car that crashes into the back of a pickup full of watermelons but I'm not really listening. All I can think about is the other side of the wall. After a bit he spots I'm not listening and says

Hey what's up?

And I'm like coke out of a shaken up bottle asking a million questions about the hotel.

What's the inside like? How many pools are there and what food do they eat? Are there any people from America there and most importantly when could I go in with him?

As usual he just rolls his eyes and gives me that annoying smug smile and I want to push him out the tree.

I was so jealous of Diego everyday he dressed up in his brown uniform and went into the hotel even though he's clearly a kid and didn't even have a job there! He told me once the story of how he ended up going to the hotel.

Carla worked there as a cleaner and when he was three or four she didn't want to leave him with his brothers so started taking him with her. Mostly she hid Diego in the cleaning trolley and would let him out when she was doing a room. She nearly got caught so after that she locked him all day in a storeroom. He got so bored one day he found an air vent that led to a courtyard and started to explore. He kept hidden at first and said he didn't speak to anyone until he was seven. By then he knew the hotel pretty well and loved hiding in the kitchen and watching the chefs rushing about.

He decided when he was older he was going to be a head chef and wear one of those big white hats. Apparently he had a great hiding place behind these stacked oil cans. He wasn't far from the main burners so could watch them all day flipping pans and shouting at the other chefs. Then one afternoon the kitchen was quiet before the evening staff arrived and the head chef Renan was cooking something for room service. He was watching from his hiding place as Renan slapped some fish and oil in a pan. He then went into the walk in fridge to get something. Just as the door closed a massive flame shot up from the back of the burners. The whole thing was on fire and not a soul was there in the kitchen. Diego didn't want to be seen but couldn't just let the place burn down. He knew what to do because he'd seen one of the chefs put out a pan fire before using this extinguisher with all this white foam in it. He ran out and grabbed the heavy extinguisher and dragged it to the burner and just at that moment Renan came round the corner with loads of vegetables in his arms and saw Diego putting it out.

I don't tell it half as well as Diego. It's hard to explain but when he tells a story it's like you were there with him.

I ask if he got in trouble but he says at first he just stood there without moving or saying anything. Renan took the extinguisher from his hands turned this big switch at the wall to stop the gas and then looked around the kitchen before taking him to this back office. Apparently he was so scared his Ma would lose her job. But then the chef put his arm around his shoulder and thanked him for saving his job. Diego and Renan were best friends after that and on his tenth birthday he gave him the porter's uniform as a present. Renan was friends with Gustavo the head of the porters so he fixed it so everyone thought he was a new staff member.

He always made excuses for why I couldn't go in with him and I think he just found my obsession with the place pretty funny which just wound me up even more. Maybe it was the beer or the party or the desperate look on my face but for a change he starts talking. It's coming up to Christmas and he tells me in the lobby there's this huge tree as tall as a house filled with lights and decorations and at the entrance they have a choir singing Christmas songs and guests in smart suits dancing at this grand Christmas ball. All of which probably sounds pretty boring and normal to you but I imagine myself in America in a long flowing dress dancing with Pa with snow outside and lights twinkling on the trees.

The day after the party when I've done all my jobs I go to see Rosa. When I get there she's asleep in her chair so I sit on her bed and watch her. She's still wearing the dress from last night and on her table are two vases full of flowers. Her mouth is open and she's snoring a bit which makes me giggle. Rosa's room was so full of stuff you could just sit and look for hours and never get bored. She only had one window so it was dark in there and smoky from the incense. In the mornings when the sun shone through the window I loved the way you could see the rays in the smoke. By the window was a tall bookcase full of old books and photo albums and when the electric was on she had her three lamps which gave the place a warm glow but there were always tons of candles in little pots and jars lit the whole time anyway. Rosa loved flowers and every bunch she got she dried them in the sun outside then hung them from the ceiling. The place was full of them. Oh and there were chests of drawers with all sorts of junk in them and piled up boxes in the corners. Most of the walls had shelves on them where she kept the old chipped plates and cups and some ornaments including the black stone horse that I played with loads that lived on the shelf above her bed. God I miss that place.

Because I don't want to wake her up I go over and get the album of her wedding day. I carefully turn the pages trying not to touch the burnt top corner which looks like someone left it too close to a fire. On the first page is a black and white photo of Rosa and Ribaldo. The edges are all brown and it's a bit faded but you can still see how beautiful she looks in her big white dress. Ribaldo is really handsome and is looking at Rosa like she's the most beautiful thing he ever saw. It's so romantic.

On the next page there's a picture of a crowd of people outside a church it's cloudy and looks like it could rain any minute. There's more of the bride and groom with an older couple who I guess are Rosa's parents.

I'm still looking at the album when she wakes up and gives me the biggest smile and waves me over for a hug. She smells of perfume and something musty like always. She whispers thank you and kisses my head and I wander off to put the kettle on the gas so she doesn't have to get up. She picks up her cake tin and pulls off the lid before passing it to me. It's full of delicious small cakes from the bakery we always got for special occasions. I take one of the chocolate ones with the yellow middle. God they were so good. What I would do for one of those right now.

I make the tea in her gold rimmed tea pot and put it on the little table with the lace tablecloth. I ask her if the people in the picture are her Ma and Pa and she nods and tells me her parents had their own finca growing all sorts but mostly maize and coffee. I think they were quite rich because they were always busy travelling all over the world. When she was my age she lived at a school run by nuns. Basically her Pa thought it was the best place for her and they learnt from the bible and did chores around the monastery. Rosa totally hated it and it put her off religion for life but she did say she learnt a lot in school. She said it was criminal that Ma couldn't afford to send me to school and that those crooks should've been paying her more. I did go to school for a while when I was younger. My Abuelita paid for me to go but she ran out of money when Pa left. School was fun. I liked learning all about new things every day. My teacher Mr Reyes was really kind and I liked the way he would wink at you when you put your hand up and got an answer right. I made some good friends but then I had to stop so I could help Ma.

You see when I was little and Pa was here we lived together all in one house in a different town quite far away but I don't remember it very well. My Uncle Carlos looked after Abuelita and for a while I remember them coming to visit all the time. Uncle Carlos was so much fun he always played games with me and would bring me a present each time they came. But then after a while they couldn't afford to come see us any more and we didn't have the money to go there. I miss them both so much I can't really think about it.

Rosa was sort of like my teacher in the afternoons. She'd help me with my reading and get down her old atlas that smelt of smoke and damp and show me maps of the world. They're some of my happiest memories sat cross legged on her bed while she told me stories or helped me with my writing her little radio always on low playing oldies tango. A lot of the time we just talked about all sorts because Rosa said there was as much learning to be done from talking things out as from books which is pretty hard to argue with.

I keep turning the pages and come to a picture of Rosa brushing a strong looking horse along its neck. I ask her where this was and she tells me that for a time she ran a stable taking American and Mexican tourists out on horse rides. She loved hearing all about their lives and meeting different people each day. She tells me how she'd had three horses at their finca when she was married. The horse in the picture was Lucy. Her favourite.

Then she starts talking about the revolution and how they lived in a huge house with loads of land and guests from all over the world coming and going. But they stopped coming when the communists started to take over. Then one day a group of scary young men came telling them they had to move out because they were taking the house and that all private land belonged to the people. She keeps her voice steady when she tells me that Ribaldo and some friends tried to fight back but all of them were killed. I can't even imagine what she must have gone through seeing the people she loved killed in front of her.

She says the communists said everything should be shared so people couldn't own a house or nice things but it turned out to be all bullshit like most things adults say. No offence. Apparently the people in the Communist Party kept all the best stuff for themselves and did all the things they told other people they couldn't do which seems pretty unfair to me but not all together unsurprising seeing what people are like generally.

All the stuff that filled her room Ribaldo sneaked out to a hidden underground bunker before he was killed. Rosa tells me she couldn't go back and get any of it for years because owning stuff was banned until Cabron took over and everyone celebrated in the streets and I'm thinking she must love Cabron but she says

They are all the same. New name same crooks in the

offices of power always has been always will be.

I didn't really get what she was on about then but it's starting to make more sense to me now. After all that's happened I suppose I'm growing up fast that's all.

Not long after Rosa's birthday it's Christmas. I meet Ma from work and we go straight to the parade. I'm worried we'll be late and miss Mary so I pull poor Ma along through the crowds. The parade starts across town but passes on the Calle Bolivar on the way to Ma's church. It's hard to get close to Mary because there were so many people but we wait on the steps by the bakery so we can look down on everything. Ten men carry her on their shoulders looking like they have to stay seriously concentrated not to just buckle under the weight. I get so excited as she appears around the corner like she's floating along the heads of the crowd. At her feet are loads of flowers and her hands are open in front of her as if she's about to catch a giant ball. But it's her face that I really want to see. I've got this thing you see with statues and wondering what they're thinking. Before you're like ok Espe's talking to statues now hear me out. It's just I like to look at their faces frozen in time and wonder what they might be thinking. Oh screw it I can't make it sound any more normal. Anyway I think Mary looked a bit like she might be embarrassed by all the fuss and while she's grateful and all she'd rather be reading a book alone without people lifting her into the air every five minutes.

Everyone in the crowd gasps and crosses themselves when they see her and once she passes we follow the crowds towards the church. Ma looks nervous when she sees the lines of military guys with their guns who I swear weren't here last year. So she takes us through the back alleys where it's quieter and we get to the church ahead of the parade and get a seat. She's pretty smart like that.

After the craziness of Borde it feels so calm in there. I love the feeling of sitting on the wooden benches looking up at the high ceilings with the light shining through the colourful windows. There's not a sound except the echo of people's footsteps. Ma knows lots of people there so she spends ages whispering to them. I look at the amazing paintings on the curved ceiling at the front and think how it must have taken them so long to do all the little details of the people in funny old cloaks.

The place fills up pretty quickly until people are standing around the edges and there isn't a space left. Then Mary arrives through the door drifting down the aisle before being put down at the front and everything goes totally silent. Back then it was the only silence I'd ever known and I swam in those couple of moments of bliss. It's funny how things can change.

Actually the church service is pretty boring to be honest. There's lots of prayers and boring speeches but I like singing the songs. In the boring bits I fill time looking at all the gold statues and carvings until it gets to my favourite bit. Going up to take communion always felt special I'm not really sure why. Credit to Ma she did give me a choice when I was little if I wanted to be baptised but to be honest I only said yes to make her happy and mostly because I knew she'd buy me a new dress to wear which is pretty hilarious.

On the way out Ma gives an extra amount to the collection that she'd saved all year for this service. Why she's giving our money to a massive building covered in statues and gold is beyond me when we could use it to buy a new saucepan to replace the one with the broken handle or get the roof repaired so we didn't have to put the bucket under it when it rained or get some new pillows that actually had some stuffing in them. But Ma says we had Jesus to thank for everything we had so the least we could do was give something back. Where do you even start arguing with that?

Later when we get back we have our Christmas Eve meal with Rosa. We pick up the food we made earlier in the day and take it over to her house and Rosa has got someone to buy her cakes from the bakery so we have dessert too. We all squeeze around her little table and pass around the tamales. Ma starts telling us how she saw some army guys near the market beat up this man who was doing nothing just waiting on the corner. Rosa gives her a look and changes the subject telling us the story about the time I climbed into an oil drum and couldn't get out. Even though I've heard it a million times the way she tells it has us in stitches.

Sometime in the night I wake up and god do I feel ill. I won't go into too much detail but I had to go to the toilets which we normally avoid doing in the dark. I haven't told you about the toilets in Borde have I? Well there were a few different toilet blocks but our closest wasn't far from the central tap. The electric is out so me and Ma are stumbling in the dark just the circle of light around us from Ma's gas lamp the glow of the candles and lamps in people's doorways and Ma holding me up by the arms. I feel so bad that I think I'm going to have to drop my pants and go in the street if we don't get there quickly.

The toilets were in a rougher part of Borde where the houses weren't so well made and people had to live with the smell. For some reason it was worse at night and the smell hits us before we can see them. Normally we only went in the day because the wooden walkway could get slippery and you needed to see what you were doing. But I'd been going there my whole life so I could've found my way up there with my eyes closed. In the day you could see the towering wall in the distance but at night it was just black.

It's quiet and I can feel Ma jumping at the smallest sounds next to me. After all the shootings she's pretty nervous of Borde at night but I'm doubled in pain and not sure which end is going first if you catch my drift.

I'm sure I'm not going to make it but we reach the first door and I grab the lamp and dash in. The toilets were basically a concrete coffin with a hole in the floor that you had to balance over. I take one look at the inside and push my way back out the door what with the floor being completely covered in shit and somehow a bird has got stuck in there and died leaving its feathers everywhere and I'm thinking could there be a worse way to go. Anyway why am I telling you this? Seriously I wish you'd stop me sometimes. So to cut a long story short it was all fine. On the way back we stop at the tap and wash our feet and hands and I don't think I've ever seen Ma so relieved to be home when we finally step through the door. She goes straight and kneels in front of Mary and closes her eyes and prays. I get into bed feeling like the world's going to end which is pretty funny looking back on it.

A couple of nights after Christmas when dinner is done and I've washed the plates in the blue plastic bowl I tell Ma I'm going to see Diego for a bit. Really I'm heading back to the wall to see what it looks like at night. I feel bad lying to Ma but she won't understand. I loved Borde in the dark. Everyone at home eating dinner sitting in doorways and the old guys playing cards sat on the benches opposite the bar and the glow of lamps from the windows. As I walk down the lanes people say hola chica or ciao Espe which gives me a warm happy feeling knowing everyone. It did have a downside because everyone sees you and then next time Ma's out they'd be like

Oh I saw little Espe last night going past our place. Where was she off to so late?

So to cover my tracks I go to the square and ask some people there if they've seen Diego. They hadn't but I knew that they'd say to check at Sancho's bike shop because if it was too dark to play football he was usually there helping out. I loved imagining a detective was following me asking people questions

Hola I'm Detective Ruiz have you seen this girl?

What Espe? Sure she was just here earlier looking for Diego.

Diego?

Yeah Diego Vidal one of Oscar's boys. I told her to check up at Sancho's bikes he's bound to be up there. She headed that way not more than twenty mins ago. Straight up there on the right.

You've been most helpful thank you sir.

Anyone watching sees me head off to Sancho's but just before I reach his workshop I cut down a thin alleyway that joined the lane behind. Everyone called it Rat Alley because there were always rats up there but I never got why everyone hates rats so much.

Did you know rats get lonely and depressed if they don't have friends about and they take care of sick rats in their group? Also they have good memories and play and sleep together although they sometimes attack other rats that aren't part of their group. That remind you of anyone? Makes you think us humans are pretty messed up when we hate something so like us doesn't it.

The problem with Rat Alley was that it flooded a lot and stank. You had to know where to walk so as soon as I step in I push each foot out to the wall then shuffle up with my legs apart so my feet stay dry. Daniela once said she saw a rat as big as a cat in the alley but I know she was lying because once she said her cousin was on tv and it turned out to be bullshit. So I get to the street on the other side and I'm careful not to be seen by hiding in the shadows. Then it's the most dangerous part. I creep past the rubbish piled up behind the bar and to my left is Andrea and Berto's house and Andrea is drinking a cola in her rocking chair so I wait in the dark at the back of the bar where I can hear music coming from inside and someone with one of those laughs that sounds a bit like a scream. I'm just thinking about doubling back when Berto shouts something from inside. Andrea ignores him at first but he shouts again and this time she rolls her eyes and gets up and shuffles in. I waste no time and dash past Andrea's chair still tipping back and forward and from there I sprint across the football pitch and reach the bushes. I bet Detective Ruiz is going to be pretty mystified when he gets to Sancho's! I imagine him stroking his big bushy moustache saying

I just don't understand where she could have got to

she gave us the slip right under our noses.

I'm about to go in when Diego appears next to me making me jump out my skin. He chuckles giving my side a squeeze and asking what I'm up to. I slap him on the shoulder and tell him off for sneaking up on me and because I can't think of an excuse why I'm sneaking about in the bushes at night and we've been friends forever I tell him I found something cool in the bushes and head in.

Rosa said once that a secret is just something we haven't shared with a close friend yet. She was right about a lot of things that lady.

So we head into the bushes me leading the way and thinking it looks a whole lot different in the dark and hoping I can find it and not rip my arms to shreds on the branches. Diego is being his usual self and taking the piss out of me but I ignore it and try to find the spot.

We reach the wall and I point to the hole and tell Diego to look but he can't see it at first so I push him up to it and show him where to look.

Ah yes the Coral Pool I don't get to go there much.

He says like it's the most normal thing in the world. I shove him out the way because I can't wait a minute longer. Lights are twinkling everywhere in the bushes and lining the path that winds through the grass. It looks like a carpet and I so desperately want to go in there and lie down on it. In Borde there wasn't any grass let alone a carpet. It's windy and the small trees are blowing about and each one has a light by the trunk so they're all lit up. I know I'm not telling you anything you don't know but it was just about the most beautiful thing I'd ever seen.

It's a little while before I see anyone but then this couple come along the path not far from the wall and I know it's stupid but I hold my breath worried they'll know we're there. They're both so glamorous. She has long blonde hair and is wearing a sparkly gold dress and high heels that clip clop on the path. She keeps giggling and he has his hand around her back just above her butt which she doesn't seem too bothered about. He's very good looking and has swooshy hair that he keeps pushing back with his free hand and something tells me he's the kind of guy who likes looking in the mirror a lot.

I tap Diego who's standing close to me and we swap places. I just watch his face in the half-light looking for clues of what might be happening and after a bit he starts grinning and whispers for me to look. They're standing not far from us kissing and her hand is across his back and he's just slightly on tiptoes as she's taller which I didn't notice at first. I feel rude watching them so I step back but I can't help but go back for another look. When they stop the man pats her on the bum and she giggles like an idiot and they walk off and Diego pushes me out the way for one last look.

Back then I'd kissed two boys. The first was Sol when we were down by the stream one afternoon. He'd told me he loved me and gave me a wooden bracelet he'd made which I thought was really sweet and he was good looking even though he had that weird head twitch thing which mum told me not to mention around his mum and dad. I asked him about it once and he went quiet and wouldn't look at me so I didn't bring it up again. He held my hand and gently kissed me. It was really nice but I was really nervous in case I was doing it wrong. We'd gone out for a couple of months but Diego teased me all the time that I was going out with the yes man because his twitch looked like he was nodding all the time. He was really mean.

The more nervous Sol was the worse it got so he just nodded away and then got angry with himself. I didn't talk to Diego for a long time. I hated him for a bit. Only a while later after Sol moved away because his dad got a job up north and Diego said sorry did we speak again.

The other boy was Felix. He was two years older than me and lived out by the main road. We go to his house one afternoon when I've finished all Ma's jobs and they've just got a tv and he says I can watch it with him which I'm really excited about because no one I knew had a tv and there might be a show set in America on. We lie on his parent's bed which has a big soft blanket with a wolf on it and watch the film. I know it's stupid but I'm always looking out for Pa in case he's there somewhere in the background walking down the wide streets or getting into those yellow taxis. After a bit Felix starts telling me how gorgeous I am and strokes my hair. Who doesn't want to hear that right? He's older and I didn't think he'd like me so I'm kind of surprised. We kiss and this time I'm not so nervous because I've done it before. But then he puts his hand down my shorts and I have to hit him hard in the face before he'll take it out. As I run back home I try not to cry but the look on his face when his hand was down there really scared me.

You know I've never told anyone about that. I'm not sure why I'm telling you maybe it's just easy to tell someone who doesn't talk back. Felix didn't even look at me after that and when I was around he'd just pretend like I didn't exist which suited me just fine.

Anyway me and Diego stay for a while at the wall watching people walk by and pretending we're off to dinner with them to a posh restaurant with waiters and silver plates.

Diego asks me if we should head back and I say I want one more look through. That's when I see him standing over by the pool. At first he has his back to me but I recognise those shoulders straight away. He turns around and there he is facing me in a smart suit casually smoking a cigarette like he didn't just vanish out of my life. And before I can think I shout out.....Pa!

I clamp my hand over my mouth and tears are rolling down my face and still he's there looking straight at me. I was young when Pa left so I don't remember him that well but I look at his pictures all the time and there's no doubt it's him. This shiver goes all through my body and I want to climb the wall and run to him but it's too high and I start to blubber nonsense and Diego's asking me a million questions.

He gently moves me to the side and looks through. And without looking from the hole he says

The guy by the pool? Wow he's really here?

We swap again and I want that moment to last forever but after a few minutes he stubs out his cigarette in one of the plant pots and strolls away. I'm a total wreck but Diego takes me gently by the shoulders and it's just light enough to see the serious look on his face.

He tells me he'll look for him tomorrow find out what room he is in that sort of thing and not to worry he won't let him leave. I give him a hug and we stay like that for a while with branches poking our sides. That's probably still the longest I've ever hugged anyone for other than Ma but it felt nice.

When we stumble out of the bushes I can see the kiosk opposite the bar is shut and that means it's past ten. Ma always asked me to be back by ten so I knew I was going to be in trouble.

When I get in Ma has her back to me and I know she's really angry when she doesn't turn around or say anything.

I say sorry I'm late as casually as I can but she still doesn't turn around and for a moment I think maybe she's heard Pa's back. I'm so excited that I nearly blurt out about seeing him but we hadn't talked about Pa in a long time. When she finally turns around she looks really upset and asks me in a soft voice where I've been. I tell her I was with Diego but she cuts me off and says Rosa's ill and she'd needed my help but no one could find me. I can't think of anything to say other than sorry and she looks me in the eye for ages like she's making her mind up about something then says she needs to go to bed. I'm feeling guilty and annoyed with myself because normally I'm back in time and I hate it when Ma's upset.

That night I can't sleep. I keep thinking Pa is just the other side of the wall and how I want to see him so badly. I'm freaking out that he might go home again before I can find him. I lie there looking up at the patterns in the wood on the ceiling and try to bring myself down.

The next day I take extra care over the work and do all the jobs around the house so Ma won't be angry. Time passes so slowly and all I can think of is Diego and whether he's found Pa. In my head I keep imagining Pa packing his bags and leaving in a taxi and it gives me this feeling like my heart has fallen into my stomach. Have you ever had that?

When all the work's done I go and see Rosa to check she's ok.

When I get there she's sat up in bed with all her lacy pillows around her reading a book.

She says ciao Angel smiling and pats the end of the bed. I ask her what the book's about and she says it's about how it doesn't matter who we are or where we come from we all need the same things. I tell Rosa I'm not sure about that because Diego tells me the people in the hotel are always really happy and relaxed and smiling. Not like Borde where people shout and get drunk and fight. I don't tell her I've seen them with my own eyes. She says it's not that people look or seem the same but that what they actually need from life is the same. Then she says something that has really stuck with me since then. She tells me that's why when people do bad things you shouldn't feel bad or hate them instead you should try to understand why they did what they did. That's pretty hard to do isn't it? But I've given it some thought and tried it out and once you get through the anger and the pain it does help make sense of things.

I ask her about the Communists who killed Ribaldo surely she hates them? She says she did once but tells me that even they were human beings being scared and all that. She described it like a yawn. When one person yawns then everybody starts right so when people do bad things more people do bad things. It's the same the other way around if you do good things other people will do good things too.

This made sense to me so after that I've tried to always do or say nice things. I figured if I did it enough the world had to eventually be a better place. I'm not sure if I still believe that now things have got complicated but I still want it to be true.

I ask Rosa how she's feeling. She's coughing a lot but she tells me not to worry it's just her lungs aren't what they were. I guess I must be looking really worried because she takes my hand and leans close to look me in the eye. Rosa had lovely brown eyes with bits of gold in them like glitter. You know if you really look closely at people's eyes they're like looking into another universe. Carlos taught me that once. He let me look closely at his eyes and he was right. Mostly people don't like it though because if you look at them too long in the eye they look away and get all funny about it. Once I told Diego about it and he looked for ages at my eyes and said they were pretty amazing. Then we played a fun game with people we came across in El Borde. Every time we saw someone we'd stop and be all polite and get them talking but look them in the eye the whole time and people were so weirded out they didn't know what to do. Diego was really good at the game he'd keep a straight face the whole time. I just got the giggles too much.

Sitting there with Rosa she asks what's bothering me. Rosa was annoying like that. She always knew what you were thinking and it was hard to keep secrets from her. I asked her about it once but she just said she could see some things other people don't see.

I really want to tell her but there was too much at stake. Instead I stare at my hands because when Rosa gets looking you in the eye it's hard not to tell the truth.

93

She's cool about it and just wraps her arms around me and gives me a little poke in the ribs which makes me giggle and I feel a bit better already just being there with her.

Diego was due back about three so I say goodbye to Rosa and go to his house feeling so nervous. When I get there Nibaldo is sitting out front kicking at the dirt. He was fifteen then and always getting in trouble. Just a couple of weeks before he got brought home by the police because they caught him and his mates robbing some homes in Otavalo where all the rich people lived. Oscar was really angry and pushed him over and he smacked the back of his head and there was blood in his hair. Diego said his dad was so angry because he had to pay the police one week's money from driving his taxi.

Nibaldo was more serious than Diego's other brothers so I never quite knew what he'd be like but I say hi and ask if Diego is home.

He says no without looking up so I go to the square to wait for him there. I sit by the tree watching people walk by feeling more and more nervous and picking at my nails. After a bit I see Alicia with her mum rushing through. I shout hi and Alicia stops and her Ma says something I can't hear but I can tell they're arguing but she comes over anyway.

She asks what I'm doing and I tell her I'm just waiting for Diego. There's a bit of an awkward silence where she stands for a bit and doesn't say anything and I'm too distracted to make conversation so I tell her to

94

sit with me. She looks like a bag of nerves as usual but then sits and her mum seeing this scuttles off with those big bags under her eyes.

I smile and she smiles back and I notice how bad her teeth are all yellow and that one missing at the top. Ma always told me to brush my teeth every day no matter what which is looking like excellent advice from where I'm sitting.

I'm so full of worry I burst out and tell her everything about the night before and she sits and listens without saying a word. She starts to say something when Diego comes whistling around the corner wearing his brown hotel uniform carrying two white fluffy towels like it was the most normal thing in the world. I abandon Alicia and run to him.

Did you find him? I blurt out my heart thumping in my ears.

Find who? He replies with that cheeky look in his eye. Seriously I could have killed him. I must have looked really annoyed because he tells me he found him sat in the piano bar this morning and followed him back to Room 2753. I start blurting all sorts of questions at him but he takes me by the shoulders and tells me he spoke to Lucas on reception who told him he's staying for another three nights. Then he says the words I'm so desperate to hear

So... let's go and find him together.

I scream in excitement and give him a massive hug and kiss him on the cheek.

Remind me to take you to the hotel more often he says so I punch him hard on the arm.

Alicia has edged over and is standing still looking awkward so I tell her the good news. Diego backs away and poor Alicia looks like a balloon with a hole in it. Without giving a shit about her feelings Diego tells me I shouldn't hang around her because she's infected and if I get too close I'll get infected too and then I'll die and so will everyone I know which when you think about it is practically the meanest thing he could say.

Alicia looks like she's going to cry or just crumble to dust and sways for a bit before turning and running.

I shout at Diego and then run after her and he just looks confused like he has no idea what he's done. Even though I'm a pretty fast runner I can't find her she's disappeared into the lanes. So after a while I walk back to the square and Diego's still there talking to some people outside the bar. He looks like he's telling one of his stories so I sit back on the wall and try to calm down.

After a bit he sees me and comes over and can see I'm angry so sits next to me and says nothing for a bit. Diego's never been good at silence so he starts again telling me how I really shouldn't hang out with her but this time in a soft voice like that's going to bring me around. Seriously! I practically lose it shouting at him and generally make a scene so everyone outside the bar is staring at me.

I'm on my feet and taking deep breaths and feeling

so angry I just want to break everything.

Diego holds his hand in the air with those two beautiful towels looking stupidly out of place on his lap. He says he's just looking out for me and that I should be careful because if you get TB it's a horrible slow death. The more he talks the more angry I get until I kick those fucking towels off his lap in fury and run. Running is still the only way I know to calm down so I bolt down random lanes pushing past people sweat and tears mixing and dripping off my nose. But he gets me thinking. What if he's right and I'm the reason Rosa's sick?

I find myself at the stream just before the wasteland and I sit on the mound in the dirt all puffed out. Over to the left I can see the overpass stretching into the distance packed with traffic as always. To the right is the patch of open ground where we got the tyres and next to that the hotel wall runs along and then bends to the right. The stream isn't exactly mountain fresh and runs all the way from the source a massive pipe in the side of the wall we found when we were kids. We had grand plans to break into the hotel through the pipe until we got there and found a solid metal grill blocking our path. Back then I didn't think anything of it but when you think it over that place was pretty out of order dumping all their shitty water in Borde.

A few minutes later Diego appears looking all sheepish. I don't know how he knew I'd be there. We played this game a few times where we'd give different bits of rubbish in the stream points and try to hit them with stones. My best shot ever was when we gave this plastic cup that was on its side 25 points to hit it or 100 points if the stone went inside. On my first go I acted all casual and said yeah no worries and just calmly chucked the stone and it landed perfectly in the cup with a splash. I pretend like it was nothing but Diego jumped to his feet and said I was the coolest girl he'd ever met which made me think he hadn't met many girls.

So he sits next to me and swats away the flies before picking up a stone and saying 75 points for the scary doll pointing down at the toy with no eyes and burn marks where hair should be. He throws a stone that falls short and splashes into the water before trying again knowing I won't be able to resist. So we sit for a while chucking stones and not talking.

Finally Diego says sorry and says let's talk about the plan for tomorrow and I nod but can't quite look at him yet. He tells me to go to the east staff entrance at twelve the next day and wait at the top of the drive by the bushes. He says a man called Sergio who drives the van delivering Pepsi will stop and pick me up and take me to a store area under the kitchens where Diego will meet me. After that the plan is to sneak into the cupboard where they keep the mops and for me to get changed into a cleaner's uniform.

Then for the most dangerous part. Avoiding the lift we have to take the back stairs and hope no staff see us and get to the cleaner's store where a woman called

Julia will meet us and smuggle me in her trolley to room 2753. All we have to do is wait for Pa to come back to his room and mission complete.

As he runs through the plan Diego's drawing lines in the dirt with a stick mapping it all out in the dust. I'm basically shit scared of every part of that plan but he makes it all sound so routine I hold it together and feel a tingle of excitement that tomorrow could be the day I see Pa again.

The sun beats down the mist, and the temperature rises. Towering poplars that line the fields whisper in the breeze. At their feet wild flowers scatter a sweet smell of blossom amongst the long grass. To the right of a cluster of farm buildings three horses, necks dropped to grass, amble their way across the field. Above them, perched on the red tiled roof of a simple wooden barn, the brightly coloured bird diligently pecks at its feathers. Abruptly he lifts his head and listens motionless, before returning to his work. Somewhere nearby, a dog barks and he dashes away on delicate wings over a concrete yard, through a small orchard (branches heavy with fruit) until he reaches the edge of a large field that curves away into the valley.

Landing on the roof of a tired tractor, he drinks from rain collected amongst the rust. Something catches his eye through the faded levers and he drops down to balance on the steering wheel. Much of the seat's padding has broken away, but sandwiched between perished foam a glint of gold catches the light. Turning his head, he looks closely for a moment before hopping closer and pulling at the diminutive gold cross but it stays wedged where it is. He tries again without success, the metal reflecting in the glossy black pools of his eyes.

On a Saturday morning towards the end of January, Alex struck out early to find some breakfast. His shoes echoed off the pavement as he passed a doorway where a thinning Christmas tree lay drunk on its side, centrepiece to forgotten in two swift weeks.

He'd given himself the day off as he was flying out to Athens on Sunday night. It was early, the streets were deserted except for a lone street cleaner who ambled along in a filthy fluorescent jacket and a flimsy pair of headphones balanced on the top of his black beanie hat. A biting wind whipped against Alex's face as he headed towards Exmouth Market, the weak winter sun attempting to push through the mist. Hands deep in the pockets of his cashmere coat, he tried to push work from his mind.

Stopping briefly, he studied himself in a car window and frowned, wondering if he should bring his fortnightly hair appointment forward. As the shadow of age grew, Alex's attempts to stay in the sun grew more desperate. Despite his disdain of anything to do with sport, he'd bought a state of the art home gym to improve his sagging physique. The thought of sweating and exercising with others turned his stomach, but at home (in the quiet of the spare room) he'd built it into his routine; although he wouldn't admit it to himself he was quite enjoying it.

Exmouth Market was just waking up. A squat man unloaded boxes from a white unmarked lorry, whilst a woman with a cigarette between her lips, dressed all in denim, swept the street outside the cafe on the corner. Alex pushed open the door to the café that was empty except for an elderly man who sat stooped in his thick coat and Russian style winter hat. He ordered breakfast and settled on one of the wooden mismatched chairs at a table facing the street. To fill the time Alex scrolled through his news feed, reading about another car factory closure and yet more misery on the international markets. He snapped his head up in alarm as the man, who'd been sat in the corner, sat lightly in the seat opposite. Unsure what to say, Alex just stared at him, unable to pull his gaze away from what looked like flakes of croissant in his wild salt and peppered beard. He wasn't as old as Alex had first thought. Laying both his fingerless glove clad hands on the table, he stared unblinkingly across at Alex with sharp pale blue eyes.

'Mmm, it's going to get interesting now, isn't it?!' he chuckled to himself, never breaking eye contact.

Alex, unnerved by the invasion of his space looked

away, only to find those eyes still contemplating him.

'What...?' Alex eventually managed, pulling his bag into his lap.

'You can't keep ignoring it, although you've done a pretty good job so far, I'll give you that.' he replied, smiling at Alex and running a hand through his unwashed hair.

He was dressed like a tramp, his clothes threadbare, dirt collecting under his long nicotine stained fingernails. He held himself with the swagger of a man thoroughly content with himself. Clearly, the man was out of his mind. Alex was accustomed to the scripted routine of slipping away from such characters. As he began to rise apologetically, a cheery woman arrived at his side.

'Eggs Florentine on sourdough and a flat white?' she said in a Bulgarian accent.

He hovered over his chair unable to pick up his bag, coat and breakfast, and unwilling to sacrifice any of them.

Unimpressed at being ignored, she tutted under her breath and dutifully slid his breakfast onto the table.

'Look, if you don't mind I'd just like to eat my breakfast in peace.' Alex said, pulling himself together.

'Peace...not easy to find, as you'd know as well as anyone.' The man said dreamily, showing no intention of moving and picking at something between his stained teeth, 'But why her? That's the fascinating part of it all, don't you think? I suppose you couldn't just keep traipsing around the world, shut uptight and expect nothing to happen.'

This last comment made Alex look up sharply from his steaming breakfast.

'What do you want?' Alex inquired, his stomach rumbling expectantly but his food sitting untouched in front of him.

'I'm just a man making conversation Alex, one fellow man to another. It's called connection and pretty common throughout the world.' He clucked nonchalantly, taking a sip of Alex's coffee before replacing it carefully back in its saucer. Leaning back in his chair, as if he were sat in his own front room, he continued, 'What you or I want is neither here or there my friend. The thickest and tallest walls are built to keep it out but you can't keep out what's already in now, can you?'

'How do you know my name?' Alex croaked, numbness seeping into his fingers. The weathered face in front of him was puzzlingly familiar, as if they'd met many years ago, and he couldn't quite locate the memory.

'You told me.' he replied matter of factly.

'But...,' was all Alex managed, losing grip on the conversation and looking pale in the face.

'Look, don't be too hard on yourself now, it's just the way some things pan out, who knows where all this comes from, no one knows is the honest truth. But it's bound to come to a head at some point, all rivers lead out to sea as you old Stanley would always say.'

Alex's eyes darted to meet those opposite him but his head was swimming and he began to feel hot and a little faint. Frantically he rose, knocking his chair over behind him as he snatched at his coat. He searched for his bag before realising he was clutching it to his chest like a rag doll.

'You're not going already are you? Here sit down and have your breakfast.' the stranger said pushing the plate towards him, 'You don't look too well fella.'

Alex staggered back bumping into a squat table piled with various board games. A simple black box with Cards Against Humanity written on it clattered loudly to the floor but he made no move to pick it up. Suddenly he was aware a classical song he recognised was playing, he couldn't remember which film he knew it from. Something didn't seem right, it was too loud, the woman's operatic voice soared filling his ears. Why had they suddenly turned the music up? He looked towards the counter for some explanation but the lady who had brought his breakfast stood motionless staring at him. Was it him or were none of them blinking? Everything seemed curiously still with the exception of his dishevelled companion who, eyes closed in apparent bliss, swayed his arms aloft as if conducting an orchestra. The enchanting voice continued to fill his ears as the sun slipped from behind a cloud, illuminating the steam from his breakfast. The delicate columns appear to twist and turn in time to the music.

Panicked, Alex turned to the door but felt as if he were walking through water. It seemed to take an age to reach it, numbness bursting into his finger tips. He yanked the door towards him, the music stopping instantly as he stumbled out, gulping down cool air.

Only when he reached the busy Farringdon Road did he stop on the edge of the curb, drawing in deep breaths. A red double decker bus pulled up in front of him so close he could have reached out and touched it. He searched about himself before remembering he'd put it in the inner pocket of his jacket. In his hand, the weight of the coin began to calm his tempestuous pulse as he flipped it methodically between his fingers.

After a few minutes, he calmed, the brick buildings coming back into focus. Suddenly he felt furious with himself. How had he been tricked so easily? He prided himself on being a tough competitor, it was part of what made him so good at his job, calm, charming but no-nonsense. Turning purposely he began striding back to the cafe, rehearsing what he would say to put him in his place. Pushing open the door a little too forcefully so it slammed against the wall (raised eyebrows from a woman in her fifties emptying a third sugar into her coffee), he found himself staring at an empty table. The man was nowhere to be seen. All that remained was his rapidly cooling breakfast and a half drunk coffee.

Legs planted like an oil rig, he stood for what felt like an eternity, while the staff behind the counter eyed him suspiciously. Colour flushing through his cheeks, he sat down, his hand trembling as he attempted to lift his knife and fork. He pushed away the plate after one mouthful; he couldn't face it. Too ashamed to get up again so soon he pulled out his phone and pretended to study it. He felt dizzy and confused, what had just happened? How on earth had that man known his name? How had he known Grandpa's name?

Reaching into his bag, he pulled out the small bottle, flipped the lid and dropped an oval shaped pill into his palm. He slipped it into his mouth and washed it down with a now cold coffee. The sleeping pills from his mother had helped him to sleep but made him far too drowsy. After a bit of internet research, he'd bought a whole load of anti-anxiety drugs that stated they also helped with sleeping. The first brand he'd tried made him feel thirsty all the time, the next one seemed to do nothing, but this current batch seemed decent. He was sleeping better and Alex had noticed his mind was much calmer after taking them.

Closing his eyes, he breathed deeply. He began running through his work calendar and task lists, checking over details in an attempt to push the harrowing encounter from his mind. Each task was broken down into a number of segments so he could keep track of exactly where he was with each one. The order of the system pleased him and he was dedicated to leaving nothing to chance.

After a while, deciding he couldn't sit at the table a minute longer, he rose and left the cafe without looking back. It felt good to be on the move, fresh air in his lungs, the winter sun on his face. He marched straight past his building in the direction of Farringdon station, upping the pace and taking a random left turn up a narrow street. At the end of the road, he turned right alongside a large window displaying high-end designer furniture. An elegantly curved armchair that somehow reminded Alex of a long legged bird, made him pause. It would look excellent in the living room, he thought to himself, turning on his heel and heading through the entrance. He didn't ask how much it was, cutting the salesman off pre-pitch, asking only when it could be delivered. Five minutes later he was back on the street. He felt better, he noted, much better.

Alex sat on the sofa in his office reading a 150 page report under the glow of a lamp. At some point, it had got dark but he couldn't remember when. This was his favourite time of the day, when the office cleared out except for a few cleaning staff. Sometimes he would walk around the building breathing in the tranquillity, no phones ringing, no one asking him questions. Once when visiting the main concourse, a darkened large open space that smelt of new carpet and plastic, he'd sat at a random desk and closed his eyes. He'd felt a deep sense of peace, just the sound of machines and the faint rush of traffic in the streets beyond. He'd stayed there a while, sat in a state of meditation, listening to the rhythmic click of the air-conditioning. When he'd opened his eyes, a worried looking woman in her fifties was staring at him, the vacuum cleaner limp in her hand. Embarrassed, he'd bolted out of the chair, hearing the sound of the vacuum igniting behind him. He was sharply interrupted from his reading by the appearance of Phil at his door.

'Golden Boy, still here I see.' he said, dropping heavily into Alex's chair behind his desk. He picked up a stone carving of a dragon that had been a gift from one of Alex's Chinese colleagues, and weighed it in his hand.

'Seeing as it's gone seven-thirty, can I pull you away from here for a drink? I've told Lisa I'm on a late one.' he quipped, winking at Alex.

Phil, in his forties, balding and with a love for mid-afternoon biscuits that was beginning to show, worked downstairs in finance. They'd met a couple of years back when working on a project together and he was now the closest thing to a friend that Alex had. On the face of it they were a strange mix; Phil, married and up to his eyeballs in kids, appeared to have little in common with Alex. There was something though in each others lives that was fascinating and alluring.

'I can't, I've not finished this report and I'm meeting the panel next Tuesday.' Alex replied apologetically.

'That's bullshit, get your coat.' Phil commanded, walking around the desk, snatching the report from Alex's hands and throwing it onto the sofa.

Alex sighed and glanced at his watch. 'Alright, meet me in the lobby in five.'

'That's the spirit!' Phil grinned, slipping out the door. Alex placed the report back on his desk, straightened his stationery and took his coat from the stand. Pulling it on he walked over to his floor to ceiling window and peered down at the street. There he was, looking straight up at him with a wry smile, same scruffy coat and hat, hand raised in a mock salute. Alex stumbled back, smacking his leg painfully on the desk and landing on the carpet. He tore at his coat, feeling hot and finding it hard to breathe. He scrambled back up on to the sofa and heaved in deep breaths. Tentatively, he got to his feet and inched his way back to the window where he stared down at an empty pavement.

'Fuck.' Alex muttered to himself, his hands shaking.

Pulling open the bottom drawer of his desk, he grabbed his bottle of pills and snatched at the lid. A deep sense of unease crept under his skin and he couldn't shake the feeling he needed to get away. He shook a few pills into his hand and swallowed them down with some water, grabbed his coat and lurched to the door.

'You ok buddy? You look like you saw a ghost!' Phil joked as Alex arrived in the lobby, sweat beading at his brow.

'I'm alright; just need a drink, come on.' Alex replied, heading out the building without waiting. He looked up and down the street but there was no sign of the man. Jogging to keep up Phil eyed him closely, 'You sure you're alright? You don't look too shit hot.'

'I'm fine.' Alex puffed irritably.

They walked side by side, hands deep in their pockets to fight back the cold. It was dry but a penetrating wind whipped down the office-lined street. A steady stream of traffic crawled at walking pace to their right giving the air a metallic grit.

They reached Vagabonds, a cosy bar tucked down a side street. Walking in off the street the place seemed tiny; just a few tables and a bar made of an old copper water tank at the far end. But downstairs was a sprawling cellar with booths and tables under the brick arches. Relieved to be out of the cold they headed straight to the bar, sidestepping three smartly dressed middle-aged women deep in conversation. Guiding their drinks down the spiral stairs, they settled in a curved booth tucked away to the left of the old cellar.

'What do you make of everything going on in Europe? You're in with those at the top, are any jobs going to go?'

'I'm sure it'll be fine...' Alex mumbled absent mindedly.

'I really can't lose this job right now, not with the price of my mortgage.'

Swiping the tapas menu to one side and resting on his elbows he studied Alex.

'You sure you're alright mate? You seem miles away.'

'It's nothing really, I feel a bit stupid to be honest.'

'No go on, tell Uncle Phil.'

Alex shifted in his seat awkwardly.

'It's just this strange man approached me the other day.'

'Right?' Phil encouraged, drawing lines in the

condensation on his pint glass.

'Yeah, he sat at my table whilst I was having breakfast last weekend, and just started talking to me like we'd known each other our whole lives or something. But the weirdest thing was he knew my name and he mentioned my grandfather's name too.'

He felt foolish telling Phil and wondered if he'd think he was making too much of it.

'Sounds like a total fruit cake if you ask me. You get all sorts in London don't you; mind you that doesn't explain how he knew your name or your Grandfather's.'

'Exactly! That's the bit that's been bothering me. But then I saw him again just now as I was leaving the office.'

'When, in the street? I didn't see him.'

'No, just as I was leaving the office I looked out the window and he was there, looking straight back up at me from the street. Scared the shit out of me.'

'Blimey.' Phil said, stroking his goatee beard thoughtfully, 'Maybe he's your long lost brother you never knew you had, that your mum secretly gave away when she was young. He's spent a lifetime tracking you down, watching your every move, the brother living the life he never had!'

'Come on, seriously though Phil, he had this look in his eye like he knew everything about me, it was very disarming.' Alex replied, whilst tidying the sugar sachets that sat in a glass in the middle of the table.

'Exactly you see, he's been watching you for years.

He knows where you live, where you work, he's just been biding his time, waiting for the right moment to approach you!' Phil laughed heartily, running a hand over his bald head.

Alex rolled his eyes and downed his wine, 'Same again?' he asked, heading for the steps, not waiting for an answer.

Upstairs was still quiet. At the bar he was met by a confident, young barman. Alex couldn't help but feel irritated by the very sight of him. Unsmiling he ordered the drinks, turned his back and leaned on the bar. Out the front window, he caught sight of a figure loitering outside in the gloom. Half spooked, half angry, he clattered outside. Looking around wildly, he saw no one, the street was empty except for a white plastic bag that cartwheeled down the middle of the street.

'For fuck's sake Alex, pull yourself together,' he lectured himself, before returning to the confused barman.

When he returned, Phil was punching at his phone, his brow creased in concentration. Feeling listless and edgy Alex placed the drinks on the table and wondered when the pills would kick in. Phil dropped his phone into his coat pocket and mumbled an apology.

'Before I forget, we're having a barbecue on the 12th if you can make it? I'm forty would you believe.' Phil said, taking his drink from Alex.

He handed him a neatly printed invitation card. Alex had never met Phil's family, in fact they'd never met other than at work or in this bar. Before he'd thought anything of it he said, 'I'd be honoured to come.'

Phil looked pleased and took a sip of his pint.

'Lisa's looking forward to meeting you too, I'm sure she doesn't even believe that you exist!'

Alex was surprised, he'd never even considered that Phil might have mentioned him to his family.

'It'll be nice to meet her too.'

Phil talked about Lisa a lot. Several times he'd told him the story of how they first met, a well rehearsed and polished performance that was as good to listen to even on the third outing. A younger and trimmer Phil had been playing trumpet in the Camden Symphony Orchestra at the time (an instrument that was now gathering a considerable amount of dust in the loft) when Lisa had come to watch their summer outdoor performance in Victoria Park. Less than an hour before they were due to start, Phil suddenly realised he'd left his trumpet in the cafe where he'd had lunch. As it turns out Lisa arrived with Sam (her housemate) shortly after and spotted the black case leaning against the wall in the corner. Having tickets for the show, they skipped coffee to take the instrument up to the park on the off chance. As luck would have it they met an out of breath, panicked Phil at the entrance to the park who stopped in his tracks, 'having seen the most beautiful woman I'd ever seen stood there holding my trumpet,' as Phil put it. When Lisa tells the story she jokes that it was the beginning of a lifetime looking after her absent minded husband.

'Turning forty, that's a big one.' Alex said, to suppress his panicked thoughts of how turning forty was only seven years away.

'I'm trying not to think about it too much but I think I've probably got to admit I'm not young any more. Unlike you my baby faced friend.'

Alex raised a brief smile. 'No girlfriend at the moment.'

'What happened to that barmaid....what was her name, Mary?'

'Maddy.'

'Yeah her, last time we had a drink you were taking her out the night after.'

'We had fun but nothing more than that really.'

'You didn't like her or she didn't like you?'

This was one of the reasons they'd become friends, Phil bulldozed through Alex's resistance oblivious to his awkward discomfort.

'She was only here for a few months then went back to the States.' Alex replied hoping he would drop it.

'Yeah long distance never works does it. Years ago I met a girl on a holiday in France. Lovely she was. We told each other the distance didn't matter and all that but it can't have been more than a month before we stopped contacting each other.'

They talked for a while longer but Alex began to feel weary and as the conversation withered, he made his excuses. Stepping out into the cold they shook hands, bid each other goodnight and walked away in different directions.

Throughout the next day, Alex felt rattled and edgy, jumping when he failed to notice Olivia approaching his desk, much to her amusement. Unable to stop himself he kept returning to the window and, convinced the pills weren't working, turned to the internet for alternatives. He clicked into one of the many sites selling prescription drugs and hovering over the various categories selected 'Anti-Anxiety'. There were plenty to choose from and he didn't have the energy to read about each one, so picked five at random and ordered five boxes of each on next day delivery. His body felt weak, as if gravity were too much for it. However much he tried to push it to one side he couldn't shake the feeling he was sliding, some unseen momentum dragging him down, like the room had suddenly been tipped to one side.

In an afternoon meeting, only when Sue Palmer from Health (hair like a manicured hedge) had nudged his arm did he come crashing back into the room, a circle of expectant faces pointed in his direction.

'Err I'm sorry...' Alex mumbled, flustered, looking for a clue in their faces.

'The Nagoya contract.' Clayton prompted, pushing his pen into the dimple of his chin.

After the meeting Clayton cornered him, waiting until just the two of them stood around the oval table.

'Everything alright Alex?'

'Yeah sure, sorry about that, a million miles away.' Alex conceded, tucking his chair under the table.

Clayton considered him for a second before adding: 'We're not putting too much on you are we? You would say wouldn't you? You've always been efficiency personified but every man has his limits.'

'No honestly, I'm fine.' Alex replied, making himself turn to look him in the eye. 'Just a little trouble sleeping of late.'

'Well, if you say so, but remember there's no shame in taking a little time off if needed. Just say the word.'

'Appreciate that Andrew, thanks.'

Clayton hesitated by the door momentarily, smiled weakly and slipped out.

Alex emailed him from the taxi on the way home, and received a quick short reply saying he could take as long as he needed. He was struck by the simplicity of something he hadn't even considered. Arriving home feeling a little better, he was pleased with himself for taking control of the situation. Two days rest, some sleep and he'd be back to his normal self, he had been working hard of late. Having eaten a Japanese salad, he flicked on the tv and watched for a while.

Later, he got ready for bed, it was still early but he was spent. He took a double dose of the sleeping pills his mother had given him, he couldn't face another night watching the clock.

Wrapped in his duvet like a child he woke with a

start, a thin strip of sunlight cut through his curtains, slicing his room in half. He was consumed with a feeling of despair from a dream. He'd been in a tall industrial building that towered over a half demolished jumble of buildings below. Sunshine streamed through small dirty windows on one side of the room and the crumbling remains of office furniture lay around him. He wasn't alone, a woman was there that he didn't recognise, but in the dream he seemed to know her. She was stood still by a closed door on the opposite wall.

Alex watched as she opened the door, a gust of wind whipping her dark hair about her shoulders. She stepped deliberately to the door frame and he saw that the door opened to nothing, just a vast drop to the ruined buildings below. Although all of this must have taken just seconds, the dream had a slowed quality about it. Alex had felt his legs begin to move as he stepped around the desk towards her. For a few seconds she balanced perfectly on the edge, as if admiring the view beyond. Then without warning she gently leaned forward, dropping away without a word.

That night it takes me ages to get to sleep. I keep running through the plan in my head. Over and over again I practice what I'll say to Pa and keep panicking that he won't recognise me or be gone before I get there.

The next day I struggle to keep my hands steady as I work through my sewing. I'm terrified I'll make a mistake and not get things done for eleven-thirty but finally I get it all done. At the last minute I grab the picture of me and Pa and put them in the top pocket of my shirt. Then I race down to the north entrance and wait behind the bushes.

So there I am a bundle of sweat and nerves crouched behind a bush and I'm thinking if anyone spots me they'll blatantly think I'm taking a shit which is just delightful. I'm early but every time I hear a car I peer through the branches to see if it's my ride. I've been there a while and still no Sergio just lots of staff walking up and down the road and one truck but it doesn't stop and anyway it has Gomez Carniceros in big blue letters on the side. I've nearly picked off all my nails when the Pepsi truck pulls up right in front of me and a short man in a stained t-shirt jumps out with a big grin on his face like we're off for a day trip to the beach not on a mission to find my long lost father.

Epse!!

He says like we were old friends and shakes my sweaty hand. I can't help staring at his beard which is the biggest I've ever seen in my life and fills most of his face and looks like it might start getting in his eyes soon if he doesn't get it under control.

He tells me to follow him and leads me around the back of the truck and opens the back door so I can climb in amongst the crates. He apologises for the darkness but says it'll only take five minutes to get there. I nod trying to look brave. It's cool inside at least and smells of plastic. I sit down with my back to some crates and watch the daylight disappear. Once inside I can't even see my legs in front of me but I keep calm by running my finger along the edge of the photo over and over. The engine starts and we get going and all I have to go on is my hearing which is a new experience.

Soon we stop again and with the engine still running I hear Sergio joking with someone which I guess must be the security guards at the gate. We lurch off again so quickly I hit the back of my head on a crate but feel relieved we're on our way. Sergio's right it isn't long before we stop and I wait and wait for him to open the back door but there's nothing except the ticking noise from the truck. I stand to stretch my legs and then sit again trying to pretend I'm not freaking the hell out. About a second before I start climbing the walls I hear voices and then Sergio pulls open the doors but it's so bright I cover my eyes and I can't see anything for what feels like forever. When I finally get used to the light Sergio and Diego help me down and we're in this massive concrete sloping yard that has a huge open store next to it that goes under the buildings. Diego shakes hands with Sergio like older men do and he shouts good luck to me as Diego leads the way into the store that's packed with boxes and crates all neatly piled up everywhere.

I follow Diego to the left past a wooden crate with giant cans of tomatoes stacked to double my height and we reach a white door. The room is full of buckets with mops upside down in them and shelves packed with big rolls of toilet paper. From behind one of the buckets Diego grabs a plastic bag and passes it to me. Inside is a neatly folded grey uniform that is quite obviously way too big for me but sometimes I'm not such an idiot that I don't know when to keep my mouth shut and be grateful. He turns away and I quickly change and although I have to roll up the trouser legs I like the feeling of the uniform.

Diego tells me if we meet anyone to let him do the talking and he looks the most serious I've ever seen him so I nod and take a deep breath. He slowly opens the door peering through the gap. There's this humming noise filling the room and so many crates of food that I can't help thinking it could feed everyone in Borde for a year. We dash quickly behind one of them before sneaking a look to see if all is quiet. I think this would be really exciting if I wasn't shitting myself so much.

We keep going before pausing again by another crate stacked with giant bags of rice and Diego points silently to the door at the far end of the room three more rows down. We reach the last row of crates and wait because we can hear some voices but they're far off and soon disappear. Then it's silent again and all I can hear is my own heartbeat and that low hum. Diego sticks his head out to check and gives me the signal to follow but we've only taken a few steps from the last crate when the door in front of us begins to open. Like lunatics we scramble back and jump behind the crate again and Diego trips over my leg and falls on top of me. What a right pair of pros. We don't dare move as the men chat and make jokes and I hold my breath until I'm sure they're gone. I'm actually really good at holding my breath. We once had a competition to see who could hold it the longest in this metal tub of water and I came second and I was the youngest. Diego's brother Victor won. He kept his head under so long everyone got all scared that he might be dead.

Here look I'll show you. Ready.....

Not
bad
hey.
Hang on
let me catch my breath.

Anyway where was I? Oh yeah so we wait a bit until it's silent and then try again and this time we get through the doors and head up the stairs. We run up them on tiptoes until I see Level 4 on a sign and Diego pushes open the door looking back at me to smile and bumps straight into a thin old leathery skinned man coming the other way.

Diego amigo where are you off to in such a hurry?

The man asks folding his arms and I think oh great we've blown it already. Diego goes all polite and apologises and then starts talking to him about plants and flowers. This does the trick as the old man looks less serious straight away and begins rambling on and I haven't got a clue what they're on about but I just keep quiet and hope he doesn't notice me. Diego listens carefully and asks questions like

Isn't that coming into flower this month?

The man's eyes are all watery and he wears a bright green all in one overall. It isn't long before Diego has him laughing and smiling and the old man looks at him like he's his long lost grandson or something and says how Diego really should join the garden team and how they need someone with his passion and I'm left wondering just how he does it. The old guy coughs into a grey handkerchief and then seems to notice me for the first time.

He apologises and asks who I am. Diego gives him the nonsense story about being a new cleaner even though I must clearly look like a child in an oversized uniform but he seems to buy it.

He bangs on about Diego being a good boy and always looking after people and tells me I'm in safe hands here and the whole time Diego is playing along pretending to be modest although we all know he's anything but.

Finally the old gardener leaves and Diego lets out a

big sigh of relief. We head down a long corridor with doors either side and I ask him where all the guests are but he tells me we're just in the bit where the staff sleep. I can't believe how big the place is. Before that the biggest building I'd been in was my old school and that was tiny compared to this.

We reach a door like all the others and Diego stops and pulls a plastic card out of his pocket that he just taps on the door and it opens. And even though we were supposed to be keeping out of sight and all I wasn't letting that bit of wizardry slide so I grab it off him and have a go myself. Inside is dark but Diego finds the light switch and I see we're in another storeroom with no windows but this one is much bigger and has cleaners trolleys parked side by side taking up most of the space. Diego points to Julia's trolley standing by the left wall and I don't say what I'm thinking which is how on God's earth am I supposed to hide in that. He opens the little cupboard door on its side and pulls out two cans of fizzy orange and hands me one and we slump down against the wall to wait.

The drink goes down a treat and I reckon Diego must have seen me looking over at the cleaning trolley because he says don't worry they're bigger than they look. He opens up the bottom cupboard which is empty and in fairness there is more room than I expected. Diego sees me looking all nervous about getting in but says he's sorry as even with the uniform we can't risk walking that far across the hotel. I ask why this woman

127

is helping us as I didn't know her and I'm a bit worried she'll change her mind or tell on me at the last minute. He tells me that she owes him a favour. Of course I should have guessed.

Rosa sometimes called Diego El Encantador and said a starving man would happily give his last grain of rice to that silver tongue. Actually I think Diego is more likely to help that man trade those last grains for a pair of sunglasses that Diego then sells to an American tourist for ten dollars as he's giving him a made up tour of the city which he's charged him thirty dollars for and it happens to stop at the starving man's shack who Diego has told the tourist is a local shaman and for another ten dollars he'll tell his future. All of which leaves the starving man with ten dollars for a few grains of rice and indebted to the selfless wonder boy who's made himself three times as much!

Julia doesn't come for a while so we sit on the cool floor and Diego asks me what I remember about my Pa. The truth is not much but I tell him about my favourite memory. This one day where we all went together with Abuelita to this park where we used to live. I was pretty young but I remember we took a picnic and we sat on the grass by this massive lake and there were flamingos in the water. It's all a bit hazy because I must have been three or something but I remember feeling so happy us being together as a family everyone relaxed and laughing and having a good time.

I'm about to say more when the door opens and we

both jump to our feet. Julia's very pretty with a wide smile and long straight hair and she's wearing lots of makeup and gold jewellery and when she hugs Diego one of her gold hoop earrings gets caught in his hair. She hugs me like we're friends already and I'm finding it pretty difficult not to look at her massive breasts seeing as they're spilling all over the place.

Diego's completely embarrassing himself laughing at everything she says and constantly looking at her. It's obvious he totally has the hots for her. I don't quite get why she's flirting right back seeing as he's just a kid but I guess she's loving the attention. I start to feel really annoyed because they're wasting time and I want to find my dad. I must look angry because Julia takes one look at me and cuts it out getting the trolley ready instead. She opens the doors and I squeeze inside and there isn't much room but I'm ready to do anything to see Pa again. Julia explains that it's quite far to reach the room as it's in another part of the hotel and as she closes the doors she says she'll try not to go over too many bumps. And I'm thinking here I go again for the second time in one day bumping along in the dark.

Julia's right it takes ages and by the time we get to the room I can't feel my arm any more. She whispers to me that we've arrived and then I hear the sound of a door opening and they wheel me in and everything's quiet. Diego opens the doors and helps me out.

I'm stood in the most beautiful room I've ever seen in my life. The floor is cool shiny marble and there's this bed almost as big as the room me and Ma share at home. On the wall is a massive tv and everything is so amazingly clean. There isn't a speck of dirt in the place and it's like it's just been made ten minutes ago. I stand there just staring feeling grubby and disgusting compared to that place. The end of the room's all window and through it is a balcony that looks out over the beautiful gardens and pools. It wasn't the same pool I could see from the wall so I turn to Diego and Julia amazed and ask how many pools there are. He says there are four if you include the kids one as if this were the most normal thing ever.

Julia has to go as she has other rooms to clean so I thank her and as she leaves the room I watch her wiggling bottom in her tight leggings and wonder if she practices that walk in front of a mirror at home. I notice Diego watching her too and he looks a bit embarrassed and starts telling me about the room. He shows me the bathroom that has this huge bath the shape of a shell and these holes at the side that make bubbles when you're in it. On a shelf there's piles of big fluffy towels and all sorts of bottles and soaps and above the bath these different coloured lights that change colour on their own. Diego says this is mood lighting for when you're in the bath. I ask him what the hell is mood lighting but he ignores me shows me the toilet instead that flushes like magic when you put your hand in front of this tiny black circle. I don't know if it's all the time cramped up in dark places but my head is spinning and

I feel like I just time travelled to the future.

We go back into the bedroom and I notice some clothes left on a chair and I pick up a shirt and think this is Pa's shirt. I start to panic wondering when Pa will come back and I'm freaking out that it could be hours and we might get found out before then.

Diego sees me looking worried and asks me what I'm going to say to him. I'd thought a lot about this the night before and realised I had so many questions but more than anything I just want to hug him and see his face...

Sorry.
Give me a minute.

It always makes me teary talking about Pa.

Ok I'm good.
Where was I? So yeah we're waiting and I put the picture of me and Pa on the bed that I brought along in case he doesn't recognise me after all this time.

Next to the bed is a silver tray with leftover food on it and just looking at the cakes and some fruit is making me hungry. Diego sees me looking and picks up two of the cakes and he shoves one in his mouth and gives me the other. I'm like what are you doing? But he says not to worry they'll just be thrown out otherwise. I can't believe they'll throw away perfectly good food but it's true! Sitting here talking to you now I find that even more difficult to make sense of.

We eat the cakes and the fruit and sit on the bed and wait. The clock shows two forty-seven and I start to worry that Pa will stay out all day and not come back til late and Ma will come home from work and wonder where I am. We run out of things to say so we sit in nervy silence.

Finally there's a click and the door swings open. We both jump to our feet and stand guiltily as Pa stops just inside the door and looks at us all confused.

Straight away I know it's not him. He's the man I'd seen through wall and up close he did look a lot like my Papa but it wasn't him.

He says something to us in English that I don't understand but I can't move or say anything I just stand there frozen. Diego totally comes to the rescue and speaks to him in the little English he knows. I go as white as a ghost and the man is asking if I'm ok and Diego tries to tell him I'm not well and grabs the tray of plates with one hand and my elbow with the other and pulls me towards the door.

In the hall Diego holds me by the shoulders and is saying something but it's like I'm not there. I'd been so sure I was going to see my Pa. Diego hugs me tight and I can't stop the tears they just fall out of me.

He takes me down a load of steps and corridors but I don't really remember it I was in such a state. I was going to see my father again. I was finally going to go with him to America and now all I had again was the picture in my pocket. I feel the pocket of the uniform for the picture and straight away realise my mistake. I have a bit of a mini meltdown then drop to the floor and sob a lot. I don't really remember what happened only that I shout at Diego and start kicking stuff and somehow he pulls me along without anyone seeing a badly disguised kid who clearly doesn't belong in the hotel losing their shit.

We ended up in the kitchens. The place is really busy with people running about all over the place and most look up and say hola to Diego as we pass. Everywhere there's big steaming pots or trays of food. Chefs are shouting orders at each other and younger boys in purple uniforms run around grabbing empty saucepans. A huge man in a white hat is arranging some food on plates and looks up and breaks into a big smile that turns him from mean looking to a friendly bear. He comes around and shakes Diego's hand and pats him on the back and asks who he has with him.

Diego's like
Renan meet Espe. Espe meet Renan.

I say hello but my eyes are all sore and I must look a right state. Renan's eyes go all big and he says

What.... the Espe?

Like I'm famous or something. Then makes me jump by shouting over my shoulder whilst holding up the biggest knife I've ever seen

Burn that sauce Emilio and I'll chop your balls off with this knife.

The man he shouts at looks shit scared and runs over to a pan and starts stirring it without looking at Renan.

Renan invites us to his office which is a small place with a couple of chairs and a desk covered in newspaper cuttings and books. Diego told me once that Renan was obsessed with what other chefs were doing and always kept anything in the paper about them. I feel so depressed I want to cry again but I just about hold it together. Diego tells Renan the whole story and that does it I'm back to being a dribbling wreck. Renan's big leather chair makes this woosh sound as he sits down but then he quickly stands up again and says leave it to him and asks Diego which room my not Pa is in.

He leaves for a bit then comes back holding two plates of food. He puts them on his desk and does this big performance of telling us what each thing is. I don't understand the most of what he's saying which doesn't help my general feeling that the world is collapsing under my feet.

My god though I'd never seen food that looked like this before it was all tiny things like a little bit of fish and meat with a toothpick through it with a drop of sauce and the smallest parsley leaf. And I'm thinking if this is the size of the meal you get when you're rich then I'm happy right where I am thanks very much. Renan takes one and puts the whole thing in his mouth and chews with his mouth open. Renan watches me carefully as I put one all in my mouth like him. It is still the most delicious thing I've ever eaten in my life which is not that surprising considering. I can't believe there are so many flavours all in one tiny thing. Seeing the delight on my face Renan says

Ah ha there we are Diego your girl knows her food.

I looked sideways at Diego because

A. I'm not his girl and

B. I'm not ever going to be someone's girl.

He looks away quickly and goes red.

To cover it he tells Renan he thinks the food's a bit too salty with a cheeky grin on his face. Renan grabs him pretending to wrestle him but just gives him a big hug instead in that way guys do because they can't just hug each other.

There's a knock at the door and Renan gets up and stands at the door talking through the gap. He shuts it again nodding looking all serious and comes over to where I'm sitting and squats down so our faces are at the same height. He's sweaty and I'm weirded out that he's so close but he says I have some food in my hair and reaches out to my ear and when he pulls his hand back my photo is right between his fingers. To this day I've no idea how he did it but I'm so grateful he did.

Renan helps us sneak back out of the hotel again. He goes out the side door of the kitchen to meet the fish man and we wait in his office. I feel this horrible ache in my chest mixed together with a kind of emptiness.

After a bit he comes back and we follow him out through the kitchen to a small yard where the man is waiting. He lets us into the back seats and asks us to squat down as we leave but says not to worry as the guards only check on the way in. We say thanks to Renan and climb in. He drops us on the main road shouting goodbye over loud pop music and together we walk back into Borde.

Only when one of the guys we sometimes play football with asks if we're both working at the hotel now do we realise I'm still wearing the cleaner uniform. We rush back to my place taking all the back alleys hoping no one sees us. I go into my room and change whilst Diego makes some tea. I put the uniform in a plastic bag and give it to him and he says he'll get my other clothes back tomorrow and I look at the clock and can't believe it's past five. I put the picture on the table and just stare at it as we sip our tea. Diego stays and helps me peel the potatoes for dinner and we don't talk much but that's ok because when you're good friends you don't always have to talk. Sharing silence is ok too.

A drip of sweat hung for an impossibly long time on the end of Jago's nose. Finally succumbing to gravity, it dropped between his stiff legs. The air was so thick and hot that he had long ago stopped wiping the sweat from himself. He could no longer judge how long they'd been in the back of the battered lorry. It had been early morning when they took their positions amongst the boxes stacked to the ceiling. Legs pulled into their chests (each of them clutching the cut off two litre plastic bottle they were given) they huddled in the small airless opening, just big enough for each of them to sit. Then, brick by brick, they were sealed in, enveloped in darkness and the heavy scent of washing powder. At first Jago had been determined not to use his bottle, deciding it was mind over matter. The shame of going, in touching distance of others, even if the darkness hid their faces, seemed too much. He was unsure how long it was before he cracked, he certainly wasn't the first, by the time his panicky fingers frantically released his belt the stale air was a mixture of urine and chemical washing powder that stuck in the back of your throat.

They had stopped four times. Each time he imagined the muffled exchange of voices would lead to their discovery. In desperation, he held his breath, praying that the faceless man opposite would control his wheezing cough. On the second occasion the back doors had sprung open, sending in a rush of fresh air that Jago had spent hours obsessively yearning for but now desperately wanted gone. The friendly, overweight driver could be heard giving details of his cargo. He kept a casual and jokey tone as he revealed the Trojan horse of brown cardboard, that stood between them and the end of their dream. Each of them waited for boxes to be pulled away to reveal five pairs of frightened eyes, squinting into the pale dawn, but the doors were slammed shut and on they rumbled. Even when the noise of the engine filled their ears none of them dared utter a whisper, too much was at stake.

To pass some time, he retreated to memories of childhood. He thought about the rain falling in the burnt orange dust of the back yard, the fig tree still glistening with water droplets. Remembering when his whole family had been out in force searching the Rojo for his mother's lost earring that she had inherited from her mother. Overturned sheets and dented cooking pots had revealed nothing. His older sister Lola, who adored him and loved to show him off to anyone who would listen, had said they would never find it. Jago remembered seeing her squatting half-heartedly looking through a pile of newspapers in the living room, her chocolate hair falling in her eyes. She was eleven then, four years Jago's senior, so unnervingly beautiful that all of Jago's friends loved her instantly. Carlos, already a head taller than Jago, would press incessantly for details.

'How does she like her eggs, because when we're married I'm going to cook her breakfast every day, just the way she likes it and bring it to her in bed if she wants.' Carlos would dreamily say, propped up on Jago's bed as they sorted through his collection of beer bottle caps.

Jago rolled his favourite across his fingers, slightly dented from where it had been opened. It had a red star on a yellow background, in the middle a small black monkey stared back at him, its tail curled around itself like a cat.

'I think her eyes are my favourite part of her; I mean I love her hair as well,' (Jago knew full well that Carlos had once stolen one of her hairs from an upturned hairbrush, left on the sink in the bathroom) 'but her eyes, wow, they just sparkle and they are brown and green at the same time, have you noticed that J?'

In truth, Lola found Jago's friend's devotion sweet and she always took the time to talk to them, despite Jago rolling his eyes as they hung on her every word. For all the attention of boys younger and often older, she had little confidence in herself and thought her hair too thick, her eyes not dark enough, her legs too long. In protection against her self-doubt, she turned to an imaginary world where animals could talk and even a missing earring was part of a greater story.

'I knew he would take something in return.' she informed Jago, without looking up from the papers.

'What?' he replied, confused.

'Tivana, he was here yesterday, I saw him on the yard wall, eating a mango. He told me a special secret but said he would need something in return.' she said, giving up on the papers and resting against the wall.

Jago sighed, he was used to this but could never keep up with who was who. 'Who's Tivana again?' he asked, pushing his hands into the cushions of the chair.

'I've told you a million times, he's the monkey prince of the Pana Kingdom but he will never be king because he had to run away after the evil monkey Tonga killed his family and stole the purple jewel of Leo. Tivana is on a quest to get it back.'

'So he took Ma's earring as part of the quest?' he offered, not wanting to upset his sister.

'Yes, I think it is a key part of the puzzle,' she speculated, looking thoughtfully into space.

Just as the day was fading with their hopes, Jago saw it, catching the afternoon sun in the dirt of the chicken coop. For a moment he savoured its sight, the glory of discovery, then heart thumping he turned to the others holding it high. The rest of that afternoon and evening had been a giddy celebration with him the hero of the hour. Drinks were passed around, music played and Jago remembered so much laughter it filled the room and burst out the backdoor and into the city beyond.

Perched on his mother's lap, centre stage, every smile and wink was for him. But above all, played and replayed, were his father's smiling eyes. For once they were full of satisfaction and praise, like a beam of sunlight momentarily cutting through the otherwise dense cloud of disappointment. Passed around like a trophy he felt such warmth and happiness he didn't want the night to end, eventually falling asleep on his father's shoulder.

His mind drifted to racing Carlos across the back lanes, both at full speed, glancing across at his furrowed brow. Those spindly legs that sprayed out to the left and right as he ran, Jago always slightly quicker than his dear friend. One hot afternoon he had raced ahead, reaching the leafy square with the stone fountain they had stolen coins out of the week before. Lola had been there, sat with a friend whose name Jago couldn't recall. Red in the face and drawing in breath, he'd dropped beside them on the cool stone bench that ran around the fountain. Hand sized leaves above gently caught the breeze, casting map-like shadows on Lola's smooth skin. As Carlos came storming into sight down the cobbled hill, all chaotic arms and legs, Lola had playfully squeezed the back of Jago's neck and proudly said to her friend. 'My brother will win gold in the Olympics one day.'

Jago remembered the swell of pride he felt at that moment, forcing his frame upright and pushing out his chest as he met his sister's kind eyes. He'd returned to those memories so often, like a worn magazine flopped open at a favourite page. Jago wished he had more of Lola but he was young, and however much he tried to recall those times it was like grasping at ash.

Inside the container, no light crept in to reveal whether it was night or day, but the temperature had dropped a little, making Jago think the sunlight might have faded. Reducing speed, they turned onto an unpaved road. Like a ship on stormy waters, the vehicle cautiously ploughed forward. Every rise and fall ached through Jago's exhausted bones. He tried to shift position to ease the discomfort but every patch of him was worn through.

Eventually, they came to an abrupt halt, the driver killing the engine. Bodies shifted positions around him as they anxiously waited, shirts clinging to backs. As the doors swung open a flood of cool air engulfed them.

'Ok my friends, we made it!' their driver announced, as he pulled away the first of the boxes.

No one moved, even when he stood before them smoking a cigarette casually, the ash falling on his stained vest. So many hours in one position left them like dripping statues with wide eyes.

Finally, a soft voice asked, 'is it safe?'

The driver chuckled turning away from them. 'Come on, come on,' he muttered passing a hand through his greasy hair.

A gust of the purest air Jago had ever tasted brought

him to his senses. He arched his back and tentatively got to his feet. Stumbling out, he staggered into the undergrowth on road legs, tripping over an exposed root before finding a spot to relieve himself. It was only once he was squatting, trousers around his knees, did he hear the sea, so close he squinted through the vegetation looking for its shape in the gloom.

When he returned, the group was nowhere to be seen so Jago headed towards the lights of the jetty. He stood briefly at the edge of the trees as an urgent wind swept across the wooden jetty, the coal-black ocean beyond swirling under a glassy skin. Despite the dancing of the trees that lined the shore, there was an eerie silence that was only broken by the regular knocking of a faded buoy against the only boat tethered, at the far end of the dock. Striding over to the others, he felt a wave of euphoria sweep over him. Maybe it was the sea air or just being on his feet again but he felt all his fear drop away. We're going to make it, he marvelled. A thought he hadn't allowed himself, until then.

'Ah here he is!' smiled the driver, to a stern looking bearded man with a rolled cigarette perched between dark thin lips. The huddled group turned to look at him and for the first time he properly took in his companions. Propped against a weathered, wooden slat hut (that quietly creaked on its aching foundations) was a scrawny boy, dressed in tattered jeans and a Hugo Boss t-shirt that he twisted and curled around his finger nervously. His untidy teeth looked like they'd been thrown in his mouth as an afterthought and the threat of a moustache lingered on his top lip. Huddled together to his left was a couple a little older than Jago. Taller than her partner, the woman had a pleasant wide face with high cheekbones, her long, oily black hair plaited down her muscular back. Gripping her hand, her upright husband stood vacantly staring forward from smoky white eyes, under the brim of a faded baseball cap. Slightly separate from the others, faced towards the ocean stood the final member of their group. Impatiently, she tapped her beaten, leather cowboy boots on the wood and returned her concentration to the water, as if searching for something on the horizon. She looked his way with dark eyes that held his gaze, making him look away.

'Right my friends, this is Ivan,' the truck driver gestured with a nod of his head, 'you're in his safe hands from here.'

'Five minutes, end of the dock.' Ivan said without smiling, the rollie still balanced on his lips.

Turning his broad shoulders away he strode back to his vessel.

'Don't mind Ivan, he's a big softy really.' the driver explained, pulling a squashed cigarette pack out of his back pocket.

'How long will it take?' enquired the woman, glancing at her husband with concern.

The driver chuckled. 'Hard to say chica, I've never

144

done the journey to the promised land! Only a few hours though, I think. You'll be there soon enough.' he added kindly, lighting his cigarette.

'Well, my work is done here, thank you for choosing Mateo Holidays. We wish you a pleasant journey to your onward destination! Best of luck to all of you.'

With that, he turned away from them and returned to his truck. Jago squinted towards the simple boat tethered at the end of the rotting wooden platform. Raised on flaking metal poles stood two bare bulbs that released a limp light. Swarming around them, drunk insects weaved in chaotic patterns frantic to escape the inky night. The woman in the cowboy boots had already made it to the end of the jetty and was exchanging a few words with their captain. Gradually they began to follow, the lady catching his eye as she passed with her husband, offering a sympathetic smile. Stretching his heavy arms, Jago yawned and picked up his small backpack, that contained all the belongings he would take to the new world. An empty water bottle, a hand sized note pad that he haphazardly scribbled thoughts in his illegible slant, a half-full bag of pumpkin seeds, three thousand US dollars, a change of clothes and a picture of a young girl smiling back at the camera, curled at the edges and beginning to fade. That line of tiny, white teeth and those questioning eyes stared out from the small plastic sandwich bag that protected it.

As they climbed aboard the restless boat, the wind

whipped hair about their faces, the thick plastic awning that covered the boat straining on its fixing. All the while a chorus of frolicking leaves competed with the roar of the sea. Finding a dry spot between a sturdy padlocked white box and a tangled orange net, Jago slouched down on the deck, his back to the sea. Their cheerless captain started the juddering engine. Their lungs filled with clean salt air laced with a scent that reminded Jago of the city. Just across from him sat the couple, sharing a guava, deep in an inaudible conversation. At the bow, the boy stood, eyes fixed out to sea, routinely pushing his unkempt hair from his face.

Quite suddenly, the woman in the cowboy boots rose from her perch at the helm and without meeting their eyes stepped briskly off the boat. Silently, they all watched her disappear down the wooden platform.

'Where's she going?' the boy asked nervously, turning to the captain.

'She decided against it.' he replied, without looking up from his instruments.

The boy continued to look at him for some time, before returning his attention to the sea. Jago exchanged glances with the woman opposite. He was suddenly overcome by doubt. Was he a fool for doing this, as Carlos had argued the day he left.

Promptly, Ivan released their moorings and steered the vessel away from the shore, cutting at an angle across the bay. Soon they were rising and falling on the formidable waves, the land shrinking behind them. Jago raised himself to his knees and squinted through the gloom to the dark regressing land. He felt that deep, heart aching sentimentality that comes with leaving one world behind. Not quite gone but yet to arrive. On the edge of the quivering diving board, a place where you are in love with your past and future. He thought of his father and riding on the lightness of the moment, made peace with him, releasing all the strain and resentment that wrapped around him, like finally removing a long, heavy, sodden coat. Only then did he realise how consumed he'd been, how anger had buzzed through him like a current.

As they rose and fell on the waves, he suddenly felt an immense lightness as if the wind might whisk him away into the night. He took a deep lungful of salt air and found himself smiling. Everything seemed sharp and different some how, as if looking through another man's eyes. The solitary lamp above the helm cast a warm glow that Jago found beautiful. Just enough light to pick out features but low enough to create mysterious shadows. Looking down at his backpack he noticed a small badge pinned to the front, put there many years before. Whilst he knew it was there, he couldn't remember the last time he'd looked at, as if his mind had removed it from his consciousness in utter boredom. Turning it to the light, he took in its detail, on a faded red background were the white letters:

It took him back to before those first elections, that feeling amongst them that all was about to change. Swept along in the euphoria, he'd handed out badges and leaflets with the troop of volunteers. Excited and scared they talked up a future of freedoms they, until recently, hadn't dared to dream of. Along with the thousands of others he'd taken to the streets, his feet barely touching the ground as the mass poured down Calle Bolivar. Across its considerable width was a sea of people, not a patch of ground in sight, thousands of hearts beating to the same tune.

Of course, Jago's father opposed the changes as if they were born to stand apart. For twenty-six years the large figure of his father had run their watering hole, known locally as Rojo because of its imposing, red metal roof. Nothing much had changed since Jago was a child, the same tired furniture, the comforting sound of rain on the roof, flaking olive walls and the long curved wooden bar. As a child, Jago had forever stood impatiently as his father stopped to talk to another person he knew.

Eternally the host, he filled the space, asking attentive questions,

'Is your mother feeling better? How is the new job going?'

People came to him for advice or a favour. Could he introduce them to so and so? He was a habitual storyteller in those unrushed deep tones of his. Jago remembered visitors bringing him gifts and singing his praises throughout Rojo, a padre to all of them. How Jago craved a father to himself, longing for one of those ambling stories to be told at his bedside. Perpetually in his father's shadow, he could never quite find the inner strength to meet the weight of his expectation. His father's friends saw him as a meek boy who, under an unkempt mop of dark hair, struggled to meet their eyes. In truth, Jago wasn't as lightweight a child as he seemed but he enjoyed time alone, finding solace unearthing stones in the yard or spying on customers from his hiding place in the bar. He loved to climb out of bed in the middle of the night and walk around the house in the darkness, stepping slowly, his fingertips his guide. In his mind, he created a map in the dark so he could tiptoe to his father's glass cabinet. Silently he'd turn the brass key opening the door (lifting it slightly to avoid its squeak) and ease out the large commemorative plate, that he was strictly forbidden to touch. His father's proudest possession felt smooth and cool in his hands as he ran his fingers around its hexagonal shape. Jago didn't need to see what was printed on it, he knew it by heart.

A hero of the Union
Awarded to:
Almando Vera
for services to our great Communist Party

Almando was proud of his work for the party. From time to time officials would come to Rojo and a great show would be made of their visit. His father would usher them into the best seats in the house evicting its resident with a wave of a hand. Backs were slapped, hands were shaken, he was one of them. Cabron's vision of a new dawn promised democracy and economic freedom, that threatened to pull the rug from his established troop and send him tumbling into the unknown.

Jago's standing on the matter infuriated his father, who saw it as a personal betrayal. On the day he discovered the Cabron posters in Jago's bag he launched at him in a rage, pinning him to the wall, sending a picture of Almando's father in military uniform staring out from long dead eyes, crashing to the floor. Wild, the vein on the right of his head ready to burst, he released a tirade of indignation, spit striking his son's face. In the aftermath, Jago gathered his possessions from a pile at the door and fled. The lonely figure of his mother, stood in the arch of the kitchen door for a long time after the back gate was slammed, the hammering of the rain on the roof all that remained, a small scrap of paper in her pocket nervously folded and unfolded.

The lanky stooped figure of Carlos happily welcomed a dripping Jago into his simple room above the mechanics where he worked. Their friendship had stayed strong all these years. At night they would take to the bustling city streets, buzzing with the scent of change, raising their drinks to Cabron. They strolled amongst the threadbare buildings, until the sun began to rise, dreaming of a future where they could earn a decent living. Carlos wanted a car, maybe a convertible, so they could cruise the city at night, music in their ears, a twinkle in their eyes. Jago thought he might buy a suit and work in an office, in a new glass tower built by Cabron.

It was the June of Jago's twenty-eighth year when Cabron finally swept to power. The Communist Party could no longer hold back the tide of change. Conversations were dominated by telling and retelling where they were when they heard. For Jago he'd woken early in last night's clothes, with a stale mouth and muddled head, his legs aching from hours of walking the night before. Stepping out to smoke a cigarette in the cool morning air, he took in the calm of the normally busy street. The grubby shutters were down on most of the shop fronts, none of the street sellers (offering bags of nuts and fresh juices) had arrived yet. For a moment he stood in the middle of the potholed road, that in a couple of hours would be choked with noise and fumes. Opposite a small kiosk was open, run by Juan, a quiet man who always looked up when speaking as if the heavens might hold the answers. Perching on a ripped leather stool he ordered a coffee, looking down at his fingers, jaundice yellow from the smoke. Too tired to hold a conversation he allowed the stream of official party announcements to wash over him as Juan tipped the spoons of Nescafe into a chipped cup for him. Quite suddenly the sound that filtered from the dust-covered radio ceased. They both raised their heads and stared at it, as if noticing it for the first time. Their eyes met in confusion and just as Juan was turning the old radio over to check it's batteries a different voice crackled into life.

'This is your president Luis Cabron....'

Even when the announcement was repeating for the third time they both remained frozen, Juan cradling the radio like an injured bird. Most of the city was still asleep, unaware that the world had changed; Jago and Juan sat opposite each other, wide eyed. The spell was only broken when a barefooted young man in a bright yellow t-shirt, came shouting hysterically down the street, 'We did it! We did it!'

The days that followed were a blur of celebrations and drinking. People took to the streets, strangers became instant friends, all barriers brought down by the jubilation of victory. Much of this joyous time was lost to Jago's memory, washed away in an alcoholic haze.

Early one hot afternoon, as Jago was taking a nap with an empty bottle of rum at his feet, Ricardo the barman from Rojo stormed into the room with a look on his handsome face that left him instantly sober.

His father had collapsed that morning in the back yard, falling with one large hand gripping his chest. Rojo had stood closed for over a week since the revolution and his father had withdrawn to its back rooms not uttering a word, even to Jago's mother. For periods of the day he took to the yard, obsessively repairing the chicken coop, that until then had been in a perpetual state of decay.

After the funeral, Jago moved back to be with his mother. She crumpled like a paper bag at her husband's death, looking out through pinhole eyes at a world she no longer recognised. Surrounded by too much liquor, Jago burned an anger fuelled fire of rage and grief that engulfed him. Regularly he woke in the middle of the afternoon to find a glass of water beside him, left by his mother.

Finally, a few weeks later, empty to the core, he stepped into the dark bar. Fine dust covered the tables, like a scene of a discovered building preserved after a volcanic eruption. Behind the bar, browned lemon slices still lay in the porcelain dish, three full ashtrays waited to be cleared and next to them sat his father's gold watch. Jago carefully picked it up and stared as the second hand worked its way around the unnumbered marks, regular and predictable. Turning it over, he read the inscription on the back that simply read 'comrade'. The watch had been given to his father by Lucio, a close friend who had disappeared, assumed dead, before Jago was born. The stories his father told of Lucio were like folklore to Jago. Heroic, lavish stories of a man overcoming all the odds. Slipping the watch into his pocket, he wandered over to a large framed photo that hung on the wall above a dark wooden table, its four

153

chairs neatly stacked underneath. In faded black and white, five rows of men stared unsmilingly back at the camera. Jago's father was sat in the second row, three from the left in a loose white shirt, much thinner but with the same serious eyes and large forehead. The picture had been taken at a banana plantation, behind them paddle-like leaves swayed against a cloudless sky. On the left side a small dog had made its way into the picture, stopping to gnaw at an itch on its back at the second the shutter opened.

Jago realised he had no idea who these people were or what his father was doing amongst them. Now he was gone he wanted to ask his father about his childhood, what life had been like when he was a young man but it was too late. Carefully he removed all the pictures from the walls, leaving pale rectangular footprints where they once stood. Then unhurriedly he righted the tables and swept the concrete floor. When he'd run a cloth around the bar and emptied the ashtrays, he raised the noisy shutters and reopened Rojo.

Without comment, as if it had been never closed, regular customers gradually trickled back in. And so Jago came to be running Rojo as if by compulsion. Ricardo returned and Carlos came most evenings after work, as they set about the task of making sense of how to run the place in the new world. The customers, cautious at first of Jago, soon lingered at the bar, clinging to its familiarity in a whirlwind of change.

As the weeks passed, Jago began to make changes.

Like many of the cafes and bars, he took advantage of the too good to be true free Pepsi plastic chairs and umbrellas, given to them by the smiling men in suits. Jago also took up their offer of two new glass fronted fridges, that he filled with their carbonated drinks. Their bright logos excited him, they looked modern and expensive amongst the Rojo's faded backdrop.

Things changed very quickly in the following months. Constructions sites began to appear with glossy posters of modern buildings coming soon. The customary Communist billboards replaced with adverts for beer and fast food. One quiet afternoon, Jago sat at a table at the back of the bar, all of its ceiling fans fighting an impossible battle against the heat. Just two men populated Rojo, nursing cold beers, staring out to the bustling street beyond. Ricardo sat beside him and helped himself to a cigarette from Jago's pack that sat on the table, his lighter neatly placed on top.

'How's it looking?' He asked, nodding his head to the large accounting book laid out in front of Jago.

Jago had spent the best part of the last hour working and reworking the figures but whatever angle you approached from they were ugly.

'Hopeless, I don't know how my father kept this place alive.' Jago admitted.

'He didn't have to, things were different. He knew all the right people, favours for favours; he never even kept the figures like you are.' Ricardo explained, gently moving his hands up and down his smooth, freshly shaved face, as if discovering a part of himself for the first time. Beards were rapidly disappearing from the young as they imitated the new arrivals on their tv screens.

Jago had turned the place upside down looking for some evidence of how Rojo was run, wishing he'd paid more attention when he was younger. But he found nothing except a wad of cash in a rusting tin, in the bottom drawer of the desk in the cramped back office. All that remained of that money was now folded in Jago's back pocket.

'These are new times Rico, the price of stock keeps going up and up and who has the money to spend, huh?'

As he said this Jago wanted a beer desperately but he wasn't going to scratch that itch, he had promised himself that much.

'True, but it'll come, Cabron will make us all rich in time.' Ricardo replied, getting up briskly from his chair to serve two young women who'd strolled into the bar laughing.

Jago was immensely grateful for Ricardo's effortless charm and laid back efficiency that had helped balance his sullen impatience. He aimlessly watched his two new customers take a seat near the centre of the room, close to one of the large pillars that rose up to the metal roof. A wry smile crept across his face as he watched the ever popular Ricardo flirt with them, pulling up a seat at their table uninvited. As he watched them, he noticed how beautiful the woman facing him was, her dark fawn eyes and thin mouth that crept up at the corners, as if in constant amusement. Jago averted his eyes as she glanced his way, looking quickly back at his numbers.

That was the first time he laid eyes on Christina but it wasn't until several weeks later that he spoke to her, despite her visiting the Rojo a few times in between. Not that Jago hadn't noticed, far from it. He was building a small obsession for the woman, that comes from a man with time on his hands. Ricardo was taking great delight in his boss's crippling discomfort each time she appeared, exaggerating his flirting with her whilst throwing Jago the occasional mischievous wink.

When finally they did stand face to face, Jago felt all the confidence drain from him. He was so lost in her wavy hair that he didn't hear the question she asked him.

'Do you have any work going here?' she repeated. 'I can clean or cook, I could serve customers.' she added to fill the void of silence.

'I don't at the moment, but why don't you leave your details in case something comes up?' he finally blurted out, scrabbling under the bar for a piece of paper and pen.

That evening as he and Carlos mulled over the day, in their usual positions looking out over the half full bar, he stared down at the scrap of paper.

'So you going to call this Christina then?' Carlos asked, taking a swig from his beer.

'Yep.' Jago replied decisively.

'Alright.' Carlos said, surprised at his friend's sudden urgency, 'what will you say to her?'

'I am going to offer her a job!'

Uttering the words aloud made the thought that had just come to him seem more concrete.

'But isn't Rojo struggling? You were only saying yesterday you might have to cut back Rico's hours.'

His mother hadn't been well, she wasn't able to do everything she used to. Jago couldn't cook to save himself and his half-hearted attempts at cleaning up left his mother frustrated.

'It's the perfect solution, Ma needs help, Christina said she is a good cook, I think it is just what this place needs. We'll just have to attract more customers, start doing food again.' Jago replied, the optimism rising in his voice.

Carlos sighed and shook his head. 'This won't end well.'

She started four days later, working a morning shift three days a week. Christina worked hard, a trait she learnt from her industrious mother, who raised her and her two sisters following the death of her father. A somewhat drifty child, she couldn't remember their 'brick house' as her elder sister Sabina had named it. As far as she was concerned she'd always lived in their two room shack, that shook when the freight trains passed, leading her mother to tape her statue of Jesus to the shelf. Despite a procession of hopeful boys always popping by, her older sister wasn't known for her common sense and ended up unhappily married to an overweight plumbing supplies shop owner eleven years her senior.

Her younger sister Bianca had nearly died on delivery but battled through a testing forty-eight hours that her mother didn't like to talk about. Their neighbour Anita however, a woman who delighted in knowing everything about everyone, told of her role in the 'miracle' with gleeful regularity. Perhaps her arduous start to life was what made Bianca such a fierce character who was regularly marched home by one of their community for fighting with one of the boys who wouldn't let her onto the roof of the station, called her a bitch, took her knife....etc etc.

Of the three, Christina was most like her mother, a resolute rule follower who believed that those who made the laws must know a whole lot more than she did. Christina's long slender fingers took effortlessly to the needlework her mother taught her. From a young age, she helped her repair and later make clothes. Fondly, she remembered hours sat huddled under their one lamp, a needle in her hand whilst her mother worked the machine. Christina was well liked amongst their groups of ramshackle houses, walls so thin that secrets evaporated like summer rain. Being dependable and honest didn't make her the most popular girl in their community but it meant those friends she did have lasted the test of time. On evenings when they climbed to the flat roof of the train station and shared a beer, Christina would decline a cigarette, dusting off a concrete block before sitting to watch the trains rumble by. Amongst the elderly in their community Christina was adored, always helpful, popping by to help cook, or just listen to their stories. She felt safe amongst those older than her, unfazed by their reminder of our impending mortality.

Meticulously she went to work cleaning Rojo,

sweating over bubbling pots, much to Jago's mother's annoyance.

'That woman has put the pans back in the wrong place and this food is too salty.'

'Give her a chance Ma, she worked really hard this morning.' Jago said, helping himself to another spoon of the delicious stew. His mother continued to grumble but didn't comment when he ladled more onto her plate.

In the months that followed, Christina became an integral part of their lives, so much so Jago wondered how they had survived without her. The backyard was swept, the junk that Jago had begun piling there cleared away. She trimmed back plants and brought order not seen since his father died. Even his mother had ceased complaining, a quiet acceptance falling over her. Christina's simple, caring nature was hard to resist as she seeped into the grain of Rojo. It had been her who had suggested that they repaint the bar, her idea to add the large potted plants that sat amongst the tables. There could be no arguing things were on the up. They were busier than ever, which Jago in devotion put down to her. He wasn't sure when she started staying all day instead of just the morning or when three days became four or five. She dropped in meals for Ma at the weekend and she would stay a while. All this time Jago never confessed his feelings to her, locking them in an already overflowing basement of suppression.

One evening she knocked on the office door and

stood in the doorway.

'I'm all done for today.'

Getting no reply, Christina watched Jago inquisitively as he gazed at a photo.

'I found it this morning, I was sure dad got rid them all,' he said holding up a faded picture of a young girl, looking directly at the camera, her hands raised above her head, mouth open in delighted surprise.

'Who's that?' Christina asked, leaning in for a closer look, 'She's beautiful.'

'That's Lola, my sister; she died when I was nine.' he answered, not taking his eye from the picture.

'Oh Jago, I'm sorry, I didn't know,' she replied in shock, her hand covering her mouth, 'what happened to her?'

Jago swallowed, his mouth suddenly dry. He hadn't talked about Lola for a long time, 'An accident. I'd bugged her to take me over to the empty warehouse, where the new petrol station is now, around the corner. I was always the baby amongst her group of friends, they looked out for me though. We'd been going to that place for months, I don't know what happened but somehow the roof collapsed.'

He held the picture closer, staring into those eyes as if looking for something he had missed all these years, 'I was knocked out. I came round as they were carrying me into the yard. All I remember is the dust, in my hair, up my nose, the water turned brown when Ma washed me. I found out later that my father and a couple of guys from the bar dug us out with their bare hands. Lola didn't make it.'

'Your poor Ma,' Christina whispered to herself.

Jago fell into a solemn silence lost in thought. Feeling awkward, Christina mumbled a goodbye and let herself out.

As time passed Jago began to sense something shift between them, their friendship breaking free of the job roles it had germinated from. Carlos began to tease him, incredulous that they had yet to get together, like the whole world could see it except them.

On the evening of the one year celebrations of the Cabron revolution, Christina worked the bar with Jago and Ricardo. The room was full to bursting, excited voices cutting through the stomping band Jago had hired for the evening. It had been declared a national holiday and the punters were in a fine mood. Tirelessly they worked for hours, serving the waves of customers that stood three or four deep at the bar. Jago hailed it 'Rojo's return.' She was alive again, bustling with energy brought by a new younger crowd.

At close to five am Jago, Christina, Ricardo and Carlos, who had weighed in to help, slouched in chairs, exhausted but exhilarated. They had taken more money in that one night than in whole months when Jago had first taken the reins. A little drunk and beyond sleep, Jago poured his friends another glass of rum.

'To Cabron!' he blurted, raising his glass.

'Cabron!' they replied in unison.

An exhausted silence fell on them.

'I need my bed.' Carlos eventually said, getting clumsily to his feet.

'I'll walk with you.' Ricardo replied quickly, downing his drink and reaching over to hug Jago.

Both Jago and Christina stood to hug their friends goodnight.

'Thanks for tonight, you saved us there!' Jago said, a hand on Carlos' shoulder.

Jago watched them leave the bar into the silent streets bathed in the weak light of a new day.

'You're lucky to have those two.' Christina said, leaning back in her chair.

'I know. I don't know what I'd do without them, or you,' he replied, looking her in the eye.

She looked away, embarrassed by the compliment.

'I'm serious,' he pressed on, 'you've really helped turn this place around.'

As he said this he gently touched her hand and left it lingering there as long as he dared.

Looking back, those times were the happiest of Jago's life. A heaviness was lifted from him. As they they ran Rojo together, he smiled and joked more than Carlos could ever remember. His mother had embraced Christina as the daughter she had lost, bringing her out of her mourning. She pinned her hair back again and rose early to make them both banana fritters and dark black coffee.

Seven months later they married, a simple gathering at the Santa Clara church just around the corner. In the evening a host of family and friends came to Rojo for a party that lasted well into the night. Jago's side of the family drank heavily, relieved that some celebration was finally cutting through the grief.

After the wedding, Christina officially moved into Rojo. They worked hard, rising at six to prepare the bar for the day. Christina and his mother decided to offer food again. Together they planned a simple but well received menu.

One morning as they all sat peeling onions in the yard, Christina cleared her throat, 'I have some news,' she said nervously to both of them, wiping her hands on her apron.

Jago wasn't sure whether he wanted a child, in truth he hadn't even given it a thought. His mother leapt from her stool to gather Christina in her arms, her face so overcome with a happiness Jago hadn't seen for many years.

Christina looked to him. 'So, are you ok with this?'

'Of course I am,' he quickly replied, moving to hold her in his arms.

Espe was born just after eight on a misty morning in April. After eighteen arduous hours of labour, Christina held in her arms her first and only child. Wrapped in a towel the newborn was handed to Jago who held her in wonder. Her button nose was perfect and he marvelled at her wild dark hair matted to her head. As he held her, stood by the fourth floor window, she briefly opened her eyes. Seeing those eyes made Jago stagger back, knocking over a chair behind him. Jago's mother quickly took her granddaughter from him. Feeling hot and faint Jago pushed his way out of the room, his head spinning, a taste of dust in his mouth. Suddenly he was violently sick across the corridor floor.

'What's happening?' Christina called out to Jago's mother, but she didn't reply. Instead, she stood motionless, staring at the bundle in her arm. She couldn't pull her herself away from the child's eyes. It was the same for anyone who had known Lola, the minute they first met Espe they stopped as if seeing a ghost, she unmistakably had her eyes.

Later, Christina tried to question Jago about what happened at the hospital but feeling foolish he covered the truth saying it was just the stress of the birth. He tried to make sense of the anger he felt, of the impending fear that gripped him every time he looked at his daughter. But despite an urgency to strike another path, he was much like his father, unequipped to navigate the tall grass of emotion that surrounded him. So he busied himself at the bar, finding reasons to stay later and later in his office. Frustrated, Christina couldn't understand his continued absence at a time when she needed him the most. When he was with them Jago was bad tempered and irritable. In spite of her father's distance, Espe was dedicated to him. As soon as she could crawl, she followed him around Rojo.

166

The more Jago knew he should be kinder to his daughter the more irritable he became. He wanted so much to hold her and make her smile but as soon as she looked at him a panic surged through him.

When Espe had been put to bed Jago often apologised for his behaviour to his wife, making excuse after excuse, but he could never find the courage to utter the truth. At first, she accepted his remorse but in time, a cold hardness seeped between them. Jago began drinking more and the closeness of their first months together faded. Unlike her son, Espe's Abuelita became devoted to her granddaughter, unable to tear herself from her side. Unconsciously, she drunk in those eyes she had been so cruelly denied.

Espe quickly grew into a confident child, who took no time in befriending new people. The customers adored her, lifting her onto their laps and cooing over her. In turn she loved the attention, boldly grabbing their faces and giggling with delight. Constantly, they complimented Christina and Jago on her.

'What a wonderful child, she is so much fun and those eyes!'

But despite a show of togetherness their marriage began to crumble. By the time Espe was up on her unsteady feet most of her parent's conversations had become short, snappy and bulging with contempt.

On a clear morning, two weeks after Espe's third birthday, two suited men came into the bar just as Ricardo was setting out ashtrays. They both shook his hand and introduced themselves as representatives from Servo. The taller of the two men, speaking perfect Spanish with an American accent, asked to see the owner.

'Sure, hang on.' Ricardo replied, heading to the back office.

'Some suits here to see you boss.' he said, leaning his head around the open office door, eyebrows raised. Jago picked himself up from behind the desk and went out to meet them. 'How can I help you?' he asked, offering them both a hand.

'Well actually, we hope we can help you,' chirped the American, 'I'm Todd Chambers from Servo, this is my partner Simon Cambasso.'

Jago had no idea what Servo was but he motioned for them to take a seat, nodding to Ricardo to bring some colas. Pulling a cigarette from a pack in his top pocket he offered one to the two men who declined.

'What's this about then?' Jago shrugged.

'We'd like to buy your bar,' declared Simon, who until now had remained quiet. He removed his sunglasses revealing serious opal eyes.

'Servo's one of the biggest American developers working here.' Todd boasted, smiling gratefully at Ricardo as he placed a cola in front of him, 'We're building two hundred and fifty million dollars worth of modern apartments across the country and are looking for sites in this part of the city.'

'Are you now?' Jago scoffed. 'And what makes you

think I want to sell?'

Todd pulled an envelope out of his jacket pocket and slid it across the table towards Jago. Resting his cigarette gently on the ashtray, Jago picked up the envelope that was made from thick, high quality paper. He turned it over and pulled out its contents. On headed paper under a Servo logo sat the figure $40,000. Jago looked up at the two calm gentlemen opposite him. Unhurried, he returned the letter to the envelope and slid it back towards them. Rising to his feet and extending a hand, Jago said, 'Thanks for coming by but like I said, I am not interested in selling.'

Both men rose, offering him firm, confident handshakes.

'Give it some thought,' asserted Todd, downing his cola.

Jago watched them stroll into the street only then noticing the envelope still lay by the ashtray.

'What was that all about?' Ricardo asked, appearing behind him.

Jago turned to face him. 'They want to buy Rojo.'

'Shit really, you selling?'

'Not a chance in hell!' Jago replied, picking up the envelope and pushing past him.

Only when he'd shut the office door and sat back behind his desk did he open the envelope again. The figure was more money than Jago had ever imagined, enough to start a new life.

It was nearly a month before Todd Chambers

appeared again. Those escaping the afternoon heat had started to slip away into the city when he stepped alone up to the bar wearing new jeans and a bright green polo shirt.

'Jago,' he beamed, as if they were old school friends, 'you got a minute? I'd like to show you something.'

'What's that?' questioned Jago, stubbing out a cigarette.

'Just around the corner, it'll only take two minutes, come on walk with me.'

Rojo was dead so Jago nodded.

'Back soon Rico,' he muttered and stepped out from the bar to follow the American.

Todd took a right turn out of the Rojo, setting a steady pace.

'You know, I am not ashamed to say it, one of the things I love about America is the comfort. Comfortable chairs, quality beds, dishwashers, microwaves, the rest of the world doesn't know what it's missing! The way I see it we've evolved into highly intelligent beings, why are we still washing up?!' Todd shouted, raising his voice over the noise of the chaotic traffic that choked the street.

Jago didn't reply. They stopped in front of a large, shiny, glass door of an only just finished six story building. Todd swiped a card and pushed open the door, standing aside to let Jago past. They stood in a silent lobby of floor-to-ceiling marble that felt wonderfully cool after the stifling afternoon heat.

'I mean, who really wants to sit in plastic chairs?' Todd continued, 'Who doesn't want a new car with air conditioning?'

He led them to an open lift at the far end of the hall, stepped inside and pressed an illuminated button with the letter P on it. They rapidly rose through the floors before stopping smoothly.

'Follow me.' Todd smiled mischievously, his eyes sparkling as the door slid open.

They walked into a spacious, open apartment at the top of the building, surrounded on all sides by glass offering panoramic views of the city beyond. Jago stood silently taking it all in. Directly in front of him, three large white leather sofas faced the wall of glass, to his left a vast open plan kitchen spilled into a dining area with a long, solid table lined with chairs.

'Impressive isn't it?' Admired Todd, 'Come and see the view.'

They walked out onto an expansive veranda that surrounded the entire apartment. Perfectly clipped shrubs were positioned in planters amongst an array of relaxed seating.

'Wow.' Jago managed, taking in the jumble of buildings below.

He had lived all his life in this city but standing there was like seeing it for the first time. He picked out the distinctive towers of the Iglesia de Maria to the west and the tree tops of the newly named Parque de Cabron. Leaning tentatively over the railing, he looked down at the vibrant street. Scooters zipped through the dense traffic, a woman carrying heavy bags weaved across the worn pavements, stopping to haggle over brightly coloured plastic goods from an animated seller. A scruffy dog, slumped by a wall chewing at something Jago couldn't make out between his paws, all oblivious to his gaze. Jago turned and looked back at the apartment unable to believe it belonged to the same world. A feeling he couldn't place crept over his skin, somewhere between exhilaration and longing. Todd strolled through to the kitchen, like it was his family home, casually retrieving a bottle of wine from a well stocked rack. Taking two glasses out of a sleek white cupboard, he laid them on the granite worktop. Disorientated, Jago drifted in to join him just as Todd finished pouring them both a glass, holding one up to him with a grin.

'Argentinian, Malbec from Mendoza, aged for twelve years, really layered taste,' he purred, taking a sip.

Without doubt it was the greatest wine Jago had ever tasted. He thought he knew a bit about wine but this was something else. Todd showed him into one of the bedrooms, that Jago decided was as big as Rojo's four back rooms together. Facing the view was an enormous bed, topped with a luxurious throw patterned with small birds in silver thread. Jago wondered who would have enough clothes to fill the mirrored, built in wardrobes that ran along one wall. Resting his glass carefully on a small table by one of the easy chairs dotted about the room, Todd removed his shoes and laid down on the bed.

'You see, there's just no going back once you lay on a bed like this!' He chuckled, gazing up at the elaborate glass light fitting that transformed the sun into rainbows dancing across the room.

'Right, your go!' he instructed Jago, jumping to his feet.

'No I'm fine really,' he protested, unsure why he was even standing in this palace with a glass of wine in his hand.

'Don't be ridiculous...here.' Todd replied assertively, taking Jago's glass from his hand and placing it on the table.

He felt foolish removing his shoes with this man he didn't know but obediently kicked them off and carefully lowered himself onto the centre of the bed. Instantly an incredible weariness overcame him, as if had he just realised he hadn't slept for weeks. He wasn't sure if it was the wine but he let his eyes flutter closed, as he sunk into a perfect synergy of softness and support. Months of the strain between him and Christina suddenly fell away. He felt weightless, as if the bed had gently risen up and on the call of a gust of wind, sailed out of the double doors, over the reclining chairs on the veranda and up high over the chessboard city. Only Todd's phone ringing brought him back to reality, making him sit bolt upright.

'Todd Chambers...yep, sure, I'm just up at Tiffany

Heights with our friend Jago. Oh really! Well there you go...sure...right. Great news, I'll let him know. Yep bye.'

'Well, that was some good news, my friend.' Todd clucked, sitting beside him and taking a delicate sip from his glass, 'Our men at the top have just upped their valuation of Rojo. Seems they didn't originally factor in the full site, just the bar. Anyway, I think you are going to be pretty pleased with what they've come back with.'

'I already told you, it's not for sale. My father created Rojo from nothing, it means too much.' Jago declared, pulling his shoes back on.

'Hear me out buddy, life is about knowing when to sell and I think when you're offered sixty-five thousand dollars for something, you gotta at least give it some thought.'

Jago's mouth dropped open a little but no sound came from it. Instead he just stared at the charming man in front of him, forty thousand had seemed incredible enough but sixty-five!

For the next few days, Jago found himself utterly distracted by his visit to Tiffany Heights. Ricardo gave up asking what was up and carried on running the bar in his increasing absence. He barely noticed Christina and Espe as his mind chewed over the offer. But as much as he tried to swim against the tide he failed to resist its power, pulling him towards a world of riches. He went through the motions of deliberating the sale, his heart was already sold, already spending the fortune on items he'd never even noticed existed. Constantly, he found himself daydreaming of being in the apartment, running a finger along its clean edges, breathing in the smell of new carpets. Rojo seemed so revoltingly shabby and worn that Jago spent less and less time there. So obsessed was he with Tiffany Heights that he half convinced himself that he would sell Rojo and move there, a glass of wine in his hands, his head in the clouds.

The deal was done quickly once he made the call. Todd came with papers to sign and a goodwill five thousand in cash, neatly bundled in a large envelope. There was paperwork to be filed and Todd estimated they would complete the sale in around five months.

Once the American had left, Jago retreated to his office, laid out the crisp notes on the desk and stared at them for a long time. Eventually, he called Carlos and arranged to meet him at nine. He took four of the thousand dollar bundles and stuffed them back into the envelope, sliding it under the heavy wooden bookcase that had once belonged to his grandfather. The other thousand he cut roughly in half, putting one pile into the top drawer of the desk, the other in his pocket.

When Christina walked into the bar looking for her husband he was nowhere to be seen.

'Where is he, Rico?' she asked, an exasperated expression on her face.

'He went out with Carlos for the evening', he replied apologetically.

'Of course he did,' she muttered, turning back to the

yard where she'd left Espe trying, without much success, to stroke one of the chickens. Christina tried to hold back the tears of frustration and loneliness but they tumbled down her cheeks regardless.

'Here…' Abuelita said, holding out a towel as Christina entered the yard.

She tried to turn away but with surprising strength the elderly lady pulled her into an embrace, gripping her shaking shoulders.

'I can't keep doing this,' she sniffed looking up into the eyes of this woman who had become like a mother.

'So much like his father,' she quietly observed, rubbing Christina's shoulder. 'He isn't a bad man.'

Straightening her back and rubbing her eyes she angrily replied, 'I know but what did I do wrong? I wish he would talk to me. Sometimes I think that he couldn't care less about me and Espe. I mean does he even give a fuck about our child?'

'Christina!' she reprimanded but then continued more softly. 'He loves her very much, but it's more complicated than that, it hurts him too much.'

At that moment, Espe grabbed at Christina's leg excitedly, 'Ma look, look!'

In one hand, she apprehensively cradled a smooth white egg as if at any moment it might jump from between her tiny fingers. But Espe was a careful and competent girl who, even at this age, took her time. She gently lowered the egg into her mother's hand, her face a picture of concentration. Passing the egg to Abuelita she scooped Espe up and held her tightly, kissing her perfect neck. Espe giggled, throwing her arms around her mother.

Resting her head against Christina's chest she asked, 'Where's daddy? I want to show him my egg.'

Christina woke alone in their bed. She wasn't sure what time it was but she could hear laughter coming from the next room. Sleepily she got to her feet and followed the sounds until she stood in the light thrown through Espe's open door. On all fours, giggling like a boy, was her very drunk husband. Espe sat up proudly on his back, shouting for him to go faster. She gleefully hugged his back as he haphazardly carried her around the room bumping into furniture.

Noticing her in the doorway Espe giggled, 'Pa is a bull, Ma!'

Jago swung around guiltily to face the door, getting onto one knee, forgetting for a moment that Espe was on his back. She toppled backwards, crashing her head onto the corner of the blue painted chest of drawers they had picked out together from the market in happier days. She hit the floor hard, an avalanche of books tumbling on to her from where they had been neatly stacked on top of the drawers. For a second there was calm, then she began to wail, a loud cry that brought her Abuelita from her bed as quickly as her old bones would permit. Christina rushed to her daughter, pulling her into a hug, inspecting her head where she had fallen. A deep red smudge had begun to work its way down the lines of her chocolate hair. Picking her up, Christina rushed her sobbing daughter out the door. Jago remained frozen on one knee in the now empty room.

When he woke the next morning, radiant sunlight streaked through the open window above their bed, a gentle breeze worked its way across the deep-set lines on his face. His head ached and waves of nausea kept him from moving. When eventually he rose fully dressed, his t-shirt mysteriously ripped at the sleeve, he staggered to the bathroom to be sick. Jago felt a misguided relief as the nausea passed and he splashed cool water on his face. It was as he stared back at his sorry reflection that he noticed the faded plastic cup on the shelf held just one solitary toothbrush.

He found his mother in the yard sitting quietly under the avocado tree sipping a glass of tea.

'They're gone,' she said without raising her eyes to meet his.

Shutting himself in his office, he sat at the desk as wave after wave of despair crashed over him. He felt regret and panic. Suddenly all he wanted was a normal morning with Espe crawling around his feet as he worked.

Jago had never been good in a crisis. He wasn't the type to grow stronger under pressure, giving himself a talking to and doing what had to be done. Instead, he drifted towards melancholy like a moth to the light. Once there, he poured himself a large drink and set in.

His mother on the other hand had no time for such behaviour, particularly considering she had just lost a daughter for the second time and now a granddaughter into the bargain.

A stiff silence formed between them, filling the empty rooms behind Rojo. An edge of decline gradually returned like a familiar old friend. Refusing to discuss the matter, he spent more and more time away. He began visiting expensive bars and then casinos. Soon the fortune under the bookcase had metamorphosed into a few hundred dollars of crumpled notes. Like everyone, he'd seen the shouty T.V adverts for personal loans. It was all too easy. Sign the form given to you by the girl with bad teeth behind the counter. Show his weathered ID and leave with the money.

His father had often said. 'When things come easy there is always a price.' But these were different times he told himself.

His newfound recklessness didn't go unnoticed. Carlos saw the signs that only a lifelong friend could. Deep Rorschach sweat patches dominated Jago's shirt as they took a weekend walk. Jago brushed off his friends gently probing questions and suggested they stop for a drink. Carlos felt helpless watching his old friend slowly come apart at the seams.

Three months after Christina and Espe left, the first letter came. The first few were opened and pinned under his father's solid glass paperweight with a ghostly image of a grand sailing ship carved inside. The rest went unopened, stuffed into an overflowing beer crate that lay on the floor behind the door. It would be wrong to say Jago didn't know he was in trouble but still he unravelled one stitch at a time, unable to catch the thread, lost in melancholy and self-loathing.

Increasingly Rico ran the bar alone. Unable to cope alone, he hired Sara, a slight seventeen-year-old history of art student, who left her eyes a little too long on Rico and wasn't a great judge of when to say goodbye at the end of shifts. But she was a hard worker and the customers liked her. At the end of each night, Rico paid her in cash out of the till as she lingered on tiptoes. At the weekends, Carlos joined them to fight back the tide but like a ship without a captain Rojo began to drift. Too tired to traipse home, Rico took to spending the night on a sleeping bag in the cramped loft room amongst stacked boxes of wine and oversized toilet rolls. Not oblivious to the stand-in captain's efforts, Jago's mother took to leaving him a morning glass of passion fruit juice and a plate of banana fritters on the top step of the wooden stairs.

When Jago hadn't been seen for two days, Rico called Carlos and they met at the corner of Calle Simon to search for their friend. Holding two takeaway coffees, Carlos arrived in tattered jeans, his flip flops slapping on the wide boulevard. It was Wednesday morning and calm set over the opening cafes and bars. Diligently their workers brushed and mopped down the footprint of pavement in front of their establishment. They worked their way through their favourite bars and cafes asking if they'd seen Jago but were met by the same apologetic shakes of heads. At Bar Loro, a spiralling filthy place with a sticky floor, the owner, a short, balding, overweight man who talked too much, told them he'd seen him last night at about 11 pm.

'Your friend was acting like a right arsehole. He got in an argument with a gringo over there by the bar, no idea over what but he was looking for trouble alright. I had to get David to haul him out in the end. The gringo was spending good money as well until your idiot friend pissed him off. I've not seen someone that drunk since my brother's wedding and that was messy. The whole family was pretty unsure when he said he was marrying a Chinese girl as you can imagine. I've always found them to be a miserable, lazy lot but she's actually really nice and pretty hot too.'

Thanking him they hastily backed out of the bar. Undeterred, the owner continued his story, turning instead to a young, nervous barman on his second full shift who stared at him with cornered-rabbit eyes.

It took them more than three hours before they finally found him, slumped asleep in the alleyway by a petrol station. He was propped up against the metal fence, his matted mop of hair resting on his wet knees. Curled up beside him was a bag-of-bones dog, that had lost a considerable amount of fur on its scab covered back. It opened one eye to survey the newcomers and beat its sorry tail in the dirt. Jago's canary yellow shirt, given to him by Christina as a birthday present two years before, was splattered with a mixture of blood, vomit and mud. One of his hands lay limp by his side, caked in dry crimson blood. With considerable difficulty, they hauled him to his feet and with an arm over each of their shoulders took him home. As they picked their way through the now busy streets, Jago sporadically groaned without ever raising his head. For all those passing knew, these two sweating men had found their friend dead. Eventually, under the midday sun they dragged him into the shut up Rojo, ignoring a man dressed all in denim, asking when they might open. They were met by Jago's mother who rushed to her son's side as they pulled him into his bedroom and laid him on the unmade bed.

When he woke, he was in just his boxer shorts under a sheet, the room dark except for a faint glow that seeped under the door. He tried to raise his head but the room began to spin dramatically. Instead he kept still and closed his eyes, letting the rhythmic sound of the ceiling fan wash over him. Momentarily he felt calm there alone in the dark, then as his mind wearily reassembled itself a surge of dread crashed through him, leaving an ache of worry in his chest. In nine days sixty thousand dollars would be deposited in his account and he would hand them the keys to their family home. It had never quite seemed the right moment to tell his mother or Rico. Becoming aware of the pain that ran from his right elbow down to his finger he glanced down and saw his hand was neatly bandaged, blood still sitting around the edges of his fingernails. He couldn't piece together much of the last couple of days but the memory of the three men who had visited him was clear enough.

'Sorry, we're closed.' he said, thinking they were customers after a late drink.

'Jago Vera?' enquired the well-built man with a soldier's haircut, on the left of the three.

'Yes?' Jago replied wearily, casting an eye over the man's black tight open polo shirt and crisply ironed beige trousers.

'We've come for some money. You haven't been big on replying to our letters and calls' he smirked.

The shortest of them, a man in his mid-forties with a

kind angular face, stood by the door, whilst the other, a towering giant, delicately inspected objects around the bar with dinner plate hands.

Jago, unsure what to do or say, hovered silently at the bar.

'Quite a little debt you've allowed to rack up my friend. Can't go on forever now can it?'

'I......' Jago began, but nothing followed.

'Look, let's keep this nice and friendly. We've got three more of these to do tonight and Rodrico's sister's getting married in the morning.' he confided, nodding over to the giant who turned from looking at the black and white picture of Cabron and grinned like a young boy.

'You owe us twelve, so I'm going to need to leave with a good portion of that so we all feel better about things, right?'

'I don't have it.' Jago eventually stuttered, 'but I will really soon, I have money coming in a few days. Here,' he offered, removing everything from the till and holding it out to them in shaking hands. 'It's only a few hundred but I have a bit more in the back, I'll give you all I have.' he pleaded, placing the cash on the bar and starting towards the back door.

Stepping assertively into his path, his polished leather shoes clicking on the concrete floor, the man held Jago's gaze for a few seconds.

'Lead the way then, let's see what we have back there.'

It was too tight for them all to fit in the small office so Jago slid around behind the desk, whilst the other two men stood awkwardly just inside the door. Jago quickly removed the remaining money from behind the bookcase and took the rest of the week's takings from the desk drawer, laying it out on its top. Flustered and with sweaty palms he counted through the notes.

'Nineteen hundred and whatever's on the bar, it's everything I have,' he said desperately, handing it to them.

At that moment, Jago's mother arrived in the corridor, in a long spotted dress, her hair pulled neatly in a bun.

'Jago? Is that you? I heard voices.' she enquired stepping towards the office.

Rising quickly to his feet, Jago replied in a loud voice, 'Yes mama, just here with some friends.'

She appeared by Rodrico in the doorway, 'Good evening,' she said greeting the two men, 'I didn't realise Jago had guests or I would have offered you something to eat. I'm sorry my son isn't always the most thoughtful at times. Are you hungry? I could have some tortillas ready in a few minutes.'

'Good evening Mrs Vega.' the man said politely, pushing the cash into his back pocket before she could see it, 'That is very kind of you. Me and Rodrico here must be going soon but I am sure we could eat something'

'Lovely, yes, come on through,' she replied full of

purpose, 'Excuse the mess, things haven't been the same since Christina left.'

The two men glanced quickly at each other before following her out into the hallway, leaving Jago stood behind his desk like a ventriloquist's dummy. Coming to his senses he rushed after them into the bright glow of the kitchen. His mother was already bent lighting the gas as he entered, talking casually to their uninvited guests.

'Lovely home you have here Mrs Vega, has it been in the family long?'

'Yes, my late husband's father ran it first as a Men's Club before Almando turned it into a bar about forty years ago. It's been through quite a lot this place.' she recounted, dropping some tortillas in a pan.

'Fascinating, and just the two of you live here now?' he continued, glancing at Rodrico as he stepped out into the backyard.

'Just us now.' she sighed reaching into the fridge, 'Jago takes care of Rojo now.'

His mother had been virtually mute since his wife and child left but she seemed to be making up for it now.

'Well, aren't you lucky to have a son like Jago here to look after you.' he said slapping him on the back and keeping a matey hand on his shoulder a little too long, 'It can be an ugly world out there.'

Rodrico returned from the yard and they all sat at the wooden table eating tortillas, chicken and avocado.

Both of the strangers complimented Jago's mother on her excellent cooking and made more small talk until Jago could bear it no longer. Pushing back his chair sharply, so it scraped loudly and rising to his feet he briskly said, 'Well, I am sure you must be late for your appointment by now.'

'Yes well, we should really be going. A pleasure to meet you Mrs Vega and thank you for the delicious food.' he said getting to his feet.

'Thank you Mrs Vega.' Rodrico parroted, quickly downing his glass of water.

Jago followed them out to the bar where the short man still stood by the door.

'We'll need the rest of that money pretty soon Jago. We'll come back in a week.' he said turning to Jago at the door, 'Good mother you got there. Make sure you look after her, won't you?'

Jago wasn't sure how much money he owed but he'd taken loans out with three different companies. That night lying in the bed he'd once shared with Christina, he felt the world cave in. He needed to escape but every way he turned he saw darkness. For two more days Jago stayed there, unable to raise his aching muscles from the bed. His mother brought him rice and beans that he barely touched and Carlos came with sympathetic eyes but Jago just turned away.

On Saturday he woke, suddenly clear on what had to be done. His bedside clock read 6.23 am as a cool breeze bellowed through his thin curtains like sails. Washing and dressing quickly he slipped out of the back gate, unable to face his mother. By the time the midday heat sent everyone into the relief of the shade, it was done. He'd rented a small flat for his mother that stood empty around the corner from Carlos, it was simple but clean with a small courtyard at the rear.

Todd Chambers had agreed to take the keys earlier than planned without question. They met at a bar on the corner of Calle Santiago. Todd was already there talking on his phone when Jago arrived. He quickly finished up the call as he approached, pocketing the phone and extending a hand in welcome.

'So how are we buddy, looking forward to the change?' Todd asked, his eyes unreadable behind expensive sunglasses.

Jago dropped into a chair beside him and ordered a coffee from the approaching waiter.

'So what's the plan, staying in the city?' Todd continued despite Jago's silence.

'I'm not sure.' Jago replied looking down at the scratched table.

'Well you have the money to start afresh; you're a lucky man Jago!' he laughed, taking a swig from his bottle of beer.

'Tell me...' Jago began, finally meeting his eyes, 'tell me about America.'

It hadn't taken long to find someone. A few questions at the bus station had led him up some steps behind the main building to a well-dressed man in his twenties (with hair that shone under the strip lights) who welcomed him into a small tiled office. The reassuring man sat, all king of his castle, behind a large glass topped desk that had an array of pictures of famous monuments around the world under it. Working with his nail at a coffee ring on the glass that hovered over the statue of liberty like a halo, Jago pressed him for details. He assured him that the journey would be by bus and then on a comfortable ferry, to a discreet port that they used near to New Orleans. He showed him laminated pictures of a deserted modern coach and a large ferry with a bar and tv.

'Much better by sea.' he said. 'Everyone is getting caught overland these days.'

He handed him a brightly coloured leaflet, with Palm Travels written at the top and a picture of a laughing couple in front of the American flag. A ticket to paradise would cost him eight thousand dollars.

It was late by the time he knocked on Carlos' door, the sound of heavy bass reverberating from the other side. Jago knocked again harder this time and the door burst open, Carlos grabbing him into a hug, a joint hanging out the corner of his smiling lips.

It took over an hour for Jago to explain everything. Carlos sat in his threadbare armchair, occasionally interrupting to clarify a point but otherwise silent. When he was finally finished Carlos looked tired, his eyes shocked with the realisation that he was losing his friend.

'Fuck, Jago.' he whispered.

Of course Carlos would do it, he would move a mother from her home, shut up Rojo for good, break the news that her only child had sold up and run without a single goodbye. Dependable, ever fucking reliable Carlos would clean up his mess, like he always had done. A silence stretched out between them, overwhelmed by a lifetime of memories and this insufficient goodbye.

'When do you go?' Carlos finally uttered, looking down at his bare feet.

'In three hours, out of town. Then a week,' he trailed off, 'I'll send money as soon as it clears.....thank you Carlos.'

'What about Christina and Espe?' Carlos eventually asked.

Reaching into his jacket pocket, Jago pulled out two envelopes, one addressed to Christina, one to Espe.

'If you can find out where they are, give these to them. They're better off without me. I'll send money when I get established.'

Jago looked down at his hands, they shook from exhaustion, 'Get Ma out tomorrow. I'll send word as soon as I arrive.'

Getting to his tired feet, Jago shuffled towards the door awkwardly, looking down at Carlos still slumped forward in his chair.

'Well, I better go.' he said so quietly he had to clear his throat and repeat himself.

Still Carlos didn't look up. Jago lingered, wanting to say something fitting but nothing seemed right. In the end, he slipped out the door, glancing back once more at the boy who had held him as he shook with rage after his sister's death, the teenager who'd pulled him drunk from the river, the man whom he was closest to in the world. Above all, Carlos would regret that moment for the rest of his life. He never saw Jago again and as much as he rewound and replayed that night he couldn't see his face as he disappeared out the door.

The solitary light from the small craft cast a glow onto the vast waves that shone like volcanic rock. Gripping the edge of the boat, fingers wrinkled, Jago couldn't tear his eyes from the swell, mesmerised by its looming form in the darkness. A large spot appeared on his shoulder, quickly followed by another. Before he had time to raise his wild eyes to the sky, the rain dropped heavily on them, leaving a million pin pricks in the angry waves. It wasn't long before he saw a collection of lights ahead glistening on the horizon. As they moved closer he could see it was another boat much larger than theirs. The others had noticed it now and they cut anxious glances to their captain but he stared forward, unconcerned. To their left, another small boat came into view and beyond them, another set of lights made their way towards the larger boat. At the front, the boy got to his unsteady feet and squinted into the downpour. As they drew closer, they could see the large boat was old and wooden, recently painted a blue that, even in the darkness, did nothing to hide its obvious decay. The simple lights of feeder boats bobbed manically as they manoeuvred towards it. He realised then that this was how they would get to America, not in a small craft with five of them, not on a large comfortable boat with T.V and bar, but in this looming monster, that sat perilously low in the water.

With considerable skill, Ivan brought them alongside the open topped boat that was bigger than Jago first thought. Rope ladders lay limp down its side at regular intervals and featureless forms could be seen scrambling up, waves leaping to meet them.

The blind man went first, his wife guiding his hands to the ropes, all the time speaking into his ear in the swirling wind. She took to the ladder almost on top of him, guiding him through each step. Unflappable at the wheel, Ivan held them close to the edge, both Jago and the young boy gripping the ladder, arms straining like branches in a storm. As the couple neared the top, Ivan's vessel was torn away from the large ship by the swell, sending Jago sprawling backwards. From the bottom of the boat, he watched in horror as a dark swell rose up and crashed over the couple but when it retreated he saw they still remained, clinging to the rope like crabs. Eventually, they both disappeared safely over the edge and Jago released a breath he didn't know he'd been holding.

A cigarette somehow still alight between his lips,

Ivan steered them back to the ladder. Taking up their positions again, soaked through, Jago nodded upwards to the boy. He stared back through petrified eyes before scrambling up the ladder, making quick work of the climb and leaping over. Time stood still for a moment as Jago paused at the bottom of the ladder, in awe at the ocean. Then he carefully rose taking a rung at a time without looking down or up. Reaching the edge surprisingly quickly, he felt hands on his arms heaving him over the edge and onto the deck. Looking around, he saw the couple and the boy had helped him over and were pulling him to his feet.

'Thank you.' he said, taking in the chaos around him.

They were stood on a wide deck that swept around the edges of the craft. It was crammed full of people who had claimed a spot on the rough wooden floor. Only close to the edge where startled bodies continued to pile, along with the occasional wave, was there any space. In the centre, stairs led to a higher deck that Jago could see was teeming as well.

'Let's find a space.' the lady said assertively, taking up her husband's arm. Jago and the boy followed as she cut a path through the huddled bodies around their feet. They weaved their way to the back, passing a stairway that led down into the hull but even the stairs were full here so they moved on. Eventually, they found an area that they could squeeze into. It was close to the shuddering engines and next to a pipe that thick dirty smoke rose from but they were grateful not to have to stand.

'This is crazy,' the young boy shouted into Jago's ear, over the storm.

Jago surveyed the crowd, hundreds of soaked bodies curled over bags silently or huddled together. An elderly man opposite him met his eye before retrieving a cap out of his bag and pulling it low over his head. To his left a mother sat with a young boy between her raised knees. He sheltered under her, eyes wide, pushing a banana into his mouth.

Reaching into his pack, Jago retrieved the photo in the sandwich bag and the packet of pumpkin seeds. He stared down at Espe as she smiled back at him. Using his sleeve he wiped at the wet surface but only made it worse. Suddenly overcome by emotion, his eyes filled with tears. How had he allowed himself to lose Espe? What was he doing here on this ship full of strangers? He felt angered by himself, he'd made a terrible mistake. If only he could turn back, gather her up in his arms again, smell her hair and say he was sorry. With tear streaked cheeks he offered the pumpkin seeds to the blind man, guiding them into his hand. Feeling the packet carefully the man smiled, the many lines vanishing briefly from his forehead. After tipping some into his hand he passed the packet to his wife and thanked Jago.

As they sat grinding the seeds with their teeth, the boat's horn sounded, cutting through the growling wind and rain. They began to move slowly away, the small feeder boat's lights diminishing. The overloaded ship diligently cut a path through the rough terrain, listing heavily from left to right.

Jago wasn't sure how long they had been on the water before he saw a commotion coming from the stairs that led down to the hold. Frantically, people were streaming out of the opening only to find there was nowhere for them to go. Those sitting around the stairway rapidly jumped to their feet to avoid being crushed. The panic spread out like a ripple on a pond as more and more bodies pushed forward. Standing on tiptoes Jago tried to see what was happening, but the nervous crowd began to push against him.

'Move back, move back!' he heard someone shout, as a back-pedalling, barefooted, stocky lady stood on his ankle.

'What's happening?' the woman to Jago's left desperately called, gripping her child tightly.

A tall, startled bald man told them that the hold had started taking on water and everyone had panicked, climbing over each other to reach the stairs. They waited for someone to tell them what to do. But as the torrential rain whipped across the sorry ship, a young girl screamed out, pointing up to the helm where the two men from the bridge could be seen trying to slip into the ships only lifeboat unnoticed. Like a fire in a room full of books, the news spread across the ship, sending them into a wild panic. Then gradually, the old vessel began slipping downward in defeat. At first, Jago didn't realise what was happening, then he noticed they were higher above the swell than before. Bodies pressed against him from all sides and a deep creaking groan came from the boat's spine. It began to angle sharply in the water as its nose dipped downwards. Water rushed hungrily across the deck sending scores of people and their belongings overboard. With one hand, Jago desperately grabbed onto a large metal ring attached to the deck, the other clutched the picture of Espe. As the ship continued its descent, he glanced up just in time to see the blind man and his wife jump hand in hand.

The water was full of people now, some sank instantly as if drawn to the looming darkness, others bobbed on the surface clutching bags. Jago considered jumping too but he'd never been the greatest swimmer, so he held on, there was little else to do. Terror spread through him, locking his muscles tight as the ship's stern continued to rise, leaving him hanging high above the gnashing waves. As if taking one last look, the vessel held its position there, like a whale's tail before diving. Jago watched helplessly as the ravenous wind whipped the photo from his hand, spinning away until it vanished from sight.

Unable to remain afloat a minute longer, the old ship slipped downward without complaint. As he hit the water, Jago released his grip from the ring but the immense force of the sinking ship pulled him with it. Opening his eyes he saw nothing but swirling darkness as he was pulled lower. Below him, the tired vessel slid towards the sea bed, trailing a million sparkling bubbles behind it. Jago reached the boundaries of his final breath but held it there regardless. Balanced on the edge of nothing, he met only one face in the darkness. Her bright eyes smiled as she held out a thin hand to him, hair dancing around her pale face. Jago reached out, taking her hand. She flashed him a knowing smile, before turning and pulling him into the darkness.

This was an unfamiliar place for Alex, a whole day stretched ahead with nothing planned. Standing in a dressing gown, nursing his third coffee and unsure what to do, he called Olivia.

'I thought you were having the day off?' she answered, without a hello.

'Morning Olivia, I just want to check you managed to move my meetings for today?'

'Yep, ten o'clock with Strategy moved to the 29th, Clayton says he'll let you know his brief, and the pm meet was just the DA so they won't miss you. Then tomorrow was only Bupa in Birmingham, Clayton's sent David instead.'

'Ok right, good.' Alex stuttered, searching for something else to say.

'Now are you going to stop talking to me and actually take some time off?' she added dryly.

'Yes, thank you Olivia, I'll see you in a couple of days.'

'Of that much we are certain.' she quipped. 'Oh and Alex?'

'Mm?'

'Make sure you actually switch off and enjoy yourself, won't you? Go shopping or something.'

'Yes. Well got to go, thanks Olivia.' Alex hastily replied ending the call.

Standing looking out onto the street below, he felt oppressed by the uniform grey sky. From where he stood he could see into the large meeting room of the advertising agency opposite. Casually dressed twenty and thirty-somethings sat around in mismatched chairs, sofas and beanbags, tapping into laptops. A young man, in ripped jeans and a cut off t-shirt that revealed tattoos down both arms, was riding a unicycle around them, seemingly unnoticed. Ego a little dented by Olivia's retort, Alex considered his options for the day. She was right, he needed to treat himself, do something he enjoyed.

He'd just put his shoes on ready to head out when the videocom buzzed.

'I'll come down,' he shouted at the screen.

Alex hated delivery people coming up to his flat with their dirty shoes and needy conversations.

'Good morning buddy,' the delivery guy chirped, putting down the two boxes at his feet, 'one more in the van, won't be a second.'

He hadn't remembered ordering this many he thought to himself, as the delivery driver reappeared with the final box.

'At least they're light.' he joked, handing Alex the machine to scribble his signature on. Completely ignoring him, Alex took the last box and pushed the door closed, cutting off his, 'You have a good day now buddy.'

'You're very welcome.' the driver muttered under his breath as he climbed back into the van. Grabbing his coffee from the cup holder he took a swig and grimaced at its cold contents. He looked at the list of deliveries and sighed.

Back in his flat, Alex retrieved a scalpel from the drawer and opened the boxes. He lined them up on the counter and wondered where they got the names from: Stilnox, Adderall, Mogadon, Xanax, Oxycodone. It suddenly came to him that he'd read something bad about Xanax in the news recently so he decided not to take that one, unless he was really desperate. Picking up the box of Adderall he looked for some information on how many he should take but couldn't find any. Deciding to go cautiously he popped one of the orange tablets from the packet and swallowed it down.

It was mid morning by the time he arrived at Westfield, just shy of two million square feet of shops and cafes tapped onto the Olympic Village. Despite the grey it was mild, a suggestion of spring in the air after so many cold days. With a spring in his step, enjoying the novelty of a day off, Alex followed the stream of people towards the entrance. The place was vast, sparkling and bright, a breathtaking number of people were gliding up escalators and drifting in and out of shops. He spent the rest of the morning buying on impulse: some new trainers (maybe he'd start running he lied to himself), a watch for Phil's birthday, the girl behind the tills weekly wage on two shirts that looked a lot like those already hanging in his wardrobe. Quickly staff spotted the well dressed man with numerous bags from expensive shops and steered him towards their top range. Not that Alex cared, he was thoroughly enjoying himself.

By lunch time the euphoria was fading and he was starting to feel shopped out. Somewhere along the way a Westfield representative, called Jenny, who had just had her number of anti-depressants upped by her doctor, offered him their 'Hands Free Service', taking his bags to a safe place so he didn't 'have the inconvenience of luggage'. A well rehearsed phrase that made Jenny despise herself just a little bit more each time she uttered it. Laden with bags, she propped up her smile and watched Alex, who hadn't even made eye contact or said thank you, saunter away.

Feeling hungry Alex settled in Café Concerto, a sparkling Gatsby of a place with a red-carpeted raised platform sporting a grand piano. A sullen, silver haired man of indeterminate age was slumped over it playing background lounge music. Alex thought the place ought to be on a cruise ship but he didn't have the legs to go elsewhere. He hadn't felt this good in ages, riding the endorphin wave of purchases through the morning he'd worked up quite an appetite. Having ordered the sea bass he sat back looking around him. Only a couple of tables were occupied, bored looking staff arriving a bit too keenly at their tables. His waitress, in a desperate attempt to cut through the boredom that stretched out endlessly in front of her, lingered when bringing his drinks, asking if he was on holiday. *On fucking holiday, Jesus Keisha,* she thought to herself, half a second later.

'No, Clerkenwell's home. This place looks a bundle of laughs to work in.' he replied, pleased for the company.

Keisha, whose habit of picking up the wrong men drove her friends crazy, smiled widely, 'Yeah, it can get pretty boring and the music sucks.' she said, dropping her voice and glancing behind her. 'Still it's a job innit and some of the customers aren't so bad.'

'I'm Alex,' he replied smiling and raising an eyebrow.

'Keisha, nice to meet you.' she returned, thinking he was a bit old but what the hell.

'Does he ever stop?' he asked, nodding his head towards piano man as he laboured through an instrumental of a Coldplay song.

'Nope, he goes for hours,' she giggled.

'Lucky you, at least I get to leave shortly.'

'Tell me about it, six more hours,' she said rolling her eyes, 'I just block it out.'

'Then we should probably have a drink when you

202

finish so you can erase it from your memory.' Alex calmly replied, holding her eye contact until she looked away.

She laughed, taken back by his confidence.

'Ok then, meet me outside at eight.'

'Look forward to it.' Alex replied, smiling.

'Well, I better do some work.' she said, not knowing what else to say and glancing back several times as she headed back to the kitchen.

'Hey, guess who's got a date tonight?' she said excitedly to Hannah, who she met coming out of the kitchen carrying three laden plates.

'What, that old guy on table seventeen?! Seriously Keisha you're such a slut.' she laughed, taking the plates to their table whilst subtly checking Alex out.

'He's kinda cute though, don't you think?'

'I think you should message your mum to tell her where you'll be just in case you end up raped and murdered at his place.' Hannah replied with a grin.

'You sick bitch!' Keisha giggled, following her into the kitchen.

Finishing his last mouthful of the fish, Alex leant back, wiping his mouth with his napkin, feeling pleased with himself. He gazed lazily out the window opposite onto the open air shopping street beyond. Sat on a bench next to an impressive olive tree, staring straight at him, was the man from the cafe. He gave a friendly wave and shook his head smiling, looking down at his unlaced boots. Without taking his eyes off him Alex sprang to his feet, knocking over his glass of water as he brushed past the table. There was no way he was getting away from him this time, Alex thought as he marched purposefully out the restaurant and over to where he sat.

'Who are you and what exactly is it you want?' he blurted a little too loudly.

'And lovely to see you again too.' the man replied, rubbing his wild beard thoughtfully.

Alex had worked over in his head all the things he would say to the man if he saw him again, but stood in front of him he forgot what they were. There was a careless disarming confidence about him.

'I go by a few names but mostly they call me Meeth.'

Calming himself Alex asked. 'Look, how do you know my name? Did we meet somewhere before that I've forgotten? And why on earth are you following me around?'

'You look a lot better than when I last saw you.' Meeth replied, pulling off his gloves. 'Had a pleasant morning, have we? You're not showing any signs of this recession everyone's talking about now are you my friend?'

Frustrated by his failure to answer his questions, Alex tried again.

'Is there something I've done to upset you somehow, because if there is I have no idea what it is. It would be decent manners to actually answer my question.'

'Well that's better Alex. I knew you had it in you

somewhere.' he smiled getting slowly to his feet, 'You've done nothing to upset me fella, I'm not that easily upset.' he chuckled, taking a half smoked cigarette from his pocket.

'You can't smoke here, it's illegal.' Alex declared automatically.

Meeth rubbed at a thick bit of skin on his yellowed finger. He seemed to be considering something.

Eventually, he looked up seriously and said, 'I don't mean to alarm you Alex but there's a fair bit riding on this and I'm not one to sit in the shadows. Whether you like it or not, something's shifting and for reasons unknown to me you've got a part to play.'

Alex glanced back through the restaurant window to see the waitress watching him, a bewildered expression on her face.

'A part to play in what exactly?'

'You'll find out soon enough and you ain't gonna like it my friend.' He lit the stub and pocketed the lighter, 'Question is have you got it in you? That's what I can't quite work out.'

'So what do you need from me?' Alex countered, determined to get to the bottom of this.

'Fuck me,' the man spluttered, laughter turning into a hacking cough, 'this ain't no business meet Alex. What you or I need ain't got nothing to do with it. The water's flowing and which way it forks is all that remains to be seen.'

Meeth was quiet for a moment as he gazed up at the

concrete sky. Alex noted the dirt under his fingernails with disgust.

'Do you remember when you were a boy Alex? Think way back. What happened to that boy, full of love, who told Francoise he wanted to save the world's sick children...where did he go?'

Without stopping, a jogger in a fluorescent jacket knocked hard into Alex's arm as he passed, causing him to spin around.

'Hey!' Alex shouted after him, annoyed, 'Watch where you're going!'

Turning back Alex found himself looking at a vacant bench. Desperately he looked around but there was no sign of him in either direction. Perplexed, he just stood there, staring at the space where Meeth had been, the smell of the tobacco still lingering in the air. An elderly woman in a camel coat, walking an impossibly small dog, eyed him suspiciously as she passed.

'Um, excuse me Alex, are you ok?' Keisha uttered, leaning half out the restaurant door starting to wonder if a drink was such a good idea.

She seemed to say something else but he couldn't understand her, as if she were suddenly speaking in a different language. He stood looking around him, a rush of heat streaming to his face. Why was everyone looking at him?

Without answering her, Alex stumbled away, a numbness spreading into his fingers. Just the mention of Francoise had sent an overwhelming cascade of emotions through him. All he could do was run, arms and legs chaotically bumping into confused shoppers. His throat closed in, he tried to swallow but couldn't. A strange buzzing filled his ears, deafening him to the world that he desperately wanted to escape. He clutched at his neck, finding it difficult to breathe. Every breath felt like he was underwater. Scrambling around in his jacket pocket, he found the Adderall and quickly swallowed a couple more tablets. He collapsed onto a bench and laid down, closing his eyes and covering his ears in a futile attempt to block out the buzzing. People streamed past him on the way to the station, too preoccupied to worry about some businessman who'd had one too many at lunch. He lay there for nearly an hour until the buzzing ebbed away. Sitting up, he cupped his head in his hands and tried to push away the thought of Meeth. Enough was enough he decided, getting to his feet and calling Olivia.

'Missing me already?' she answered.

'No, not really, but I need you to pay my bill at Café Concerto at Westfield and have my shopping collected and delivered to the flat.'

'So you went shopping...hang on, did you run out without paying the bill?'

'Look, I've got to go, just get it done.'

'Yes your majesty.' he heard her say as he cut off the call.

Back at the flat he stripped to his boxers and studied himself in the mirror before heading to the spare room to begin a workout. Whenever Meeth sneaked back into his mind he ran harder on the treadmill or lifted weights more quickly. Suddenly everything seemed simple, he felt a clarity of thought and purpose. He just needed to take control. Clearly, he told himself, one Adderall hadn't been enough but since taking those two he felt great. For over two hours he pushed his body hard, congratulating himself.

The party was in full swing when Alex arrived, a little late. In truth, he wasn't late, he couldn't bear being late. In the hope that he wouldn't have to spend hours with people he didn't know, he'd decided to arrive at 3.30 pm, an hour and a half after the invite time. Wispy marbled clouds occasionally obscured the spring sun as the guests entered into the spirit of summer, even if it wasn't quite warm enough.

Finding no answer at the front door of Phil's new build, he ventured around the back, nodding to the friendly neighbour cleaning his car outside his identical house, bubbles riding the slalom through the fresh brick paving. Alex appreciated the order and neatness of the place, the fresh paintwork and immaculate lawns. A delicious smell greeted him as he located the back gate, puffs of smoke drifting up on the gentle breeze. Stopping for a moment at the boundary, Alex watched kids storm over the clipped grass. One chubby, red cheeked girl of seven or eight wielded a plastic sword that she brought down with considerable force on any children surrounding her. A trio of huddled boys approached her with caution, brightly coloured water pistols raised. A large deck struck out from the back of the house rimmed by neat shrubs on a carpet of loose bark. The deck was filled with people holding glasses, a babble of conversation mixing with barely audible music.

'Alex, you made it!' Phil smiled, appearing from the crowd wearing a World's Best Dad apron and holding a bottle of beer.

'Happy birthday.' Alex replied, holding out a bag.

'Hey you shouldn't have,' he laughed, pulling the gift out the bag and ripping off the paper.

'Holy shit, this is awesome but way too much.' He reached to give him a hug, half stopped awkwardly, then opted to drape a matey arm around his shoulder instead, 'Come on, I'll get you a drink and introduce you.'

They squeezed their way through guests to the end of the deck where a large plastic bin was filled with ice and various bottles of beer. Phil grabbed one, opened it and held it out to Alex, not asking what he wanted.

'Hey Sarah, come here and meet Alex.'

'Ah the famous Alex, I was beginning to wonder if Phil's been having an affair.' she joked, poking her husband playfully in the side. She brushed her straight black hair from her eyes and winked at Alex.

'And look at what he got me.'

'Expensive gifts, you two are having an affair aren't you?' she laughed, knocking back a hefty swig of her beer.

'What can I say, he's a very attractive man your husband.' Alex replied, liking her instantly.

'Isn't he just,' she giggled, putting an arm around his back and kissing his broad neck.

'Nice place you have here.' Alex said looking across the garden.

'Yeah we love it, bought it off the plans, wide halls for Callum as well and we had the lift added.' she replied before shrieking with delight, excusing herself and running off to hug a woman in a long navy dress who'd appeared at the gate.

The afternoon was much more enjoyable than Alex had expected. Phil, a considerate host, introduced him to a few people who had been warm and friendly once they worked their way through the tedious script of questions about work. For a large bulk of the afternoon he spoke to an interesting couple from Albania, in their fifties and immaculately dressed but still in their coats. Having taken two trips to Tirana last year Alex was quick to tell them how much he'd enjoyed the city. They spoke passionately about Tirana, making Alex realise how little he'd really seen of the place. Sure he'd taken a walk around a couple of the tourist sights on an afternoon off but the rest had been the inside of the Sheraton. Their conversation was interrupted by Callum, Phil's eldest son of twelve working his way across the deck in his wheelchair, a large rectangular cake covered in lit candles perched on his lap. Making space for him to pass, the guests broke into song, twinkling eyes turned to locate Phil. They found him face down in the grass, a pile of giggling children on his back. Heaving his wardrobe-like frame upright, the kids tumbled onto the grass. Pushing his bright blue glasses back on straight, Ben, Phil's youngest (and absolute last he'd told Alex), clutched resolutely to his dad's leg. He stayed by his side as he blew out the candles and hugged Callum, trying not to squash the cake. Alex couldn't help making comparisons to his last birthday which he'd spent at work. He hadn't told anyone because he didn't like a fuss. When he eventually got home at eight, he'd opened the cards from his parents and his Aunt Susan, who he hadn't seen for six years, but never missed his birthday. Propped on the counter they'd looked so pathetic that Alex had put them straight into the recycling the following morning.

In search of the toilet, Alex slipped away from the noise and headed inside. Stepping into the hall, he felt relieved to be alone and stood there briefly, gazing absent mindedly at the family portraits that lined the walls. A large framed photo of the whole family somewhere abroad caught his eye. Phil wearing a ridiculous oversized sombrero beamed at the camera, carrying a much younger looking Ben. Callum was in front, his expression hidden behind sunglasses, a basketball on his lap. Sarah in a summer dress had Evie resting against her, hands raised in celebration. Behind them were palms and they stood on a wide boulevard. Alex stepped closer to see if he could work out where the picture was taken, he thought he remembered Phil mention something about a family holiday to Miami once.

'Venice Beach,' a voice said making him jump back in surprise, 'two years ago.'

He hadn't noticed Evie sitting on the second step of the stairs, knees drawn up to her chin.

Unsure how to talk to an eleven-year-old, Alex said nothing for a moment. Her long mousey hair dropped in front of her freckled cheeks as she looked down at a spot on the wooden floor.

'You ok?' Alex finally managed. 'There's cake outside.'

She ignored him and picked at a toenail. Spying the downstairs toilet near the front door Alex stepped towards it but stopped when Evie asked, 'Who're you?'

'I'm Alex.' he replied, turning to face her. She looked up and briefly met his gaze, 'How come you're in here?'

'I was supposed to take the cake out, mum said I could when we made it together.'

'I wonder why she changed her mind?' Alex speculated, perching on a bench opposite the stairs, surrounded by shoes.

Evie flicked her hair back in a way she'd seen older girls do, 'What Callum wants, Callum gets.'

Pulling herself upright she studied the man in front

of her, 'Do you always dress like you're going to work?'

'Err, yes I guess so.' Alex mumbled in response.

'Do you have a wife?'

Surprised by the question, Alex coloured a little, looking down at his shoes, 'No I don't.'

He felt uncomfortable and sat upright as if to leave.

'Sorry, I didn't mean to embarrass you.' Evie quickly said, watching him closely.

'Really, it's fine,' he replied, pulling himself together, 'are you married?'

Snorting with laughter she replied, 'I'm never getting married, I'm going to spend my life rescuing dolphins, just as soon as I get out of here.'

'Don't you like it here then?'

'You try living with two idiot brothers, one who's a little shit and steals my stuff and the other who can't do wrong.' she said sitting up arching her back like a cat. 'Do you have any brothers or sisters?'

'No, my parents didn't want any more, I'm not entirely sure they wanted me either to be totally honest.'

'Lucky you.'

'Actually I think I would've quite liked a sibling, it was a bit lonely on my own all the time.' he admitted, surprising himself.

'I reckon you'd be a nice brother.'

Alex looked up and saw she was looking straight at him.

He stood, a little too quickly, nearly losing his

balance on a pair of bright pink trainers.

'Sorry, they must be yours, I better get back.'

'No worries, they're a bit small now anyway.'

At the doorway to the kitchen, Alex turned and looked back, 'Nice to meet you.'

'Bye,' Evie said, watching him go.

Alex met Sarah in the kitchen pulling another bag of ice from the freezer, 'Ah there you are!' she said, slicing the top of the bag with some scissors, 'Did you have any cake?'

'No, I'm fine thanks, full from those kebabs. They were delicious, thank you.'

'Flattery will get you everywhere,' she laughed, pouring the ice into a large bucket and leaning against the counter to face him, 'you plan to have kids one day Alex?'

'Er probably not...I mean it's not something I've really thought about that much to be honest.' he replied, finding a clean glass and emptying the last of a bottle of red, 'I'm away a lot, and pretty sure I'd need a partner first.'

'I'm sure you'll meet the right one eventually. Come on, let's get this ice outside,' she smiled, leading the way back outside.

A few people were beginning to drift away, a soft light filling the garden, wisps of clouds criss-crossing like webs over a sky gradually losing its colour. The deck was still well occupied but the lawn was silent, scattered with abandoned inflatables and toys.

Later, Alex and the last few guests helped ferry the many glasses into the kitchen. Despite hardly having dunked his soft hands in a sink his entire life, Alex found himself washing glasses, shirt sleeves rolled up to the elbows.

'The problem is we've just not got the strength and depth for promotion this season,' a drunk Phil lectured, picking up another glass and drying it badly on an already wet tea towel.

'I don't know what that means.' Alex replied with a smile.

'Yeah, yeah you don't like football. Basically it means we don't have enough good players. But I'm still determined for you to come to a game some time; I reckon you'll love it once you get into it.'

'Maybe, but I might need to know the rules first.' Alex laughed, thinking he should put less washing up liquid in next time he did this.

'My husband boring you with football as well, Alex?' Sarah asked as she walked in carrying two large bowls, 'I find the best thing is to completely ignore him, just pretend he doesn't exist.'

'Hey it's my birthday, I'll talk about football all I like.' Phil chuckled, grabbing Sarah around the waist.

As Alex finished the last glass he realised all the other guest were gone. He suddenly felt embarrassed, an imposter in this family's home.

'God I must be drunk, I've become the guest that won't leave.' he said, hastily drying his hands and searching for his jacket.

'Don't be stupid, you've been washing up and it's been lovely having you here.' Sarah insisted. 'The kids are about to put on a film, why don't you stay and watch it?'

'No, really, thank you, I'd better be going. Great party.'

Finding his jacket on the back of a chair he pulled it on and edged to the front door.

'Thanks for coming buddy and for the watch; I love it.' Phil beamed, shaking his hand and bumping drunkenly into the dresser in the hall.

'Lovely to meet you Alex.' Sarah said, kissing him on the cheek. 'Come for Sunday lunch some time soon.'

'That'd be lovely, thanks.' Alex replied, opening the front door.

'Bye Alex,' Evie shouted from the living room.

'Well someone's made an impression with Little Miss Grump.' Sarah remarked, looking surprised.

It was getting dark and the temperature had dropped. Alex took a few steps and looked back at the house. Every window glowed and through the lounge window he saw Phil collapse onto the sofa, Ben climbing into his lap. Callum sat expressionless on the other sofa and Evie stared at her phone, crosslegged in an armchair. Sarah stepped into the room and caught sight of him through the window and waved. Embarrassed, he waved as he expeditiously turned and paced away. But as he buried his hands in his pockets he felt strangely emotional about that scene through the window, half wondering if he should have stayed.

About twenty minutes later as he waited on the busy platform for the train, he began to feel a mixture of loneliness and irritation. He got up from the bench and moved away from the teenagers playing music loudly on their phones only to find himself next to a couple in their fifties kissing intensely, the woman's hand gradually slipping downwards. Only at the very far end of the platform did he find a little quiet but by then the tips of his fingers were tingling despite the coin's reassuring weight in his hand. It was only then that he realised he hadn't taken any Adderall since this morning. Normally he had some at lunch and late afternoon; no wonder he was feeling a little off. The train had arrived so he ushered himself into the largely empty first class and took a window seat. Picking up a discarded newspaper he skimmed the lead story with the headline: *HERE WE GO AGAIN – MARKETS ON THE BRINK* before deciding it was too depressing. Instead he swallowed down two tablets, sitting back and closing his eyes as the shadow of the city slipped by.

Three weeks after the party on a warm Saturday afternoon, Alex sat wedged in the corner where he could view the half-full cafe. A late afternoon sun filtered through the windows, bathing the relaxed crowd in a dreamy golden light. Waiting for his coffee to arrive, he watched two twenty-something friends, heads bent forward, deep in conversation over their shared pot of tea. To his left, a concerned looking woman peered at her laptop, chin balanced on her wrist, a cold half drunk coffee beside her. He hadn't been back here since his meeting with Meeth but he'd resolved not to try to avoid him anymore. He seemed to have found him when he wanted anyway. Phil and Evie arrived soon afterwards, Phil breaking into a smile on spotting Alex in the far corner. For a large man he was surprisingly graceful, removing his coat he slipped between tightly packed tables with ease, Evie following behind him apprehensively.

'Hi buddy.' Phil smiled, shaking Alex's hand as he rose from his seat.

'How was the show?' Alex asked both Phil and Evie as they joined him at the table.

'Totally awesome.' Evie replied, perching on a wooden stool, 'I didn't want it to end.'

Phil looked pleased with himself, he'd booked tickets to Swan Lake at Sadlers Wells as a surprise for Evie. After the BBQ, Alex had told him about his conversation with her and ever since Phil had been all out not to lose his daughter to a growing resentment. When Phil had mentioned Alex lived around the corner, Evie had insisted they meet him after the show. I don't know how you managed it but she thinks you're great. Any tips on how to stop her hating my guts would be very welcome! Phil had said in his email.

'What do you want sweety?' Phil asked, rising to go

to the counter.

'Dad don't call me that, I'm not five.' she sighed, rolling her eyes dramatically, 'I'll have an orange juice please.'

'You should be nicer to your dad.' Alex said, once Phil had made his way to the counter.

'I know, I can't help myself sometimes.' she giggled, placing a large glossy programme on the table.

'How are you?' Alex asked to fill a brief silence.

'Good thanks. Did you tell my dad I wasn't happy at his birthday?'

Alex couldn't help feeling he'd betrayed her trust, 'Yeah sorry, was that the wrong thing to do?'

'Na it's fine, he's just been ridiculously nice to me since, it's hilarious. Thanks though, I'm loving it!' she whispered. 'You still not found a wife yet?' Evie teased, scratching her neck, leaving a red mark.

'No, it seems I'm not husband material.'

'Well I wonder what you're doing wrong? Do you want a wife?' she questioned, fixing him with eyes the colour of bark.

'Maybe. I'm not sure, I guess so, it's not something I've thought about much to be honest.' he replied, not used to being questioned so directly.

'Well that might just be the problem.' she said leaning back, hand on chin, like a detective having solved a great mystery.

Alex laughed heartily as Phil returned to the table balancing a tray with Evie's orange, two coffees and three generous slices of cake.

'Evie is just explaining to me why my relationships are such a complete disaster!'

'Oh really?' Phil remarked, eyebrows raised in surprise, 'And why is that?'

'None of your business.' Evie quickly replied, tucking her tea coloured hair behind her ears.

They talked about the show and Evie's two goals she'd scored for the school football team last week, that she was unable to describe without Phil excitedly butting in with extra details.

At school, Alex had played some rugby but he'd always been in the bottom group of misfits roughly grouped into: the geeks - who seemed blissfully unaware this world had given them limbs. The physically challenged, like Luke Farrow, who despite a rugged determination (and a specially made shoe), couldn't make up ground with one leg shorter than the other. And finally the others, a group of those who knew that sport was a big thing to almost everyone else, tried briefly to engage, but ultimately just weren't feeling it. This is where Alex found himself for much of his school life at Sudbury School for Boys, a lumbering old institution so smothered in tradition its privileged young boys could barely breathe.

When he was ten, with a whole summer holiday looming, his mother had somewhat optimistically enrolled him in tennis lessons at her club. Eager to please, Alex, lanky anaemic legs in new specially bought shorts and shoes, laboured for an entire summer, gripping the racket with two hands, desperately attempting a return on his mother's deep rooted investment. He never once moaned about going but as the leaf edges began to turn singed brown and school returned, the lessons were quietly dropped. His mother, forever the rock, never mentioned it, just one crisp Saturday morning they were going to Aunty Dolores' instead and that was that.

To change the subject, Alex asked Evie about the show and then listened contently as she went into enthusiastic detail. He could have happily sat and listened to her all afternoon but Phil glanced at the watch Alex had given him for his birthday and said they needed to get going to catch their train.

'Before I forget, Sarah asked if you'd like to come for lunch on Sunday the twenty-third? No big deal if you can't, just a family lunch.'

'I'd love to.' said Alex, before Phil could finish.

'You don't have to wear a shirt and jacket when you come, dad will probably just be wearing one of his stained t-shirts anyway.' Evie smirked, pulling on her coat.

'Evie! Don't be so rude. Sorry Alex.'

'It's alright, I'm already used to your daughter taking the piss out of me.' Alex chuckled affectionately, as they filed out the door.

Three redundant chimneys stretch up into the cloudless sky as the sprawling industrial works slip absent-mindedly to rust. Escaping the oppressive heat, a man sits with his back to the wall amongst the pipes and levers. From his pack, he takes a creased paper bag and getting to his aching feet, walks over to the control panel opposite him. Instinctively, he pushes at the many buttons and switches randomly. Nothing happens, except one of the buttons gives way, falling through the rusted casing. Gently he pours the birdseed into his coarse hand and sprinkles it onto the flat top of the panel. He adds two more handfuls before picking thoughtfully at his dirt filled nails. Then without a sound, he returns to the wall and waits. Staring intently through the gaping mouth of the open loading bay, he holds his breath in anticipation.

It's only a few minutes before the bird comes darting through the opening and lands on a pipe that hangs from the ceiling. Cocking his head he eyes the offering below, ruffling his bright feathers before landing acrobatically on the control panel. This is what the man was waiting for and what brings him back again and again. To be close to this living being, to share this moment, just a metre or so apart. Fleetingly their eyes meet and the man wonders what the bird thinks as it stares back at him. Then snatching at the seed he swoops away leaving the man alone again with his silence.

Just after Rosa got ill me and Ma are at the market getting some food for dinner and some medicine herbs for Rosa. We go to the same stall as always for our veg. The woman who ran it always looked the same with her long black hair tied back and rosy cheeks and purple top with a stained blue apron over it. I wonder how she gets so much stuff in her space as it's packed with overflowing baskets of peppers and onions and carrots and tomatoes and herbs and some things I don't know the name of and it's all piled high like a colourful hillside of veg. At the back towering above everything are wicker baskets of all shapes and sizes. She doesn't smile much but Ma said she does the freshest fruit and veg. Apparently she was the cheapest too and Ma was always worrying about the price rises.

We leave the stall and work our way through the crowds without saying much. The bag of vegetables is cutting into my hand and is really heavy so I try not to think about how far we have to walk home. The medicine stall is in the far corner of the market under the canopies that keep off the hot sun. It's quieter up there and smells of incense mixed with rotting fruit.

We find the medicine place between a book stall that looks like someone threw the books into a pile randomly and one selling religious statues of all shapes and sizes. There are all sorts of different coloured powders in bags at the front and the back is lined with jars full of all sorts of herbs and dried plants. I don't notice the old man at first he's so small and has wispy long hair and little round glasses. He appears as if by magic and asks what we need. There's something about his eyes that freak me out. They're like black dots and I get this feeling he can read my thoughts so I look away. Ma asks him for something to help Rosa's lungs and he asks a few questions before heaping a whole load of god knows what into a plastic bag and tells Ma that Rosa should mix it with water and drink three times a day. It could be coloured cement dust for all we know but Ma pays him anyway and we head home. I have this uncomfortable feeling all over my body. I can't help thinking Diego might be right. What if I gave this to Rosa? How can I tell Ma it's my fault she's sick? I feel like my chest is on fire and pain is just cutting through me and I feel so angry with myself.

When we get there later that afternoon Rosa is in bed and her eyes are closed. Ma rushes over to her and puts a hand on her arm and whispers her name.

Don't worry Christina I'm not dead yet. Rosa says

without opening her eyes and Ma looks totally terrified but Rosa squeezes her hand and smiles. Ma starts unpacking things from the market and I go over and sit with Rosa. I take her hand in mine and her skin looks like scrunched up paper and I can see all her veins underneath. I spot my reflection in her gold wedding ring and I look a total state. She told me once that Ribaldo used a piece of thread to hang it from a tree so it dangled down in the middle of the path where they walked together every day. She saw it shining in the sun and when she turned around to tell Ribaldo he was down on one knee looking up at her.

Ma has to head home for a bit to finish the trousers she's working on and asks if I'm coming but I tell her I'll stay for a bit. When Ma's gone I sit for a while by Rosa's side picking my nails with worry and listening to the radio coming from someone's room nearby. Rosa opens her eyes and asks me to help her sit up so I put her cushions behind her and she takes a sip of water from the glass with the flowers on it. She looks me straight in the eye and says

Angel I'm going to have to go soon.

I stupidly ask her where she's going not getting what she means. She says she isn't sure but that we won't see each other again after that. I just freeze and don't know what to say. My eyes fill with tears and I bite my lip and taste metal in my mouth. She pulls me into a hug and I cry so much I make her top wet. When I pull myself together I feel all shaky and she brushes my hair out of my eyes. I blubber something about being sorry and that she seemed so lonely and everyone was being so horrid to her I just wanted to be her friend and then just sob and sob resting my head on Rosa's lap.

When I calm down Rosa pulls me up and looks me in the eye and says

Espe I'm not dying of TB. You haven't caught it and this isn't your fault.

I don't believe her and explain how she got sick so soon after I hung out with Alicia and Diego told me this story. She puts her finger on my lips and tells me her lungs are shot and that she doesn't have the strength to face what's coming. When Rosa says this she looks into the distance like she's looking out the window at someone far off. I ask her what she means as she isn't making a whole lot of sense but she just says the new world will be no place for her and she's seen too many changes. I'm thinking maybe her fever has got worse and she's losing it but she looks back at me her eyes all serious and I don't have a clue what she was talking about. I do now of course. Even saying it out loud to you gives me this weird feeling like the world is moving under my feet.

That's when she grabs me either side of the face and tells me I need to be strong and that whatever the world throws at me I should take time to know myself and always be ready for change. Then she lets go of me and slowly lies back down and closes her eyes. I sit there in her dark little room on the wooden stool wondering what on earth all that meant.

Later that night I'm so churned up I can't take it a minute longer so blurt out to Ma that I'd hung out with Alicia and how it's all my fault. She hugs me and laughs and tells me it's not TB and it's definitely not my fault. She says Rosa will get better soon but she doesn't look at me when she says it so I know she's lying. She just slips into her chair and carries on sewing and I think I've never seen Ma looking so tired.

For the next few days I go and see Rosa as soon as my work's done. She mostly just lies there with her eyes closed making big wheezing breaths. I decide I'm not going to keep any more secrets from her so I sit by her side and tell her about the hotel and the letter and how much I want to go and live in America with Pa. Just like I told you. I make sure I don't miss anything out and I'm sure I feel Rosa squeeze my hand when I get a bit emotional talking about it all. When I finish it seems really quiet and all I can hear is the sound a black bug is making as it crashes into the mesh on the window over and over again. It's never silent in Borde and I feel like the whole place has been listening to my story their ears pressed against the walls.

A few nights later I wake in the middle of the night to see the gas lamp on in the other room. Ma's bed's empty and I find her kneeling in front of her little statue of Jesus. She has lines across her forehead that straighten out when she sees me. I go over and sit on her lap like I did when I was little and she puts her arms around me.

Rosa's going to die soon isn't she? I ask.

Ma goes all still and doesn't say anything. So I ask how long and she whispers so quietly I almost don't hear her say she doesn't know but not long.

The next day Ma surprises me and sends a message into work with some of the other girls that she's unwell. All the woman from Borde that worked at the Laundry stuck together so she knew she could trust them. Ma says the sewing can wait so we head out early to see Rosa. It's rained in the night and outside our door a brown puddle is full of rainbow colours from Thiago's motorbike. Ma always moaned because it made so much noise when he started it up and he would rev it for ages before going. It broke down a lot and he was always out front fixing it with greasy hands. The path in front of our place wasn't very wide and Ma'd tell him he shouldn't ride it up there but he always did anyway.

When we pass Nef's place Diego comes running out and asks how Rosa is. We hadn't seen much of each other lately and I can't find the words to tell him so I say I have to go. He asks if she needs anything from the hotel but I tell him Ma has already got a doctor out and she said Rosa should go to the hospital but really there was nothing they could do. The hospital was way too expensive and anyway Rosa told Ma she didn't want to leave her room.

Ma has disappeared around the corner so I run to catch up. When I reach Rosa's she's standing outside talking to Carmela her neighbour. Ma didn't like her much because she was always gossiping and Ma doesn't have time for gossip but today they were being friendly because Rosa was more important than all that. Carmela always kept the front of her place spotless even though the rest of the path had rubbish all over it. She tucks her grey hair behind her ears and leans on her broom and I'm thinking how's she going to brush a wet path. Carmela has been keeping an eye on Rosa when we weren't there and stops talking when she sees me and starts talking to me like I'm five or something in this stupid baby voice. I mean how old do I have to be before she thinks I can join in a normal conversation!

I ignore her and go straight inside where my eyes take a minute to get used to the dark. Rosa's in the same position as yesterday eyes closed and her head up on two pillows. I don't realise I'm holding my breath until I see her chest slowly going up and down. I touch her arm and I'm waiting for her to open her eyes and say something funny or pull me into a hug but she just lies there making a strange noise with each breath like she swallowed a stone or something. Her face looks thin and her skin is kind of clear and yellow. I don't know how long I stand there but after a while I feel Ma's hand on my shoulder. I start to think about the world without Rosa and my legs feel so weak like they might just give way so I try to push it out of my head. Ma looks at me and asks if I remembered when I was little and ran away and Rosa found me hidden at the back of

Sancho's workshop behind those two old doors. I laugh and remember I'd been so angry at Ma for not letting me come to a party at the bar. I wouldn't come out at first but Rosa just sat on a stool opposite me and started telling me a story about how when she was younger she had been to the mountains in Chile and how in spring the whole mountainside was covered in wildflowers and she made it sound so magical I forgot all about everything and wanted to hear more. Ma says she was so worried but eventually found me sat on her lap in the workshop like nothing had ever happened.

We go on like this for a while remembering and telling stories until we have nothing left to say and then just sit beside her bed. Mum's on Rosa's chair me on the little red stool. I don't know how long we stay there like that but at some point Carmela comes in with two plates of rice and beans and puts them on the table without saying a word. Neither of us can think about eating so they sit there untouched. The whole time Rosa's slow noisy breathing continues. Sometimes it seems to stop and Ma and I look quickly up at each other then her chest rises again and we let out a sigh of relief. Then a cold shiver creeps all over my body and I can't stop crying and Ma just holds me and we cry and cry until there's nothing left. I realise at one point it's become night because we're sitting in the dark and Ma put the lamps on. We haven't said anything to each other for hours and I almost feel like I've forgotten how to speak. There is nothing except Rosa's breathing rattling slowly in and out.

Then something changes she suddenly sounds different. Each breath became longer and both Ma and I jump to our feet without knowing why. I look at Ma and she nods.

Goodbye Rosa. We love you.

I almost shout. Then we tell her over and over how much we love her and I know it sounds weird but I see something in her face change like it just wasn't Rosa anymore and she breathes in and out takes one more breath...

I'm sorry...

This the first time I've ever talked about this. I don't remember much after that other than me and Ma holding each other our bodies shaking and strange noises coming from us that I've never heard before.

At some point I fall asleep and wake up in my bed confused. It's hot and sweaty and for a moment I listen to the sound of voices around me and then I remember and it's like someone's punched me in the stomach and pain fills every part of me. Ma hears me crying and comes in and sits on the edge of the bed and strokes my hair and holds me.

Sometime later when I get up I find Ma sewing under the light of the lamp. She looks up and I notice dark rings around her eyes and we sit silently for a bit then she asks softly if I want some time alone with Rosa before they take her.

The whole world feels different as we walk over. It's hard to explain but it's like I'm seeing everything for the first time. People are talking to us but I don't hear their voices. Instead I can only focus on small things I've never noticed before. I see two lines of ants moving up a wooden plank like traffic and a puzzled looking face in the cracked plaster next to Raul's Radio shop. A bit further on I notice a ring around the sun that's a bit like a rainbow but goes around it in a full circle. I try to show Ma but she doesn't hear me.

We stand for a moment outside Rosa's closed door and Ma's looking at me and starts to say something but I reach forward and push it open and go inside. The lamps are on but it's still dark in there compared to the bright sun and my heart's beating so fast I can feel my fingers throbbing. Even though no incense is burning it still smells of frankincense and I look at the jumble of furniture crammed into that small space and it hits me this is the last time I'll stand under those dried flowers.

When my eyes get used to the light I stand by Rosa's bed and don't feel scared any more. Her face is waxy and it's Rosa but at the same time it's not her at all. Ma says she's in heaven now so I guess she just left her body behind and didn't need it. I don't know if I believe in any of that. Diego says religion is made up stories and people are stupid to believe it. He says clever people believe in science because it can prove things and science helps us make all the amazing things we have like phones and computers and that. But that theory isn't looking so bulletproof now either is it. Truth is I don't know what to believe any more.

I'm only a kid and have time to work this stuff out right? I asked Rosa once if she was a Christian but she said she didn't like religion much because it was mostly run by greedy selfish men. She told me that it didn't matter what religion you're from it's all the same really. Which got me thinking about how people believe in different gods and what if they're wrong. You'd feel pretty stupid when you die. I said this to Rosa but she told me it didn't matter because there was no difference between us all whether we believe in one thing or another. She said we all want the same thing we all want to love and be loved. I realise then I won't be having any more chats with Rosa and then cry for a bit sitting on the stool holding her hand.

I notice her red nail varnish is chipped so I go over to the yellow plastic basket on the dresser and find her nail varnish. Next to it there's a small vase with a tiny hummingbird on it and I remember Rosa told me once that they're the only birds that can fly backwards. I'd never been out of the city at that time and was desperate to see one. I carefully paint each of her nails moving around the bed to do the other hand which seems stupid I know but she did always liked to keep her nails neat. Once they're done I put the varnish back and take one last look around her room and that's when I notice the torn out page tucked under a glass of water. Rosa wouldn't have liked it that dark during the day so I pull back her thick curtains and a patch of sun sparkles off the kettle and stretches across her faded rug. I sit in her chair and pick up the page as I watch the dust dance in the light. She'd underlined a few lines near the bottom and I've memorised them just like Pa's letter because you just don't know what's going to happen. It went like this:

People who do bad things are just people who might not have been loved and are likely to be lonely and afraid. To hate them is selfish; instead we should pity them. Too much time is spent looking at the differences between us; old - young; rich – poor; black - white; beautiful – ugly; that we forget to see how we are all really the same, struggling with the same things. For all our walls, physical or not, they are all imagined. It suits us sometimes to think we are different from others but in reality - it is all just a trick of the light.

I have to admit when I first read that I didn't understand any of it and I'm not sure I totally do now but lately it's been making more sense. Maybe it's because I'm a bit older.

You know even now I can't believe she's gone. I can't shake a feeling that she just went away for a while and one day she'll just walk around the corner and be back the same as she always was.

Things get pretty bad after Rosa. At first I just thought I was messed up in the head about it all. I guess I wasn't really noticing what other people were doing and was too wrapped up in my thoughts. It's only when Ma tells me there's no work to do that it hits me. There was always sewing to be done and more than we could manage most days. Ma would often work late to finish a piece for someone because she was the best in Borde and never wanted to let anyone down. Ma won't look at me when she tells me. Instead she turns her back and picks up and refolds clothes that are already neat.

But we've always got work!

I stupidly say. Ma's quiet for a bit then says she's sure things will pick up soon. We don't get to talk about it any more because there's a knock at the door and Diego pops his head in. For some reason Ma seems super pleased to see him and makes a big fuss putting on tea and getting out the biscuits she'd told me we weren't allowed to eat like an hour before. Diego makes me laugh by sitting at the table then brushing his shoulders and moving a pretend crown on his head when Ma's back is turned. I realise it's the first time I've laughed in a while and it feels good. Ma asks him loads about how he and his family are like he's just returned from overseas or something and I think she might be losing it because she's always liked Diego but not this much. He plays along like nothing's different and tells her how delicious the biscuits are and asks is that a new dress because she looks great. God he's such an embarrassing salesman sometimes.

Later on we head out for a walk and because Ma seems anxious I promise I'll be back early. As we walk I ask what that was all that about and Diego says it's not surprising really with all the stuff people have been saying so I stop and grab his arm and I'm like

What stuff?

He looks surprised and goes quiet and then all flustered pulls a magazine for me from his backpack. He starts babbling about how it was in Spanish and looks like it's never been read and how he'd found it by the pool and had to sneak it past Victor. I kick him hard in the shins.

That does the trick and he holds his hands up and says let's go to the mound by the stream to talk. We walk quickly in silence and Diego leads us the long way round rather than through the square which I think is weird until we sit on the bank and he starts talking.

He comes right out with it and says Borde thinks me

and Ma have TB. I just stare at him not believing what he's said. Apparently the rumour was that I caught it from Alicia and gave it to Rosa who died from it because she was old and so people were avoiding us big time. Diego's Ma even said he shouldn't come and see us! I sit silent for a bit and my eyes fill with tears not because of the stupid things he said but because it brings back Rosa dying and I've been trying really hard not to think about it. Diego doesn't say anything but just puts his arm around me and I let him.

Thinking about what he's said I get more and more angry. Why are some people so stupid? Did I look sick? Did Ma look sick? What was wrong with these people? Just because I was friends with Alicia who didn't even have TB. Mierda.

I kick at a rusty oil can and it hurts which just makes me angrier so I start off down the slope towards the wasteland totally fucking fuming. Diego knows how I can get angry sometimes especially since that time years ago with Matias. He tripped me up on purpose and I dropped some repaired clothes I was delivering in the mud. I'd spent all morning finishing one of those pieces and Ma was really stressed about money. Diego loves to tell that story because he had to pull me off him. I felt bad afterwards because I broke Matias' nose and there was blood everywhere. I didn't mean to I just kind of lose control sometimes.

I jump the stream and sprint into the wasteland and feel like I want to run away from everything and never come back. I've always been a fast runner so Diego struggles to keep up. I run past two older boys who are smoking drugs sat against a half collapsed wall. I know it's drugs because I recognise the disgusting smell from when we first got to Borde and next door these men were coming and going dealing drugs. We could smell it in our place because it would come through the holes in the wall and Ma tried to have a go at them but they got rude and one of them pointed a gun at her so we left that night with all our stuff.

A bit further on I trip on a piece of rusty wire and graze my hands on the concrete but I'm too mad to care. The wasteland was full of bushes and junk and under the flyover were two old tumble down buildings. No one could put homes on there because in the wet season it flooded and washed them all away. Rosa told me one time the water got so high it came all the way into Borde and everyone had to rebuild their homes. I reach the first building and stop and catch my breath. I'm all puffed out and in the distance I hear Diego calling me but I don't answer. There's a window still left on the side of the building that's pretty smashed up but I hurl some rocks at it anyway. I'm so angry at the people of Borde who I thought were my friends. How dare they spread rumours? How dare they avoid me and Alicia for no reason? How could the world be so unfair? Each stone I throw harder than the last until I drop to the ground and sob. I feel someone hugging me and I push them off but Diego just puts his arms around me again and I struggle and shout at him to leave me alone but he ignores me and keeps holding me until I give in and just cry into his shoulder.

By the time I've calmed down the sun's low in the sky like a perfect orange ball in the haze between the concrete flyover and the hotel wall. We sit for a bit kicking at the dirt and listening to the rumble of the traffic. Eventually Diego says we should head back and I nod. My legs feel wobbly and tired and I'm overcome with guilt. I can't help feeling I've ruined everything for Ma and after she told me not to go near Alicia. Diego tries to make me feel better by saying it's not my fault and that people are just scared but it didn't change the facts. I'd messed up.

Alicia told me that her Ma wanted to move away because of the way they'd been treated. I didn't want to have to move because Borde was my home but we're not always in control of life it seems. Diego says not to worry he'll come up with a plan but seriously how do you change that many people's minds? When we were younger I used to think me and Diego could do anything. We'd always have a plan to solve every problem and usually they worked. Diego would come up with some crazy idea that seemed impossible. Like the time I said I wanted to save the pig that was tied up out the back of Restaurante La Barraca on Bolivar.

We'd climbed up on the big wall and could see it tied up by it's leg to a metal pole in the backyard. We knew what was going to happen because once we'd been sat there and seen them take another pig inside and heard it squealing for its life. I know it sounds funny but it was like I could feel some of its pain like it was being tortured or something. I'll never forget the noises it made. I haven't eaten meat since that day even now when food is hard to find. Ma got really annoyed with me for a while but I've survived this long haven't I? Diego laughed it off and said he could never give up meat but I know he was pretty freaked by it. So anyway he comes up with this plan to save the pig. The problem is there's a high wall all around the back yard so the only way to get it out is through the restaurant. Somehow he manages to get two smoke bombs from someone and when I ask him he just winks and says he has his ways.

The plan works perfectly. I wait on the wall with the rope ladder we'd made until I see the smoke. Diego goes around the front and sets off the smoke bombs and shouts fire so everybody clears out the building. From the wall I hear the shouting and drop the ladder and climb down. The pig stares at me suspiciously with its little black eyes. Close up he's bigger than I thought and I'm suddenly quite scared. I try to stroke him but he isn't into that so I start untying him but he keeps wriggling about. Once he's free he runs into the corner of the yard and doesn't move. Luckily we'd thought of this and I'd brought three apples for him to eat. I give him one and he munches it up happily then starts following me as I hold out another. I lead him through

243

the kitchen into the restaurant keeping one eye on the pig and trying to see where to go in the smoke. It hurts my eyes and I nearly trip over a couple of times but I make it out to the street. All the time Diego's distracting everyone shouting that he'd seen a man throw a petrol bomb through the door and there he is down the street. He points into the traffic and everyone looks that way as I lead the pig away. It's perfect. No one sees me except this mad old guy with no teeth who's sitting begging on the street who laughs and claps his hands. Once I've got the pig out of there I realise that we hadn't thought about what we'd do with it but it doesn't matter because it's like the pig knows it's free and he just runs off into the traffic and disappears. We sprint all the way back to Borde laughing telling and retelling the soon to be famous story of when Espe and Diego saved the pig.

As we cross back over the stream trying not to get our feet wet Diego says he'll come by in the morning and talk about it more but I really don't see the point. We could see the lights coming on at Sancho's and could hear a child crying in one of the houses nearby and somehow it seemed different stepping back into Borde feeling betrayed by your own. It'd been quiet out there on the wasteland and I felt like I wanted to turn back. Ma once told me how when her and Pa ran the bar they used to have a garden and you could sit out there and hear birds singing in the morning. She told me how she would sit under this fig tree in peace and drink a coffee. I only have one memory of that place and that's of the chickens. Apparently I named one of them Blanca. Seriously imaginative top marks Espe. I tried to pick her up but she pecked my hand and gave me a right fright. That's all I remember.

We walk the rest of the way in silence keeping off the busy paths and not looking at people as they pass by. We reach my place and I turn to go but Diego calls me back. He's holding out the magazine and I smile and take it and without thinking reached forward and kiss his cheek then turn quickly so I won't see the look on his face.

I feel so ashamed when I walk in. Ma's chopping some sweet potato but quickly puts the knife down and gives me the biggest hug and I never want her to let me go. All teary I tell her I'm so sorry and that it's all my fault. Ma's great she isn't having any of it and says I was just being kind and she shouldn't have told me to stay away from Alicia. She tells me things happen for a reason we have to trust in God's plan. I'm relieved but I don't trust God. Not the God that let Rosa die and does nothing whilst all the bad things happen in the world. Obviously I didn't say that to Ma. She tuts when I start looking through my magazine but doesn't say anything and goes back to making dinner. After a bit she notices my hands and helps me clean them up and it stings like hell but feels good to be looked after.

After dinner Ma goes to her machine like always even though she doesn't have work. She tells me she's going to make me some new trousers to replace the ones with the holes in the knees and that she's sorry she hadn't had time before. I actually like the holes because I'd seen people in the magazines with rips on their knees but I keep that to myself. I go into the other room and lie on my bed and read taking my time turning each page enjoying all the pictures. There's a whole page on makeup and although Ma doesn't wear makeup I once tried some on with Camilla who lived around the corner. She's older and had a boyfriend who Ma said was bad news. It felt good to try it and she said I looked pretty but Ma got annoyed when I got back and made me wipe it all off. I guess it's not easy to see your little girl growing up.

That night I don't sleep well. I dream I'm walking through this abandoned town with pavements that have plants growing up through them. It's proper spooky like everyone just left leaving everything where it was. I go into a shop with dirty windows except for this one bit where it's been wiped away. Everything's normal inside except it's dark and there's food and household things like brushes pegs and soaps all covered in a thick layer of dust. I pick up a pack of biscuits and brush off the dirt and leave some money on the filthy counter. I don't feel scared just a bit confused about it all. When I go back outside I catch a glimpse of someone in the road up ahead but I can't see who they are because the sun's shining in my eyes. I call out to them but they disappear around the corner so I run as fast as I can to catch them up. When I reach the corner I'm looking at exactly the same street I'd just been in. I'm pretty freaked out and walk over to the shop again and through the dirty window I can see something moving inside. That's when I get this tingling feeling creeping down my neck as I slowly wipe away a patch of dirt with my sleeve and put my face up to the glass. There standing just where I'd been was me picking up the same pack of biscuits. It was so weird to see yourself like that it made me think that we look in mirrors but we never really see ourselves like others do. Anyway I jump back in shock and then just run. I was proper terrified. I get to the end of the street and hear someone call out and right then I wake up sat right up in my bed in the dark sweating like mad. After that I can't sleep. For hours I lie there listening to sirens from the main street and twice I hear gunshots which was the first time for a long time. When I think about that dream now it makes me question so much my head hurts.

In the morning when Ma goes to work I don't have any sewing to do so I spend extra time cleaning the place up instead. I take a rag and polish the statue of Jesus and the sewing machine and open the window so I can smack the dust from the cushions. I brush the floors and clean the little mirror with the cracked corner that hung in the bedroom. No one comes past and I keep on cleaning pretending I'm not waiting for Diego to come and rescue me. I've pretty much given up on him when he makes me jump by standing at the open window with a grin on his face.

Come on you can't hide in there all day!

He tells me but I'm scared to face people thinking everyone's going to be looking at me. When he finally convinces me to leave it's not as bad as I imagined. Most people ignore us as we pass and anyway it seems unusually quiet as we head up to the square. Turns out people had more on their minds than little old me that day. The bar's overflowing with people all trying to catch sight of the tv and on the edge of the crowd I see Gismar stood on tiptoes on a chair. I hadn't seen the bar like that since the World Cup. Diego marches off to have a look but I'm scared people will shout at me if I go near them. Diego notices I'm not with him and turns back and says if I act like I've got TB that's hardly going to help is it. I had to hand it to him he had a point.

I try to act normal and head over. We climb on two barrels by the door and if I lean to the left I can just see the tv fixed to the wall. The volume's at full blast but people are shouting excitedly so I can't hear a thing. On the screen people are going crazy smashing windows of buildings and throwing rocks and bottles at the police. They show buildings on fire and long lines of white people carrying loads of bags going somewhere.

Europe's going crazy! The gringos are losing it!

This woman shouts and they all laugh and it seems like everyone's enjoying watching someone else's world go to shit. Then the places on the screen change and there's lots of black faces but they're fighting too. On the screen this woman is shouting and holding up a flag that's on fire and I recognise it from my magazines and I know straight away where it is. They show someone driving a car into a big glass shop front and it smashes everywhere and people run in from all sides and grab boxes and run out again. I wonder about Pa and I hope he's safe and not in one of those burning buildings.

We watch for a while longer but it's the same thing over and over so we go and sit under the tree. I ask him why he thought all those people are fighting and he says he isn't sure but heard it had something to do with rich people losing all their money. I think about Pa and if he lost all his money how would he be able to fly back here and come and get me. I guess it was about then that I started to lose faith in his glorious return although I didn't realise it at the time.

Diego pulls a seed pod from the tree and touches my cheek with it. When we were younger we used to play a game with those pods. You'd take one each and open it and the one with the most seeds was the winner and you'd give the person with the least a silly dare like pretend you were a chicken or something stupid. It was a lot of fun because you never knew what you'd get. He splits the pod open with his thumb nail and it breaks perfectly in two and there's five flat seeds inside. I reach up and grab a pod myself and split it open but mine only has three.

Diego raises an eyebrow and pulls a bag of balloons from his pocket and holds them up and says

I dare you to blow all these up.

I just look at him confused but he asks how someone with TB and weak lungs could blow up all thirty balloons. He drops the bag in my lap and folds his arms looking all proud of himself. He leads me over to the bar and I sit opposite the crowd. I feel like a total idiot sat there in the sun blowing up balloons and after the third one I start to feel a bit light headed but Diego doesn't let me stop. He walks over to the bar and starts shouting

Hey look free balloons! Espe's just blowing them up and giving them away!

Some young kids I didn't know who are bored of playing around their Ma's feet come over and take a couple and throw them in the air. I get into a rhythm working out when to take a breath and how long to pause between each balloon. Soon I have them all around me as I sit on the dirt and more and more people come over to see what's going on. Little Maya walks over for a balloon but her Ma rushes out and grabs her. She glances at me in disgust and hurries off. I can see Diego's enjoying this. He starts shouting

Free balloons everyone. Come get them before they're gone. Look at her go she's a machine. I wish I had a pair of lungs as healthy as hers. Looks like she's going to blow up all thirty!

He dances around the crowd handing out balloons chatting and laughing with people. I feel embarrassed but I can't stop so I just look at the ground and move on to the next one. Diego carries on like a football

250

commentator

This must be some sort of world record. No one's ever blown up this many balloons in one go.

He gets the crowd counting each one as I get close to the end twenty-three....twenty-four.....twenty-five.

Now there's a crowd standing around me cheering me on and my head's spinning and I wish I'd sat in the shade. Diego's in full flow

Only a girl in peak condition could manage something like this. That's number twenty-seven who wants it? Just three to go.

The crowd starts cheering me on like I'm at the Olympics or something. I reach the last one and wait for a minute to try and stop my head spinning. I want to lie down and my mouth's dry but it's gone quiet and I look up to see a group of expectant faces. I don't want to let them down so I pick up the last balloon and stretch it a little before putting it to my mouth. I blow as hard as I can but I just hit a wall and nothing happens. Then after what seems like forever it bursts into shape filling up like the other twenty-nine. I tie it and hand it to Diego who lifts it in the air like a trophy. Everyone cheers and comes and pats me on the back like I actually did something important. Taking in big gulps of air I have to smile. Diego doesn't half know how to work a crowd.

It's hard to say whether the balloon trick worked or whether people were just to caught up in all the craziness going on but either way people seemed better towards us. Diego said that everyone all over the world was going crazy but Borde seemed the same as ever to me. Until that Sunday.

At two in the afternoon Cabron is on tv making some big speech. Ma says she'll go to the bar to watch it and Diego tries to get me to go but I don't want to. I'm so bored of hearing all about this stuff and just want to be alone so I go to the wall.

The wind's got up as I cross the football pitch and dust swirls around in tornadoes so I have to cover my eyes. I look back but no one's around to see me crawl in. Looking through the hotel looks as calm as ever. Under this tree with lots of red flowers hanging from it like lanterns is a woman with long blond hair sitting reading a book. She's wearing a white dress that flaps in the wind and she has big sunglasses pushed up on her head. I daydream that I go over and sit with her and she tells me what the book's about and I don't know how long I would have stood there if I hadn't heard that noise. It's deep and seems to rock the ground. I'd never heard anything like it.

As I scramble out of the bush I can see smoke in the sky in the distance and I hear three gunshots close by that echo off the hotel wall. For a few seconds afterwards there's silence like I've never heard in Borde and I can't move my feet. Then there's another two shots and I'm on the move pumping my legs as fast as I can. Everyone's rushing around and generally losing their shit and I don't know what to do but I know I have to find Ma. When I get to the bar it's cleared out and as I step closer I see the tables and chairs are tipped all over the place and my brain's saying Espe get out of here now but my feet are still walking and by then it's too late. I can't see their faces because they're both lying face down which let's be honest is never a good sign and it's only when I notice the reflection of the tv glinting off the floor do I see all that blood.

I feel someone grab my arm from behind and I spin around. Diego's eyes are wild and he doesn't need to say anything for me to scramble after him getting the fuck away from there.

I find Ma stuffing clothes into a bag and when I come through the door she makes a noise like an injured dog before grabbing me and hugging me so tight it hurts.

That's when we hear the second blast. I feel the vibration all through my body. Mary topples over and falls hard on to the floor and smashes into three pieces. If that wasn't a sign of things to come I don't know what is. Ma starts to move towards it but then turns back to me and shouts that we've got to go. The air smells of smoke and dust and I freeze too panicked to move. Ma screams at me which does the trick and I rush into my room and stuff some clothes in the backpack we use to carry the vegetables back from the market. I throw in my hairbrush and toothbrush and quickly throw in dad's letter and the picture of us and head for the door. We bump into an out of breath Diego and he says he's going to the hotel. Ma nods and we sprint after him.

Diego's house is total chaos as his Pa's still at work in the city and two of his brothers are missing. Carla's slumped on the floor sobbing and shouting Oscar's name a lot and Nibaldo's throwing bags out the door. The smoke gets thicker and a couple holding their baby run by screaming

It's on fire get out it's all on fire!

There are no more decisions to be made then. We just go. Diego leads us through the smoke and I try to keep up with him glancing behind me to make sure Ma's keeping up. Twice I fall bumping into other people who suddenly appear out of the smoke both of them with the same crazy look on their faces.

The second person is Alicia's mum. She doesn't seem to recognise me but Alicia takes my hand and pulls me to my feet and for what feels like forever but was probably just a second we stare into each other's eyes. Then she lets go of my hand and disappears into the smoke. For a long time there wasn't a day that went by where I didn't wonder where she went and why I just stood there saying nothing rather than asking her to come with us.

We run past the toilets and everyone's going in the opposite direction and the further we go the less people we see. Finally I realise we're at the abandoned building on the northern edge. There's no way out of Borde from here it's a dead end. Diego leads us through the building to the far corner where the air is a little clearer and plastic bottles and all sorts of rubbish are scattered across the concrete floor. Diego stops at what looks like a pile of old wood and starts throwing it aside. We help him clear it and then he grabs a thin sheet of wood that was under it and chucks it to one side. We waste no time heading down a dark set of stairs that were hidden underneath. Me and Ma hold hands as we go down into the dark and it smells nearly as bad as the toilets.

When we reach the bottom I can feel water seeping through my trainers and I hear glass crunch under someone's feet behind me. A light blinds me for a moment then sweeps away. As my eyes adjust I can see Diego's shining a torch ahead to show the corridor comes to a dead end and I'm thinking oh great now what. Holding the torch between his teeth he pulls away a crate that's resting on the far wall. Behind it is a large hole in the wall and we can hear a rumbling of machines on the other side. Nibaldo goes first ducking his head and crawling through. I go next following the light on the other side. I can hear Ma call my name behind me as I come out into a large room full of pipes and strange machines. I shout back to Ma that all is good and she soon appears blinking into the light.

When we're all through we collapse on the floor of what Diego tells us is the boiler room. It'd all happened so fast. Me and Ma are silent but Diego and his brother are telling Carla how as soon as things settle down they'll go back out and look for Oscar and Victor and Gismar. They keep saying it over and over. I lie back on

Ma and she puts her arms around me. After a bit everyone just goes quiet except the hum of the machines.

Nibaldo stands up and bangs his head and says a word I won't repeat but Ma tuts. Classic Ma our home is on fire and she's worrying about swear words. Diego breaks the silence saying he's going to head up into the hotel to find out what's going on and get us some food and water. He looks over at Carla but she's got her head in her hands and isn't listening. I hear Ma whispering a prayer under her breath and when I turn to look her eyes are closed and she's holding the cross around her neck in her fist. I can't help wondering what happened to all our friends. Did they all get out? I think I knew even then that we wouldn't be going back. Rosa comes into my head then and I feel guilty for being pleased she's dead. There's no way she would have been able to escape in time. Even though I'm sweating in there I feel a shiver run down my neck when I remember what she'd said one of the last times I spoke to her.

Diego's gone for a long time. It's hard to say what time it is because there's no windows but when he finally appears down the metal steps he has a hotel uniform on and a man is with him.

Diego introduces Hugo who he says will help us carry our stuff up to some rooms in the staff block where we could stay. Usually Diego is such a showoff and loves announcing good things he's done but this time he just speaks quietly and then goes to whisper something to Carla. Ma asks Diego if there's any news from Borde. Hugo tells us the hotel's in lockdown and that they have their own security team patrolling the walls and a lot of men on the gates. He seems nice and has a friendly smile.

Nibaldo says he wants to go out straight away to look for the others. The three of them argue about what they should do and Diego says they should wait but his brother says he doesn't get to make all the decisions. In the end they decide they'll all come up to the rooms so Nibaldo knows where they are and then he can head back out. With that settled we set off in single file following Hugo through the maze of pipes.

Once we've climbed the steps it opens out and we end up in a large area in front of a lift so big you could drive a car into it. Diego says when we reach the staff floor to follow him quickly so we don't get spotted but when we pass people they don't seem to care about us anyway. The room's on a corridor like the one I'd seen when I was there before. Hugo unlocks the door and we pile in. Inside is bigger than I expected and there's windows along one side that look out on a wall of another building. Four single beds are spread out around the room each one with a set of drawers next to them. We all stand around looking at the bare room half relieved half totally freaked out.

Ma says me and her can share so we claim a bed and straight off Nibaldo drops his bag on the nearest bed and gives Carla a hug and heads back out the door. Ma goes over to Carla and sits next to her and she looks like about the most sad woman that ever lived.

I go over to the window but there isn't anything to see except a wall and some gravel below. I press my head to the glass and looked up at the slither of sky. It's nearly dark and I see a single star shining amongst the light blue. I stay there for a while watching as it gets darker and slowly the star is joined by others but none as bright as the first.

Nibaldo doesn't come back that night. Diego brings us some food up from the kitchen and we scoff it down in silence. Me and Ma squeeze into a single bed and even though there isn't much room I think it might just be the most comfortable bed I've ever slept in. I feel bad for thinking that and wonder where everyone else from Borde was sleeping or if they were even alive. Carla's sat up on her bed hugging her knees as I fall asleep. At some point in the night I wake and see her still in exactly the same position. She looks like someone turned her to stone. I look over to Diego's bed but the covers are pulled back and he's nowhere to be seen.

When I wake again the sun's reflecting off the white wall and filling the room with bright sunlight. Carla lies across Ma's lap and she's stroking her hair like when I was ill. I get out of bed and Ma turns her head towards me and puts a finger to her lips. Carla has her eyes closed but she still looks sad. Diego told us not to leave the room so I just sit and stare at the blank walls until he comes back.

When finally the door clicks open I hope it might be like the daydream I'd been having where Oscar and the brothers all come in joking and slapping each other's backs but it was just Hugo. He's holding a bag with some bread and fruit in for us and some bottles of water. He passes it to me smiles and I notice the birthmark on his neck that spreads down under his collar like a map.

He sits on the bed next to me and asks how I'm bearing up. Adults say the funniest things sometimes. Other than the fact that we had to leave our home because it's all on fire and people are shooting guns about the place and half my friends are probably dead and we're now hiding in a hotel with no idea what will happen next I'm fine thanks....you? He was just being kind though I get that.

I feel tiny sitting next to Hugo. He has broad shoulders and a bit of grey in his hair but he looks quite young other than that. I ask where Diego is. He says he'd been down to the gate to speak to the security guys about letting his Pa's taxi in if it turned up and was now helping out down in the kitchens. They were short staffed as lots of people had rushed home to their families and they still had to cook enough to feed all the guests. I ask if I can go down and help but he says it's best if I stay put. What about your family? I ask before I can stop my stupid mouth and he tells me they're all in Argentina and he doesn't know what's happening there as he can't get through. With that he stands up and tells me there's a bathroom I can use to wash up at the end of the hall. I'm desperate for a pee so I follow him out and he grabs me a towel from a pile by the door and passes it to me telling me there's soap inside while pointing to the door opposite.

I can't believe it when I go in. I'm stood so long staring at it I nearly pee myself. There's a proper flushing toilet with a toilet seat just like in the films. In the middle of the whole world falling apart and arguing over god knows what I sit down to have a pee for the first time in my life. No squatting over a hole like normal trying to make sure none of your clothes touch the floor and breathing through your mouth. The whole room's covered in shiny clean white tiles that you could pretty much see yourself in. There's a sink too with hot and cold taps. Ok I'd used a sink before but never one this pretty. I look at myself in the mirror over the sink and my face has black marks on it and my hair's all over the place and covered in ash. I feel dirty stood in that perfect room. I notice the mud under my fingernails and I spend ages picking it out under warm soapy water. I strip off all my clothes and stand in the big white bath staring at it. I have no idea how to turn the shower on.

Normally at home I wash standing in the big plastic bowl which is a whole lot less confusing. I turn one of the silver knobs but nothing happened so I try the other and water comes flying out so quickly I scream in surprise. After a minute it gets warm and it's amazing but then it gets really hot and burns me. I work it out in the end. I've never washed in hot water before so I like it quite cold and I stay under the shower for a long time scrubbing myself clean and daydreaming about all sorts until I hear a knock on the door.

It's Ma coming to check I haven't drowned I've been so long. She opens the door a little and pushes a clean t-shirt and shorts through the gap. I'm relieved because I feel so clean I don't want to get back into those dirty clothes. When I've dried off and dressed I rub a gap in the steamed up mirror and look at myself. My cheeks are red and my hair's spiky and wet. I feel so good I can't help smiling. I know what you're thinking what a selfish bitch enjoying myself so much in there whilst Diego's brothers were missing and god knows what was happening outside.

When I get back to the room Diego's there and he gives me a tired looking smile. He looks surprised when I go straight up and hug him. He smells of fried food and sweat. We sit for a while on his bed not saying much. Carla's still asleep and Ma's lying down on our bed staring up at the ceiling. That's when we hear them. Three sharp bursts of gunfire that have us on our feet. Ma grabs our bag and shakes Carla. She tries to push her away pulling the sheet back over herself but Diego shouts at her and runs over to pull her upright. She starts screaming and totally loses it but Diego drags her out the door.

We're only just into the corridor when this high pitch alarm goes off that's like someone drilling into your head. Lots of people are coming out all the staff rooms and walking down the corridor about as fast as they can without breaking into a run. Then there's another burst of gunshots that sound pretty close to me and I look at Ma but she's just staring straight ahead holding my hand tight. We don't wait for the lift instead we follow the horde down some stairs until we reach a wide hallway that's so totally packed everyone has stopped. We get a bit further and then there's just too many people to get through. It gets more and more crowded and I'm used to being all packed together because of the market but this is different because everyone's in such a hurry and starting to freak out. We stand there for a moment not sure what to do next. That's when I look down and see something strange at my feet.

Through the window, Andrew watched the thin afternoon sun fall over the car park filled with spotless, expensive cars. A boy, who Andrew thought must be a similar age to Simon, his youngest, hopped towards the entrance in his Sunday best shirt. Summer was slipping from their grasp, a chill creeping into the late afternoon, bringing with it a bluish light that descended over orange tinged leaves.

Inside, well dressed families were slouching back stuffed with beef, gravy and high quality desserts. Amongst the content diners there seemed little concern for the chaos across Europe as the global markets sank to yet another low. This was not your All You Can Eat Carvery with psychedelic carpets and a lingering odour of stale beer. Fully booked and with enough exposed brick to please any modern diner, The Swan was a long way from its humble beginnings.

Andrew sat in the snug, just past the glass walled wine cellar, where customers were encouraged to take a

'Wine Tour' so they could fully appreciate why their bottle cost £47. Despite the crowds, the snug was deserted, the crackling open fire punctuating the hum of voices. Andrew always arrived early. Years ago he'd read a quote from the Dalai Lama where he was asked why he was always so calm. In response, he'd said it was because he always left fifteen minutes early.

Andrew had arrived early ever since. He pushed himself back into the tall chair and drew in this rare moment of solitude. Sipping his wine, he considered the elaborately gold-framed painting, on the opposite wall above the warm glow of the lamp, that sat on the table with the yachting magazines. It was of a chaotic war scene, some on horseback, swinging bayonets at each other in a melee of flags, smoke and pirate hats. Andrew couldn't help wondering how you kept a hat on whilst clambering over your dead friends to stab a stranger. The day had been dominated by the financial crisis. As ever the media were whipping everyone into a panic but Andrew had made it clear he felt Ampulex just needed to rise above it, after all it wasn't as if this hadn't happened before. They just had to be ready to pounce on the opportunities and be the company that was smart enough to make money out of the crisis.

Eventually, Ethan heaved himself through the oak door frame and gave a wave, tucking his tie under his considerable stomach. Andrew rose on muscular cyclist legs and they shook hands warmly.

'Lovely place this, did you know it was a brothel in

the 19th century? One of the finest apparently.' he chuckled, his double chins on the move.

'Really?' Andrew replied, pouring another glass of wine from the bottle and placing it in front of his guest.

'Good to see you Ethan, how's Patrica?'

'A total fucking nightmare as ever!' Ethan said, without a shade of irony as he gulped his wine.

'The kids?' Andrew enquired, sitting back down.

'Oliver is finally getting somewhere at HSBC but Lucy wants to become a teacher apparently. How are your lot?'

'Very well thanks, madness as ever.' Andrew admitted, thinking how he couldn't wait for their house move so they would have more room for the little scamps.

'Well you did have four, but with a wife as lovely as Amelia I can't say I blame you.' Ethan scoffed.

Drinks in hands, a young couple lingered in the doorway indecisively, before disappearing back where they'd come from.

'So how are you feeling about the change? I have to say we're all very excited about having you on board.' Andrew said, topping up their glasses and crossing his legs to reveal pink socks.

'Very kind of you to say so Andrew; I'm looking forward to it. I've been an MP long enough, thirty-two years this winter. The party's in a good state, it feels like the right time. One thing I won't miss though are the public events, god what a bunch of bloody whingers.

How are things at Ampulex? Not too affected by the hooha I hope?'

'Our share price has dropped this week like everyone else's because of Italy's wobble but we're keeping a close eye. Generally, it's been a great year so far. When you come in next month I'll give you the full tour and you can meet the others on the board. Your input's going to be really valuable.'

Rain began to tap against the windows, even though a patch of blue sky could be seen above the trees.

'Actually there's something on the horizon that might be up your street. I didn't mention it before in case it didn't happen, but West Midlands Police have had approval to put out a one point five billion pound contract, over seven years I believe. Pretty much everything's on offer apparently.' Ethan whispered, leaning forward until his stomach worked its way around the lip of the table.

Andrew couldn't help but notice a button had come loose revealing a grotesquely hairy belly.

'I'll let you know more when I get it, but James and I go way back and he's on the board that makes the final decision.' he said, leaning back in his chair and looking pleased with himself.

'Sounds spectacular. You're going to be Ampulex's biggest asset if you're not careful.' Andrew chimed, raising his glass to meet Ethan's.

'Tip of the iceberg; it's all going that way.' Ethan stated, studying his fingernails. 'Mind you Europe needs to get its bloody act together in the meantime. Too many idiots who think they can go on spending in this climate. Just look at Portugal.' Ethan said, swallowing a belch, 'we'll be alright, my lot have got their heads screwed on. It'll take more than a few idiot Italians to bring us to our knees, onwards and upwards I say.'

Alex was six hours and twenty-four minutes into a flight across the Atlantic Ocean. Below him was a whole lot of sea and not a lot else. He peered out of the small window at the night sky, candyfloss clouds bathed in a silvery light. He'd gone over his notes as much as he could. The negotiations should, he thought, be fairly straight forward. Ampulex had agreed a deal to build and run an initial three new schools in the city of Santa Domina and surrounding district, training teachers, supplying the books, the lot. This was a big deal for them; their first education contract in Latin America. Looking at the profiles of the five government officials he would be meeting, he didn't see too much trouble getting the thing signed. One had previously voted against the deal but had changed his mind. With experience had come the knowledge that this was just as big a deal for those he was meeting. Alex knew Ampulex was offering a golden ticket to fix whatever mess the local government had previously mismanaged. This was very much a 'throw some money at the problem' type of a solution and Alex knew there was just as much riding on this for the men (and occasionally women) that sat around the table. As ever with these things he was the face of Ampulex, and as long as he listened attentively and showed respect, the thing got done.

Clayton had met with him on Tuesday, in the face of Italy's financial collapse and the resulting market slump, to shore up any questions the group might have about the drop in Ampulex's share price. There wasn't anything Alex hadn't considered in Clayton's brief; the drop in oil price was affecting the market as a whole; China's devaluation of the Yuan hadn't helped but the European Union had a bailout package ready to go, just as it had for Greece, Ireland and Portugal before them. Clayton repeated the same mantra several times; this was a global problem affecting everyone and Ampulex was in a strong position etc.

Closing his eyes, Alex eased back in his seat and sighed. He tried listening to some music to block out the incessant hum but he couldn't settle on a track and eventually pulled the headphones off and stared into space.

He thought again about the argument and chastised himself. Tethered to an anchor of guilt he obsessed over the details, self resentment growing. In the last few months he'd spent plenty of weekends with Phil and Sarah; watching Evie play football, joining them for Sunday lunch, helping Phil (mostly by passing him tools) to build the new summer house. He was like a long forgotten uncle, who suddenly back in town, was integrated into the family seamlessly. Alex hadn't really stopped to consider it until now but he had enjoyed being with them. Callum had been a little cold at first, but a couple of games of basketball later he began to thaw. When he arrived one afternoon with four tubs of icecream Evie tried to hug him.

'It's just a hug Alex, come on you can do it!' She'd smirked as he'd stood uncomfortably in the hall.

It was the thought of not seeing her any more that was the core of his anguish.

The first few weeks taking Adderall had been fantastic. Alex could hardly remember feeling better. Rather than just taking them when he felt troubled, he decided to set into a routine of taking them regularly. One 10mg tablet first thing, another at lunch. At work he felt energised and focused, even Phil said he'd seemed a lot cheerier of late. When over a lunchtime coffee Phil asked about Meeth, Alex laughed, realising he hadn't even thought about him for ages. The whole thing seemed a bit silly to him now. Why had he let some nutter rattle him so much?

But somewhere around the start of June as an early heatwave hit London and everyone seeped to the parks in search of some air, he noticed a change. Around midday, a wave of exhaustion would hit him and he became irritable. Twice he snapped at Olivia so maliciously that even she looked shocked, dropping two envelopes on his desk and walking out without a word. Realising the cause of his exhaustion he moved his second tablet to eleven am. That did the trick, but he found he had to add a third dose around four in the afternoon to get through.

His increasing self-medication didn't escape the notice of Sarah, who having an addict for a sister, knew what she was seeing.

'And what exactly are we guzzling there?' she questioned, one eyebrow raised, hands on hips, as she appeared silently in the doorway of the lounge.

'Just a headache,' he mumbled pathetically, pushing his little solid silver pill box (he'd treated himself to from an antique shop in Madrid) into his jacket pocket.

'Seriously though Al, keep it in check.' she'd said softly, 'I've enough of that shit in my family as it is.'

He started to reply but she was gone, leaving him feeling foolish. After that he'd been more careful, popping to the toilet before 'recharging' as he'd started thinking of it. Sarah though wasn't that easily fooled. Across the laden Sunday lunch table, he would catch her watching him in a way that troubled him. Clearly she'd spoken to Phil about it at some point. As they stood waiting to pick up their take out curry from the Raj Palace just up the road (new curry house: all mirrors and blue lights), Phil pitched in with all the subtly of a Hollywood blockbuster.

'So... Sarah's asked me to check if you're a drug addict.'

'What?' Alex replied, as they waited on the faux leather sofa clad waiting area next to a couple, heads bowed over their phones as if in mourning.

'Yep, she's got you down as a right pill popper.' he chuckled, looking up from his Men's Fitness magazine.

'I was on some antibiotics recently for an ear infection.' Alex lied effortlessly, 'Maybe it was because of that.'

'Ah there we go, mystery solved! I told her it would probably be something like that...Jesus look at the guys in here, how depressing.'

Unimpressed by her husband's detective work, Sarah took matters into her own hands. By now Alex came to visit them on most weekends, when he was in the country. With summer in full swing, they invited him along to their time share in the Chiltern Hills, that they were visiting for Evie's birthday. At first Alex had declined, feeling a little intrusive and apprehensive that he might be coerced into all manner of outdoor activities. But he was no match for Evie's ruthless persuasion.

'So basically you don't care enough about me to come, is that it?' she mocked, arms folded and fixing him a furious stare.

'No no, it's not that, it's just there's a lot on at work,' he attempted weakly.

'Are you away?'

'Well no, just...'

'In which case you're coming; you don't have to work at the weekends you know. If you don't come I'll never speak to you again.' she said dramatically, turning on her heels and disappearing into the garden.

It was already hot on the morning Alex pulled into the complex. Twelve large wooden cabins dotted around a lake that glistened peacefully. Pulling over at the entrance he took his late morning dose, before going in search of Cabin 8.

A gentle breeze danced through the willow trees as he climbed out of the car, the sound of water birds in the distance.

'Please tell me you brought shorts?' Sarah joked, climbing out of a hammock and kissing him on both cheeks.

'Yes, in the case. I might have packed a little too much.' he admitted, embarrassed as he pulled two family sized cases from the boot.

'Wow, you coming for the month? Come on, I'll show you your room.'

He followed her through the front door and into a spacious lounge, bi-fold doors leading out onto a patio and a shaded lawn, from which a wooden jetty stretched out into the water. At the end of it, silhouetted by the sun, he could see Evie running and jumping into the lake, Ben watching from the edge.

They spent the rest of the day sitting, sipping gin and tonics in the shade and taking turns to lose to Callum at chess. At lunch, Evie's mockery eventually became too much and Alex jettisoned the office wear for shorts, a slightly less smart shirt and a pair of summer loafers, all bought for the trip. She wanted him to come swimming but he hadn't brought his swimwear and there was no way he was going in that dirty lake.

Sleeping at the cabin was challenging for Alex. He slept in two places, his apartment and hotel rooms. Even after he'd straightened the pictures and hidden all the trinkets in the wardrobe, the room still grated him. And sharing a bathroom filled him with anxiety he did his best not to show.

Struggling to sleep, he tiptoed downstairs and slipped out the back door. It was a warm night and the nearly full moon cast long shadows. For a while he stood at the end of the jetty, listening to the gentle ripples of the water and watching the colourless reeds dance. Hearing a noise out in the middle of the lake, he squinted in the gloom. At first he saw nothing, but gradually the knock of wood on wood grew louder. He leaned forward, straining to make out the small rowboat that gradually came into view. As it drew a little closer, Alex could see two oars dipping into mercury, ripples ebbing away across the lake, the silhouetted back of someone at the helm, methodically working the oars. Then thirty metres or so from the shore they stopped, letting the oars go limp in the oarlocks, and getting to their feet. Somehow the boat didn't rock as the man stepped up onto the seat and waved both his arms over his head in Alex's direction. Paralysed, Alex watched on as he balanced calmly for a moment before diving elegantly into the water. That was enough for Alex. He turned and ran as fast as his legs would carry him back to the house. Back in his room, he pushed a tablet into his shaking hand and gulped it down in search of peace.

When he finally emerged the next morning, Sarah and Phil were tidying away the plates from breakfast. Happy birthday banners and balloons decorated the kitchen.

'There he is, sleepyhead. I thought you weren't much of a sleeper?' Sarah joked, sticking two croissants on a plate and holding them out for him.

'No I'm fine thank you.' Alex replied, 'Where's Evie?'

'Right here, is that for me?' she grinned, appearing behind him.

Alex handed her the wrapped box, 'Happy birthday, I hope you like it.'

She ripped off the paper and then began jumping excitedly on the spot, 'Thank you thank you!'

'Here look.' Alex said, helping her pull the skateboard out of the box. The underside design he'd had personalised in black and green with octopus tentacles (her favourite colours and animal) and her name was written in graffiti style writing.

Evie held the board in silence for a minute before placing it carefully on the table and throwing both arms around his waist. Alex hugged her and felt pleased with himself.

'Hey, did you just hug me back?' she teased, letting go of him, 'Wow progress.'

'Great present mate.' Phil said, handing Alex a black

coffee which he accepted gratefully.

Only when they headed outside to sit by the lake did Alex remember last night, but he quickly took the penny from his pocket and tried to push it from his mind.

'What have you got there?' Callum asked looking up from his book.

'It's a 1933 One Penny. It was my grandfather's.'

'Cool, can I see?' he asked, wheeling himself closer.

Alex placed it gingerly into his palm. It had been quite some time since he'd allowed anyone to touch it.

'Why do you have it here?' he questioned, flipping it between hands.

'I always keep it with me.'

'Like a lucky omen?'

'Yeah I guess.' Alex replied, accepting the coin back and pushing it into his pocket.

Alex made it to just before lunch before noticing his skin begin to prickle. He slipped away to his room to take his second dose. Sat out under the shadow of the willow, a warm breeze blowing the weekend papers, Alex realised this was the most relaxed he'd been for quite some time amongst this laid back family, who'd taken him in like a lost orphan. He felt something unfamiliar that he took to be happiness at the pleasantness of the day, but was more than that. It was belonging.

That was until around four when, as the fatigue struck, he returned to his room to take his next dose.

Alex just stared in confusion at the empty inner pocket of his case. Desperately, he began pulling clothes out and throwing them to the floor. He searched the drawers and cupboard, even the bathroom, but to no avail. Panic swelled through him as he searched again and again, more and more frantically. In a rage, he threw the empty case at the wall, narrowly missing a framed print of two pheasants.

'Everything alright?' Sarah enquired, standing in the doorway.

'Where are they?' Alex shouted, jumping to his feet.

'If you didn't have a problem it wouldn't matter would it?' she replied, standing her ground.

'Look alright, alright, just give them back for fucks sake.'

'On the condition you admit you have a problem and promise me you'll get help. The clinic my sister used really helped her.'

Her words were like nails scratched down a blackboard, he needed them to stop.

'Just give them back to me you fucking bitch.' he exploded, kicking at his case as it got under his feet.

'You can kick and scream all you like but we care about you; I'm trying to help you.' Sarah said, backing away down the corridor.

'What's going on?' Phil asked appearing behind her.

'Nothing don't worry, Alex just couldn't find something.' she replied, holding Alex's stare.

'For the last time give me my fucking pills back

now.'

'Hey buddy, let's chill out here and mind your language.'

Ignoring him, Alex pushed past them both and stomped into their bedroom and began pulling clothes out of the drawers.

'They're not in here Alex, Jesus will you pull it together.' Sarah said, looking at Phil for what to do.

'I don't care about you or your pathetic little family's crusade to save me, you can all go fuck yourself.' Alex seethed, his eyes pools of fury, spit gathering at the corners of his mouth.

'Alright, that's enough mate.' Phil warned, placing a hand on Alex's shoulder just as he swung an arm back that caught him full in the face.

Phil dropped to his knees clutching his jaw.

'Get out of this house.' Sarah ordered. She pulled the boxes from her back pocket and threw them at him, 'Take you're precious pills and don't come back.'

Snatching them from the floor and quickly pushing a pill into his mouth, he staggered down the stairs, fatigue overwhelming him.

'What's going on?' Evie asked, appearing from the kitchen, the board he'd given her limp in her hand.

Stood facing her, he didn't know what to say. He started to say something but stopped. He felt a fool. Grabbing his keys from the hall table, he swept out of the door without looking back.

At some point, he'd drifted off and was woken by a woman in bright red lipstick and a crisply ironed uniform gently shaking his arm.

'We're making our descent now sir, if you could fasten your seatbelt.' she smiled, 'Can I get you anything to drink?'

Alex shook his head and blinked into the dry air that had glued his mouth shut.

'Actually, a glass of water please.' he asked as she half turned away. She returned moments later and Alex greedily emptied it and asked for another. The sun was streaking through the windows on the opposite side of the cabin, leaving illuminated patterns on the lockers above. Sliding open the shutter, he examined the dense forest below. To his right he could see a small town, where the trees came to an abrupt end, its roads like arteries leading to the centre. Gradually, as they dropped, the land became more populated and he could see the sprawl of the city beyond. Soon they reached his favourite part of plane journeys (and why he always asked for a window seat) when they were just high enough to take in the vastness of it all, but low enough to see the details of swimming pools tucked behind model houses or miniature cows in fields. He looked directly down to see a matchbox sized pickup truck moving down an impossibly long straight road. Then as the city swelled, they drifted over what Alex first took to be a rubbish dump, but as they descended lower, realised was a patchwork of metal roofs and plastic tarps endlessly linked. As they dropped so low he wondered if they would land on top of them, he caught a glimpse of a dark waterway cutting through it, children splashing and playing in the rubbish-lined water. Then in a blink of an eye they were down, bumping onto the tarmac and heavily applying the brakes.

The heat hit him as he followed the young man (who had been holding a piece of cardboard with Alex's name in capitals) through the sliding doors out to his car. On spotting Alex, he had shaken his hand enthusiastically, flashing him a smile that lit up his face and introduced himself as Rafael.

'Welcome to Santa Domina sir, I know you're going to have a wonderful time here in my city.'

'Gracias,' replied Alex, already sweating under his jacket.

'You speak Spanish?'

'Si lo mejor que pueda'

'But please, if you don't mind, speak in English; I don't get to speak very often. Now please you must step inside my car, it is fully air condition, nice and cold like your country,' he continued, holding the door open for Alex and laughing at his own joke. Once he'd packed the bags in the back, they pulled away from the concrete terminal. Rafael was every bit the tour guide, turning (with a little too much regularity for Alex's comfort) in his seat to tell him about every passing point of interest. Alex, struggling to match his driver's energy, watched in horror as Rafael turned back, just in the nick of time, to avoid an oncoming cement truck. As they worked their way into the city the traffic came to a standstill.

'Is the traffic always this bad?' Alex asked, trying to push his tired mind into some sort of conversation.

'No, today there is a bus strike in one part of the city, they park buses across the roads so no one can pass.'

'Wow that must be annoying.' Alex replied, starting to feel cold from the air conditioning.

'This one's not so bad,' Rafael shrugged, pulling the car forward a fraction into a space that wasn't there, 'last month it was the whole city, this time only where the owners of the bus company live.'

Through the windows Alex watched people going about their business along the busy street. A pair of elderly ladies in Nike trainers carrying heavy bags of vegetables, a wiry moustached man with a three metre length of pipe over his shoulder, three giggling schoolgirls in uniform, arms flung over each other's shoulders. They stopped outside a modest car mechanics, tyres and oily car parts spilled out onto the pavement in front. Inside, Alex could see a chaos of machinery piled up in every corner. In the middle a car was raised, a shadowy figure working underneath. Standing in the entrance, looking out on the traffic was a slim, stooped man, a cigarette between his lips. His clothes were oil streaked and he plucked at his smoke with black greasy hands. Alex shifted in his seat as the man continued to stare straight at him but he soon realised he couldn't be seen through the dark glass. Grinding the stub of his cigarette under his foot, the man spat on the ground, turned and disappeared into the workshop.

They inched forward as a scooter pulled alongside with what seemed to Alex to be a whole family on board. A balding man with a serious expression and thick eyebrows was steering them through the gridlock, a young boy balancing between his knees holding on to the handlebars. Behind him, his wife sat side on in jeans and a bright yellow t-shirt, an immaculately turned out girl in pigtails on her lap.

For Alex, this was his experience of all the places he visited. As he was ferried from airport to five star hotel, from hotel to meeting room, through a one way mirror he glimpsed a world he never quite experienced. He'd visited every continent, had spent the best part of the last seven years touching down in new locations, a plethora of customs, politics, celebrations, food. Alex was a man who had been everywhere and seen nothing.

Taped to the dashboard, Alex noticed a picture of Rafael, clean shaven in a striped shirt grinning madly in the middle of a large group of people.

'Is that your family?' Alex enquired, gesturing to the picture.

'Ah yes,' he replied proudly, pulling off the picture and passing it back to Alex, 'I am a lucky man, no?'

Staring back at him Rafael glowed, his arm resting gently on a plump woman's shoulder to his left, who held a young baby in her arms. Around his legs were two boys, one clinging possessively to his hand. To his right stood an older couple, he took to be his parents and behind him stood two other couples and one teenager who stared back with serious eyes.

'This is your wife next to you here and your children?' Alex asked, realising he hadn't even considered he would be old enough to have children.

'Isn't she beautiful. We met as kids, I always knew she would be my wife, even back then.' he explained, turning again in his seat, 'We married at eighteen and that's Leo, Oscar and baby Maria. She's ten months now.'

'They're beautiful.' Alex offered, struck by the contrast with the picture of him and his parents with clipped smiles, in the silver frame that his mother kept on the table in the hall.

'May I ask how old you are Rafael?' he said, leaning forward between the front seats.

'How old do you think, my friend?' Rafael replied, a sparkle in his eye.

Alex smiled and rubbed his chin in consideration, 'Twenty-five?'

'Ha not yet, but close, twenty-three.'

They rolled forward at a snail's pace and Alex thought about what he was doing at twenty-three.

'How old are your children?' Rafael asked, honking his horn at no one in particular.

'I don't have any.' Alex replied, feeling a flush rise in

his cheeks.

'You and your wife don't want them?'

'Actually I'm not married.' Alex mumbled. He didn't know why he suddenly felt foolish, like he had missed a major global event that everyone else was talking about. They stopped again and Rafael pulled himself fully around in his seat and looked at Alex as if to reconsider the man sat in the back of his car.

'Ah!' Rafael said, realisation spreading across his face like a flame across paper, 'You're homo yes, you like the boys.' Rafael was pleased he'd remembered the word in English. 'You have a picture of your boyfriend?' he asked smiling.

'No, it's not that, I'm not gay.'

'Ha, it's no problem here, we like homos in our city.

'No really, I had a girlfriend until recently, it just didn't work out.' Alex said desperately.

Rafael paused puzzled, then finally asked, 'You don't want to have a family?'

'Well, it's not that, I just haven't met the right person yet and my job takes me away a lot which doesn't help I suppose.'

'Not everyone likes children, it's not for everyone.' Rafael offered, not wanting to offend his guest.

'It's just I hadn't really considered it yet.. I'm just not ready yet I guess.' Alex tried to explain. Eyes back on the road, Rafael nodded in understanding.

A silence fell over them that left Alex self-conscious. He took out his phone and looked through a couple of emails. Then on impulse, he brought up a picture of Evie that she had taken of herself sneakily when he had left his phone in their kitchen. He'd discovered it the next day whilst sat at his desk. Terry, a stocky man in his fifties with an explorers beard, had stuck his head through the door to ask a question, to find Alex sat grinning from ear to ear.

Leaning forward, Alex held the picture for his driver to see.

'This is Evie,' he said. When Rafael glanced at him puzzled, he added surprising himself, 'she's my best friend's daughter, we're close.'

Rafael nodded again but silently, then eventually asked, 'Like an uncle?'

'Yes exactly, I spend a lot of time with them as a family.'

'Very nice, beautiful girl.' Rafael added, as the traffic started to pick up pace.

The pain of that lie cut through Alex, he hadn't spoken to them since that weekend. He knew he should call and apologise but the shame was too much. For the rest of the journey, Alex felt subdued. Rafael occasionally broke the silence to point out the entrance to the famous Parque de Cabron or to show him where he'd lived as a child. Finally they pulled up to a large double gate, a sign saying 'Bienviendos al Hotel Castillo'. Hoisting his trousers over his considerable stomach, a uniformed security guard appeared and spoke to Rafael in Spanish before glancing into the back of the car and then waving them through. They pulled in front of a grand curved entrance of the modern building that was almost all glass with a nod to a colonial past.

'Here we are, this is the best hotel in the city, you'll have a great time. Many famous people staying. Last year we had Tom Cruise!' Rafael added proudly. Alex stepped out of the chilled car into the blistering heat, shook hands with Rafael and thanked him before turning towards the entrance where three staff, in starched brown uniforms, swept to meet him.

The lobby was a vast room, with a ceiling four stories high that encompassed a bar to his left. A selection of sofas and armchairs surrounded a glass statue (twice Alex's height) of a woman reaching to the heavens. A well groomed man, who told Alex a name he'd already forgotten, ushered him into one of the chairs and offered him a drink. Alex ordered an espresso and soda water, sinking into a long mauve sofa. This was where he felt most relaxed, a home from home. No one knew him here, he could just vanish into the background. His greeter had disappeared with his passport to the long arcing reception on the far wall and a young waitress had placed his drinks on a coffee table, flashing him a smile beneath shy eyes. Alex sighed, feeling the need for a shower. Eventually, the man returned handing back his passport, rising on tiptoes and asking Alex to follow him to his room.

That evening, after ordering room service, Alex sat,

eyes sore from the air conditioning, watching the BBC News Channel. Interspersed with wobbly shots of rioters throwing bottles and lines of heavily armoured police were reporters with serious faces. Transfixed he watched the scrolling bar at the bottom of the screen;

63 dead in Italy. Mass looting across Europe. EU to announce rescue package in the next hour. Markets in meltdown. 63 dead in Italy...

Numb with tiredness, he'd watched for over an hour, finally stabbing at the mute button when a headache began it's piercing ascent. He tried to convince his body it was now eleven pm, not six in the morning. It was a battle he wasn't winning. He poured himself another drink and sunk a tablet. Eventually he slept, although he wasn't sure when.

Startled, he woke to his phone ringing, his left arm dead, and dribble on his creased shirt. Rising abruptly to his feet, he looked about for the source of the noise before locating it on the glass coffee table. He was just in time to see it was Clayton but it rang off the second he tried to answer. A thin light seeped through the curtains, the lamp and television still on from the night before. The phone rang again and this time he snatched at it.

'Morning Andrew.'
'Alex, sorry did I wake you?'

'No, it's fine.' Alex lied, 'Everything alright?'

'Have you been watching?' Clayton asked.

'Yes, awful business in Italy.' Alex replied, stepping back in to look at the television.

'I'm afraid it's got a bit worse than that.' Clayton said softly.

Alex stared at the screen that announced in large capitals:

GLOBAL MARKET MELTDOWN: SPAIN AND ITALY BANKRUPT

'Things have been pretty disastrous in the last few hours, Spain and Italy have gone under and there's a lot of fear around the EU. The markets are in total shreds and Japan is on the brink. There's wide spread panic but everyone just needs to calm down; if we can ride out the next couple of days we'll be ok. The EU is bailing them out and the Americans have pledged support. It's a gloomy picture but we'll find a way.' He pressed on in absence of a reply. 'Look Alex, the important thing here is that we manage this carefully. Like everyone else our share price has taken a battering, and I'd be lying if I said this isn't going to affect us going forward. But you'll need to go above and beyond to reassure worried minds today. There are some pretty big companies in trouble and we need to let them know we're not one of them. You know what you're doing Alex, but don't be afraid to offer a little more if you have to, we can get things moving quickly, just make sure the big ones are signed........Alex?'

'Umm yes?' Alex mumbled attempting to focus. 'Did you get all that?' Clayton questioned, sounding concerned.

'Yes, don't worry, leave it to me. How are things in the office?'

'Naturally everyone's a bit rattled but the media circus will die down in a week or two. Look I'm going to have to go, call me if you need anything, alright?'

'Ok, bye Andrew.'

Ignoring the tv, Alex drifted over to the window and pulled the curtains aside. Desperate for some air, he yanked open the glass door and stepped out onto the third floor balcony, the fine curtains lifting theatrically as a warm breeze rushed in. The sun wasn't yet up but a shallow light illuminated the well kept gardens below. Birds Alex didn't recognise energetically darted amongst the foliage. He placed both hands on the railing, as if to steady himself and heaved in a deep breath. To his right a pool glowed without a ripple, surrounded by empty sunbeds. He pulled off his socks and threw them into a corner, enjoying the cool feel of the marble underfoot. The sense of calm order struck Alex as obscene in comparison to his stuffy room. Unable to bring himself to go back inside, he stood there for some time, watching a young man in green uniform diligently sweeping the path below. Thin clouds that hugged the horizon began to fill with light, as he looked down at his hands he saw the Penny there in his palm. He hadn't remembered taking it from his pocket. The weight of it was reassuring, as he ran the tip of his index finger gently across its markings.

Only then did he remember his parents were in Spain, visiting friends. He tried his dad's mobile but it went straight to answer phone. His mother's rang and rang but nobody answered. They'd be fine he reasoned, punching a quick email and sending it to them both.

Back on the sofa, he sat for a while watching the carnage unfold, nursing a strong coffee. Interview after interview of politicians from across the world talked up a good game, calling for calm, announcing a raft of measures to steady the sinking ship. All this juxtaposed perfectly with the shrieking residents of European nations surging through the streets, camera angles dropping chaotically to the sound of gunshots.

Eventually, Alex couldn't stomach any more. After a shower and change of clothes, he headed down to a tranquil breakfast room that showed little apprehension of the morning's news. The guests sipped their morning coffees and tucked into pastries and fresh fruits from the buffet. Sat at a table he tried his parents again and then Phil but both gave him unable to connect messages. He thought to check Phil's social media pages but the last thing he'd posted was: *Holy fuck* and that was more than twenty-four hours ago.

A panic seeped under Alex's skin. He felt a drop of sweat run down his back, as he tried not to think about all the terrifying possibilities. Feeling sketchy, he decided to double his morning dose. He tried to eat some breakfast but it all seemed tasteless so he abandoned it and went to the waiting car.

They crawled through the morning traffic, coming to a halt behind a large truck carrying gas bottles. Alex rubbed his tired eyes and tried to focus on the meeting ahead. After talking to Andrew he'd pulled up Ampulex's official statement to use in the meeting. Like Andrew had said, things would calm down. It might even work in their favour if competition was light in the aftermath, Alex thought. After they hadn't moved for several minutes, he asked the driver what was happening but he just shrugged his shoulders. In one hand Alex clutched his phone, in the other he flipped the coin over and over. An email notification appeared and Alex pounced on it. It was from Andrew:

phones are down meeting cancelled im getting you out wait at the hotel until I get back to you

The panic began to flood in then. As much as anything it was the unpunctuated rushed email from Andrew that scared him. His mind went into freefall: what if he couldn't get home, his parents, the lack of control had him gasping for breath in the back seat. Feeling trapped and light headed, he pulled clumsily at the door handle but it was locked. The driver eyed him with concern in the mirror and said, 'It's not safe to get out here.'

Alex clamped his eyes shut and took deep breaths, head back against the rest, his right hand clenched into a fist around the coin.

'Back to the hotel.' he barked, without opening his eyes.

'Yes sir...are you ok? You want to open the window?'

He didn't push the strange foreigner when no reply came.

When more than three hours later they finally pulled up to the now closed hotel gates, Alex didn't think he'd ever be so relieved to see two men with automatic weapons over their shoulders.

One of them approached the window and said, 'Name?' in a surprisingly crisp English accent.

'Alex Hampton' he replied quickly.

The man radioed through, speaking quickly in Spanish. For a few seconds, there was quiet calm as they waited for a reply. A deep, distant boom filled the silence, vibrating through their feet and making them all at once look in the direction it had come from. They exchanged concerned glances before the radio crackled a response. The gates opened and they were ushered through.

Standing just inside the entrance to the cavernous lobby, Alex clutched his work bag like a swimming aid. The world outside was going to shit but inside the Hotel Castillo a stubborn resistance was being held to the world's troubles. At the bar, gentle music played, as the guests sipped their drinks in twos and threes. A few people were talking animatedly at the reception desk but otherwise it was business as usual. A staff member, whose badge announced he was Antonio, approached Alex as he hovered by the door and asked if sir would like a drink on the house. Alex stared at the thin fluff on Antonio's top lip and tried to arrange his mouth into a reply. Undeterred, Antonio gestured towards the bar trying to guide him away from the door. There was little else to do but accept his invitation.

Slipping onto a bar stool, he ordered a mojito, downed it and ordered another. His mind was retreating rapidly as it looked to pull the shutters down on reality. He slipped two Adderall onto his tongue and decided to stay put. The afternoon rolled on and the bar started to fill out. There was only so long you could sit in your room watching parts of the world collapse in on themselves. Eventually you needed to see other human beings and talk yourself down from the ledge.

By the time a broad shouldered man hauled himself onto the stool next to him, Alex was thoroughly drunk and had given up trying to call anyone. He'd scrolled the news sites for a while but now even the internet was creaking under the weight.

'A whole lot of shit's going down out there.' the man said, without turning to look at Alex.

'Mm.' Alex half-heartedly replied.

'It's been coming though, we got to be more blinkered than a wagon horse.' he chuckled.

Alex turned to take him in fully, black cargo trousers

with zipped pockets, heavy looking boots. Alex wondered if he had stepped out in today's heat?

'Nathan.' he said, offering a firm no nonsense handshake.

'Alex....what do you mean, it's been coming?'

'Well, if you keep digging dirt out the basement to build extra rooms, you gotta leave the house something to stand on.' he explained, removing a baseball cap that read River Falls and placing it on the counter. He ran a palm over his shaved head and turned in his stool, looking at Alex's blank expression before trying again.

'It's like that thing where they say children can see all sorts that we can't because they have no reference on what should and shouldn't be there. By the time we're adults our subconscious has got it all worked out, we barely need to look any more, we know what a bar looks like, we've seen a million, our brains can fill in the gaps. No need to actually look. So when something is there that's out of place, doesn't make sense, our minds just filter it out, simple.'

Alex still didn't have a clue what he was talking about and was distracted trying to guess Nathan's age. He estimated he was somewhere between thirty and fifty, his skin looked weathered which made Alex lean towards the latter, but something in his eyes and smile made him think he was younger. He knew he was supposed to say something right now, that was how conversation worked, but Alex was sloshed and never had been much of one for riddles anyway.

'So what's here we can't see?' was the best he could manage.

'Everything. It's a global consciousness thing we don't want to face, who and what we are, why would we, it's too fucking depressing for one.' With that he necked his only just arrived whisky and ordered another, raising his eyebrows in question to Alex.

'I'll have the same, thanks.' Alex replied, pulling himself upright on the stool. 'Are you telling me you saw all this coming?'

'You don't know the half of it.' he replied, rubbing a hand through his thick ginger beard. 'I've spent the last seven years prepping for this exact moment.'

Alex had now set on early forties and was considering his origin, Northern Europe, maybe Norway he guessed.

'Why are you here then?' Alex asked, confused.

'Well exactly, life fucks you sideways like that. Came into town yesterday for some supplies, truck broke down, all routes out are blocked and here I am, checked in to the only hotel in town with a wall around it.'

'Where do you live normally?' Alex asked.

'Place at the foot of the mountains, three hours drive from here, stream on site, off grid, everything I need.'

'So you've been living there because...' Alex trailed off as the waiter placed their drinks on napkins in front of them.

'Look, I don't know anything about you or your life but most folks here have no fucking idea what's happening in the world. They bumble along making and spending money with no clue that our existence is about as solid as a brick balancing on an eggshell. But then you can't blame people, it's too much to take in. I mean, it took me long enough to accept what had to be done. When I first moved out here I thought Nathan what the fuck are you doing? But the more I read the more I was convinced. I got myself ready for what might come, grew my own food, drank spring water, kept a couple of goats, hard graft. And then, the moment comes and here I am sat in denial headquarters having a drink with you, I might as well just have stayed in Denmark.'

Ah close, thought Alex.

Just then another boom shook the building, everyone freezing momentarily before looking at each other to see if it was time to panic yet. It was the second since he'd been at the gate.

'Well this isn't quite what I had in mind either.' Alex replied, 'but I'm sure everything will calm down in the next couple of days if we sit tight.'

'You really believe that bullshit?' Nathan roared, fixing him a disbelieving stare. Alex looked down at a bit of stray spit that landed on his shirt and seeped into the cotton, 'Life isn't a movie where the army rolls in and we all send up a cheer and fiesta into the night!'

'So what's going to happen then?' Alex asked, slurring his words slightly, after they'd sat for a moment in silence.

'I have absolutely no idea, my guess is we're completely fucked.'

'To being royally fucked.' Alex chimed raising his glass. Nathan cracked a smile, like the sun breaking through storm clouds, and raised his glass before downing its contents.

Much later, solidly drunk and a little unsteady on his feet, Alex staggered back to his room. A message on the in-hotel tv system announced that until further notice all guests were to stay in the hotel for their own safety. In need of air, Alex crashed out onto the balcony and sat on one of the loungers. To his right, he could see the illuminated wall that ran around the hotel and beyond. The air smelt of burning plastic; the sound of birds chirping excitedly from the gardens was punctuated by the rattle of gunfire. A couple of hours ago when he'd checked at reception for any messages from Andrew, they'd reassured him that the hotel was well guarded and that the safety of their guests was paramount. Unnerved by the gunfire, he retreated to the safety of his room. He didn't turn on the television, instead he lay down fully clothed on the bed. In minutes he was asleep.

Just after first light, not quite asleep yet not fully awake, he lay listening to the rain intensify like a cheer. There was something peaceful about it, a calming simplicity that held Alex. For a moment he didn't think anything, just allowed the sound to pass through him, eyes half closed, under crisp clean sheets. Like a tap where the water takes time to work its way through the pipes, he was held peacefully in that anomaly we call time. Then inevitably the world came rushing back in, casting a shadow with its heavy burdens. In the months that followed, Alex would often think back to that moment.

The fire alarm was the first indication that something wasn't right. Alex dressed quickly and stepped out blinking into the hallway. He followed the other confused looking guests down the corridor. The alarm continued at unbearable piercing intervals, stoking the flames of his raging hangover. He felt into to his pocket for his pill box but realised he'd left it in the room. Stopping abruptly, a tall well dressed lady in her sixties bumped into him, pushing past him without a word. He considered going back but the corridor was packed. He pressed his index fingers into his temples and reluctantly followed the masses down the stairs and into the wide corridor that led out to the pools. People spilled into the space from every stairway, staff and guests alike. They ground to a halt as the sheer numbers bottlenecked before flowing out the open doors. Alex stood stiff, suppressing his rising panic. He hated big crowds, he had learnt to manage them to a degree but largely avoided them.

Clutching the coin in his right fist, he waited as they edged forward, feeling the weight of expectation at his back. Ahead of him he noticed the man from the bar last night, the back of his shaved head high above the others. Habitually he rolled his thumb along the edge of the Penny, just as a woman behind him tripped, pushing him forward. He helped her up, gripping her forearm and she thanked him in Spanish. As he turned to face the doors, he realised the coin wasn't in his hand any more. Distraught, he scanned the floor but he couldn't see it. In a space that wasn't really there, Alex squatted down to try and get a better view through the forest of legs. He looked to his right through the gap between a brown uniformed leg and a flowing summer dress adorned with hummingbirds, and saw a girl staring straight back at him. She held his gaze and slowly lifted her hand like a question, revealing the coin held between thumb and forefinger. Alex nodded but what he said next was lost in the deafening sound of gunfire. It rattled off the marble walls and no one in the hall needed telling this time, it was inside the hotel. As Alex tried to get to his feet, he was shoved forward as the hysterical crowd charged. He looked to the girl but could no longer see her through the mass of limbs. Somebody stood on his left leg and he felt a knee in his back, he let out a scream nobody heard and attempted to claw himself upright. Desperately, he scanned the horde but there was no sign of her.

A second round of gunfire, closer this time, rang out as he bulldozed his way to where the girl had been. Those heading out to the pools suddenly changed their minds, turning to head back where they had come from. The people behind them hadn't witnessed what was happening outside but the terror in their eyes was enough to make them turn and run too. Amongst the chaos, screams were drowned out by gunfire, this time right on top of them. That's when he saw her by the descending stairway, she half turned as she fell, dropping abruptly downwards. Above her head, on the wall of the stairwell, three holes suddenly appeared amongst a cloud of fine plaster. Alex, like those around him, fell to his knees, both hands covering his head. More shots rang and then nothing.

On his hands and knees, he crawled over to the girl who lay face down on the floor. He didn't feel the kicks and shoves as the panicked throng started to move again, his whole being was focused on the back of her head. Gripping her shoulders he turned her over without thinking about what he might find. Her eyes were closed and one small line of concern was etched across her forehead as if she were contemplating something. Awkwardly, he picked her up and attempted to carry her towards the stairs. Straight away he tripped nearly dropping her, a hand instinctively plummeting to the floor to steady himself. It slid on something wet and he nearly stumbled downwards. He looked to see what he had fallen over and quickly looked away, but there's no erasing something once seen, however briefly.

He pushed on down the stairs not knowing where they were going, anywhere just not in that hallway. Feeling her body twitch, he looked down to find her blinking up at him. She smiled as he paused for breath at the bottom of the stairs.

'Are you alright?' Alex asked, but she didn't answer. Instead she took his hand and carefully placed something in it, closing his fingers around it. The last thing he remembered was looking down at the coin in his open palm, Britannia proudly holding her trident aloft. At that precise moment the first of two explosive devices detonated, destroying most of the west side of the once grand hotel. A noise so loud it etched through every muscle. Then it all came crashing down, rubble, dust and finally silence.

873 days later

On the west side of the settlement, the paved road abruptly comes to an end, the dust track splits through overgrown fields before disappearing into the forest. A simple house, the colour of old paper, with a hole in the roof (that two pale doves playfully soar in and out of) sits silently overlooking the shelving bay. Its garden, once someone's pride and joy, gradually suffocates itself. Vines have begun their ascent of the walls, as nature reclaims what is hers.

What a project we undertook, eyes on the heavens, a lie encased in glass and stone, our wheezing children trampled unnoticed at our feet in the dash for the heavens. It would be wrong to say we didn't love her but love is complicated like that. We shackled her in our gardens, slashed and dug so that we could build more and more icons of our own greatness. It is this that is the unspoken unity of a divided species, to discover, catalogue, claim every last molecule of this Earth and make it ours. Only then would we be the gods we secretly saw ourselves to be.

At the edge of the garden, a flaking wooden fence disappearing into foliage, leans towards the ocean. Attached to it a gate flaps apathetically in the warm breeze. Landing lightly a stone's throw away, the colourful bird pecks at dry grass poking up through the fine sand. Gripping a suitable piece in its beak, it looks briefly up to the house before darting away in the direction of the town. It follows the potholed road, resting briefly on top of an electricity pylon. Below, the pavement is overrun by knee high plants, scattered with white and yellow flowers. Catching unseen currents, it pushes on towards the once busy seafront, landing on the roof of a museum piece car, neatly parked outside a beachfront cafe. There aren't many cars left in the town but this one is fascinatingly untouched, windows intact, not a dent in sight. Its flat tyres and dust-covered exterior the only give away of its long abandoned state.

Seeing something of interest, our feathered friend zips off over the collapsed roof of the bar, landing on one of the few tables not overturned. Rusting chair legs point to the heavens, as a part-submerged hardback diary's pages flap urgently in the sea air. Momentarily the wind drops and the pages settle like a falling feather to reveal: *Martha 11.30* scrawled in pink pen at an angle under a heading of *September 27th*. A gust of wind sends the pages back into a dance. The bird briefly drops his length of grass to peck at something on the tabletop, before snatching it back up and heading inland.

Drifting over forgotten streets he circles the deserted main square. A fountain full of leaves stands at its centre, topped by a statue of a forgotten saint looking down his absent nose at the scorched remains of a once impressive church. Facing it, three storey colonial houses stare down the burnt-out south of the town without comment. Once vibrant and bustling, the square is cloaked in silence, except for the faint hush of the sea. Outside a restaurant, its glass front an angry mouth of sharp teeth, lies a child's toy pushchair on its side. Still strapped in, an expressionless doll stares forward as if in shock. Not far away two leather suitcases rest on the cobbled stones. One case sits upright, its buckle still neatly fastened. The other lies open, its contents spread haphazardly; a pair of nylon brown trousers and faded yellow shorts hanging half in, half out. Inside, an open album reveals three neatly placed photos and a faded space that held a fourth. In the first is a woman in her late twenties, sunglasses holding her hair back, with a look on her face that says she doesn't want the picture taken. Next to it is a picture of another woman in a swimsuit laughing, the sun sparkling off the water behind her. In the third they are together, beaming, arms around each other's shoulders, sat at a table in a bar. Upturned to the sun, the contrast has drained from them; soon nothing will remain except the shadow of a memory.

Banking sharply right, he flutters on over red tiled rooftops before landing gracefully on the top bar of a metal climbing frame. From his safe height he watches a group of coati, tails raised, with their long snouts snuffling amongst the long grass for lizards and insects. The playground is much as it was, the one remaining lonely swing moving gently back and forth in the dry breeze. The metal slide glints in the sun, facing the low building that had once been the school. The double doors facing the playground stand open, as they had every playtime before the whistle was blown, calling the children to line up class by class. But none of this is of any consequence to him.

He darts directly through the open doors, down the corridor lined with rubbish and tatty books, and into a classroom to his right. Once through the gap, where the door had been, he heads straight to the far side of the room, over the teacher's shit splattered desk. Chairs and desks lie overturned, their legs tangled. Book pages curl like wood shavings amongst the smell of decay. To the right of the desk by the window is a low sideboard still populated with plastic drawers adorned with labels that read: Thais, Camilo, Gaby. Above them is a fish tank half filled with green liquid. Next to it a pot of beautifully sharp pencils sits collecting dust. Finally, he lands on a high shelf where, in the gloom, he adds the grass to the construction site of his nest. Then without fanfare, launches from the shelf, flying back down the corridor and out the doors. He rests in the branches of a tree, its silvery leaves like fish scales in the wind, and sets to the task of pruning his feathers.

Below, a faded blue plastic bag is drawing circles in the dirt, rising and falling on invisible strings. Rapidly it ascends, filling like a sail and whips away towards the ocean. It snags momentarily on a wire fence before continuing its intoxicated dance across the street beyond a row of larger houses and onto the beach where it catches on a fallen tree branch, on the edge of the waterline. Frantically it flaps, as if to escape, before the wind drops and it sinks deflated. The bay is scattered with gifts left in dedication by the sea: a handleless plastic bucket, cracked and faded; a rusted metal tin that had once held biscuits; a piece of shredded green plastic sheeting, that floats down the beach like a jellyfish. Objects that belonged to a different time, remains of humanity's hay day, a time where nothing was ever too much.

At the top of the beach, under the shade of a palm, two figures sit side by side escaping the midday heat. Espe had watched him for a short while from the window of the house, before heading out and sitting gently in the sand next to him. He didn't register her arrival, instead continued to stare out at the horizon. She was used to him being like this, she hadn't known any different. Only because he'd been carrying a wallet at the beginning did she even know his name. One night when they'd sheltered in an abandoned house on the outskirts of the city, she'd asked if she could look at it. Curiously, Espe had looked through the strange cards, taking each one out and studying them. One of them had a picture of him on it and the words Alex Hampton.

She'd only heard his voice once when he'd cried out something she couldn't understand as they slept in a small hamlet of trees one night. So surprised was Espe that she ran over to him, in the hope he would say more but he turned away from her and dropped back into silence. After that night she knew he could speak, just that he didn't want to and she was fine with that. But that afternoon, seeing him sat alone, she had an idea.

She ties her long, stiff hair back in a bun to keep it out of her eyes and pushes her toes into the sand.

'We've been together for a while now and looked out for each other haven't we? There's been so much running we haven't had a chance to stop. You don't really know much about me so I'd like to tell you. Would that be ok?' Espe says, looking up, hoping for a reaction.

She doesn't get one. Alex's weather beaten face (brown from the sun, cracked lips from the sea air barely visible under his wild black beard) continues to face outwards towards the ocean. Espe pauses wondering what to tell him, before seeing a worn car tyre draped in seaweed over to her right. She goes right back to the beginning and tells her story. All of it, from life in Borde right up until they met.

'Did I ever tell you about the tyre races we used to have in Borde? Well basically they were about the most fun thing you could do as a kid living in a place where people made their own houses and the roofs leaked when it rained and nobody had any money. Not that it mattered in the end anyway. Before each race I was sure I would win but then my Ma did call me Esperanza so maybe hope is just who I am.

So I'm stood in a line with Sol and Diego up where the path widened out just past Jana's place where she's always sat out front smoking. Sol looks nervous as usual but Diego's all cocky looking and catches my eye before drawing a finger across his throat and even though I am really trying hard to focus I can't help but laugh. As usual we got the tyres from the bit of wasteland just past the last houses where a whole load of crap was dumped and we weren't supposed to go but always did anyway. I'm stood there trying not to look at Diego and instead keeping my eyes on Nef's door...'

It takes Espe over two hours to tell it all. Suddenly exhausted, she falls silent, watching a stilted bird land in the shallows. She'd talked so much her cheekbones hurt but she felt better. Alex remained silent the whole time offering nothing in return, until he reached out and took her hand as she described Rosa's death. As if it might escape, Espe holds it in both hands.

'Do you remember the explosion?' she asks looking at him. He pulls his knees up to his chest and gently shakes his head.

'Apparently there were two explosions but I only remember one. I was still watching you just standing there when the wall behind you collapsed. I think the gunshots made me deaf because I don't remember any sound. I was thrown across the floor and curled up into a ball. When I looked back it was like you'd just vanished; all I could see was dust and rock. I remember screaming but no sound came out. There was so much dust it made it hard to breathe and there was this weird chemical smell. Ma was right beside me shaking my arms and saying something to me but I just saw her lips moving. I looked for Diego and Carla but couldn't see them. Ma tried to pull me down the corridor away from the rubble but I pushed her away and crawled over to where you'd been a minute ago. I'm still getting nightmares about what I saw.' Espe picks at her nails anxiously, 'It's always the boy, he's still covered in dust and his neck is all twisted the way it was. The worst is his eyes, I wish he'd just close them.'

Alex turns to look at her, Espe smiles, not letting go of his rough hand.

'It's ok. I'm used to them now.'

For a little while, they both just watch the ocean lapping unhurriedly in front of them. Reluctantly, she lets go of his hand. Alex picks up a handful of sand and lets it run between his fingers as he listens to the sound of the sea. After the chaos of the city there had been silence, so much silence. Turning towards him she notices his eyes are closed, both hands resting lightly on his chest. From the corner of his eye a fugitive tear blinks into the light, pausing fleetingly, before dashing across open ground for the safety of his wiry beard.

They couldn't say whether they'd stay. It seemed a good spot but so had the deserted farmhouse before they'd found the barn. The house was a grand ambassador of a once wealthy elite, stretching an afternoon shadow towards the sea, glass still in the shuttered windows, sheets on the beds and stairs that complained all the way to the fourth floor. They'd cleared the rubbish, righted the fine woven armchairs and brushed out the sand. In the garden, they'd even hacked back the plants so you could sit on the rusted swing chair and look out to the tanker that sat motionless a kilometre from the shore. Upon arrival they'd found the heavy front door ajar. Slouching in they'd dropped their bags wearily on the tiled floor and stood in silence. The sorry group had walked non stop, barely spending more than a night in one place. Dust worked into every crease mixing with sweat. They gave in to it, their resolve evaporated. Seeing no one, they'd long given up talking. What was there left to say? Yet still their footprints pushed into the dust of forgotten roads and muddy river banks as if leaving a final vestige.

It was Diego who saw it first, extending a scrawny arm to point at the slip of opal on the horizon. At first, Espe didn't know what she was looking at. Their pace quickened as they pushed into a salty breeze, the end of the line in sight. They could go no further to escape themselves. A lifetime ago Espe had dreamt many times of that moment, following the mass of blue to the horizon, dipping her toes into the gentle surf. The beach was no less beautiful than she'd imagined; tree branches bowing to meet the water before thinning out to reveal a shallow cove of amber sand. Long shadows stretched like totems as Espe soothed her blistered feet. It was without doubt the most beautiful thing she'd ever seen, but she felt nothing.

It had been different the day they found the farmhouse, five months on the run, the chaos of the city behind them. Like children at Christmas, they'd darted from room to room, discovering fresh clothes still hanging in the wardrobes, new books to read in a wall to ceiling bookcase by the wood burner. There were even a few large, tough carrots growing in the fields. Christina found eggs from a surprisingly healthy looking brood of hens and most exciting of all, running water actually flowing from taps. That evening with aching legs and flush from the bottle of red they'd found in the cellar, they unbolted the gate, allowing a little hope to slip through. Between slurps of carrot soup, they talked up a simple life where they woke each morning in the same place, maybe even tending to some crops, building up a steady supply of food. In the store at the side of the house Carla found grain, not all of it lost to mice. Christina suggested planting some wheat, maybe in time they could grind some and make flour for tortillas. Resting back in her chair, Espe fell quiet watching her mother across the table sipping wine, a flush of pink rising in her cheeks. She was in animated discussion with Carla about the merit of killing one of the chickens. Espe thought how nice it was to see Carla smile again, but couldn't help wondering where the smiling parents and three young children in the photo on the hall table had gone. Why would they just up and leave when they had food and a nice house, miles from anywhere? In Espe's head, something didn't fit.

Leaving the city had been hardest on Carla and Diego. In that first week, they just walked away from the smoke and gunfire. Stationary cars clogged the streets, smashed shop windows were smashed and panic swelled. Christina questioned whether they should be bringing along this silent, dull-eyed gringo who they knew nothing about, but Espe's declaration that he'd saved her life silenced her. It seemed the whole city was on foot, like rats from a sinking ship. Belongings bindled in bedsheets, families scuttled in clusters dragging along wide-eyed children. When night fell they slept where they could, at first in parks or doorways. Later Diego climbed through an upstairs window to let them into an abandoned house. On the eighth night, the electricity dropped out and never returned.

The following morning Carla watched through the

crack of a door as Alex rifled through drawers in one of the bedrooms. As she watched he suddenly paused, holding up a small pill bottle in the gloom of the pulled curtains before whipping off the lid and downing the contents. She kept it to herself that first time. She couldn't pretend she hadn't slipped away when they'd first arrived to search the kitchen for a drink. But as the days passed and they went from house to house, she watched him more closely. She saw his pattern, the desperate eyes, sweat beading on his brow followed by his long sleeps during the day. Sometimes there were moments of calmness where he would help barricade the door or come into the kitchen to help chop some onions.

One day soon after, it rained heavily, creating rivers cascading down the streets. They decided to stay put for another day; they had a bit of food and ached with tiredness. Alex, on the other hand, became agitated, pacing the room in trousers a little short for him. Without a word, he began to pull away the barricade on the door, desperate to get out. Diego tried to stop him, shouting at him and pulling at his arms. Undeterred, Alex pushed him away, shuffling the heavy dresser from the door. In a rage, Diego jumped to his feet and pushed Alex hard from behind so he caught his stubbled chin on the dresser's edge. Just as the rest of them came into the room to see what the noise was about, an out of control Alex turned on Diego, pinning him to the floor. Diego spluttered, his arms and legs working like an upturned beetle under Alex's weight. After what seemed an eternity finally Alex let go, stumbling out the door into the pouring rain.

They stood for a moment in shock, staring at the open door before Carla dropped to the floor to comfort Diego, whilst Espe and Christina slammed it shut. Sitting around the kitchen table, they tried to work out what had just happened.

'Let's leave right now, find a new place to shelter and be rid of that gringo.' Carla spat, slamming a hand down on the table. 'He's a dangerous druggy. I tried to warn you he's trouble.'

Espe attempted to interject but Carla cut her off, 'I've seem him, sneaking around, going through the cupboards looking for anything to shove down his throat. He could have killed Diego! Why are we even discussing this?'

'Yeah that's something you'd know all about isn't Carla but then that's just a harmless drink right?'

'Espe enough!' reprimanded Christina.

They fell quiet for a moment, listening to the sound of the rain hammering on the tin roof. Then the conversation continued. Espe fought Alex's corner. He had saved her life, they couldn't just abandon him, he had no one. The debate raged on. Her cheeks flushed with anger, gripping the edges of the table, Espe was fighting a losing battle. Everyone else was in agreement, they would ask him to go.

As Espe tried again to convince them, Alex slipped

quietly through the door. He was soaked to the skin, blood from the cut on his chin smudged across his shirt. He stood stationary without looking at them, a pool of water forming at his feet.

Breaking an awkward silence, Carla scraped back her chair and rose, pointed at the door and told him to go. He glanced briefly in the direction of Espe and then turned to go. But Espe was on her feet and by his side in a second, tears of frustration clouding her vision. She grabbed his arm and stood next to him, announcing that if he was going she was too. Alex looked down at her in confusion, unsure what to do. Christina, Diego and Carla all took turns to try to reason with her but, they'd seen that look in her eyes before.

In the end they had to ask him back in, and to shut the door before more water rushed into the house. Shivering, hair plastered to his head, Alex stood sheepishly away from the others. Espe was like a guardian at his side. Whilst they argued loudly about what to do, Espe reached up and stabbed at his shoulder making him look at her, then whispered, 'No más drogas.'

It was only slight, but that nod of the head told Espe he could understand everything they said. There was such fire in her eyes and strength in that face, Alex couldn't let her down.

Things were tense for the next few days but they pushed on to the edges of the city. Reaching the suburbs things seemed calmer, the occasional gun shots were always in the distance. Over the neat houses with their well tended gardens, a towering plume of black smoke could be seen from the direction from which they had come. Exhausted, the five of them rested on a triangle of ground at the end of the quiet residential street. The subject couldn't be avoided much longer, but how could they rush Carla and Diego? Startling them, a solidly built man greeted them with a smile of crooked teeth. He announced that he lived a couple of houses up the street and asked where they were heading – offering them lunch with him and his wife.

The house was cool after the street and they were met by a squat, trampled woman of few words who ushered them towards the living room. Victor lowered himself into a recliner that sighed under his weight while his wife Julia brought plastic chairs that they perched on. Awkward silences were punctuated with kind comments about the bizarre collection of Elvis memorabilia that filled the walls. Over lunch they shared their experiences in the city and Victor told them all he'd discovered from the television, before the electricity went. He told them how economies in Europe had collapsed like dominoes and that the world markets went into freefall. All across the world there was widespread civil unrest, a fragile system brought to its knees. Cabron had called for calm and a stop to the looting, insisting the military would restore order. But a few days later he vanished from the screens, replaced by an army general. A couple of days after that the power went and never came back.

After a delicious meal, that they praised an embarrassed Julia for repeatedly, Victor offered for them to stay. They had two spare rooms since their daughter moved away.

For most of the eleven days they stayed, Alex lay under a blanket in the simple whitewashed bedroom he and Diego shared. After the first night, Diego had taken to the sofa, unable to bear the tossing and turning for another night. On that first day, Christina had warned their hosts about the erratic foreigner and Julia had removed all the medicines in the house to a hidden location. This hadn't stopped Alex looking of course. Just after breakfast on their first morning there, Espe found Alex pacing in the garden and told him to sit down and listen. He did as he was told. Espe sat cross-legged opposite him with a determined look in her eye.

'I know you're totally addicted to those things but you're coming off them now. I don't know much about this stuff but I'm guessing it's going to be really tough and you're going to go a bit nuts and want to break out and get some more. But listen to me,' she said, grabbing his arm, making him look up from his hands, 'you need to do this. You can't keep letting it rule you and anyway I'm worried about you, ok?'

Alex looked back at his hands without a sound, as a pleasant smell of fried food drifted from the open door of the kitchen.

'I'm going to help you. I know I'm just a stupid kid

but I'm all you've got and we're safe here and we've got food and somewhere to sleep. Carla said that you'd need to stay in your room mostly because you'll get a bit crazy and weak. I'll bring you food and water and anything else you need but you've got to promise me you'll do this.' she leaned forward and held his face between her hands, 'Promise me you'll do this.'

Alex looked into her eyes and nodded faintly.

'Come on then.' she said, pulling him to his feet by the hand, 'You've got to give me your stash and don't go shrugging your shoulders and pretending you don't have some because I mean it.'

Alex traipsed behind Espe as she led the way to his room and stood expectantly with her hands on her hips whilst he searched through his bag. He sheepishly handed her two boxes.

'Is that all of it?'

Alex hesitated before taking out a half empty strip from the front pocket of his bag, then seeing the look on her face passed her one more from his trouser pocket. Sitting on the bed, he held his head in his hands and stared at a hairline crack in the floor tile.

Sitting lightly next to him clutching the pills, she thought for a moment then said, 'Back there at the hotel you saved me and you didn't have to do that, we didn't know each other. You could have just run and left me there and really it wouldn't have been your fault because I was just another person in the world and we can't help everyone can we? So now I'm helping you, not because I have to or anything like that, but because I want to and now everything's all fucked up we have to look out for each other. All the others didn't want you with us, which I don't blame them for really but I know you're good. So don't let me down ok?'

Leaving him, she slipped out the room, heading straight into the bathroom where she popped the pills out one by one and washed them down the sink.

For the next few days, Alex didn't move from his bed. He shook and turned milky pale, his hair matted with sweat. Victor took to calling him El Fantasma Gringo chuckling at his own joke. Espe dutifully checked in on him every hour and brought him food that he scoffed down in increasing quantities. His eyes glazed over and his short breathing was drowned out by the ticking of the clock on the far wall. Alex's body worked its way through an appalling withdrawal. He clawed at the skin on his forearms drawing blood that Espe dabbed with damp cotton wool. He suffered terrible nightmares and fits of intense anger. Following the anger, a numb depression consumed him. Turned to face the wall, he gave up on everything. He felt himself sink slowly like a brick thrown in the ocean, the light gradually fading above. But Espe perched on a stall by his side whispering encouragement, gently lifting his hand away from picking at his wounds. Christina gave up asking her to come to join the others for dinner, bringing a plate to her instead, placing it on the small bedside table and kissing the top of her head. Alex didn't move or open his eyes and if it hadn't been for his shallow breath and the occasional shivers you might have taken him for dead. Petrified he would stop breathing, Espe slept fully clothed on the bed vacated by Diego.

Days passed like this until one morning Espe woke to find his bed empty. She jumped to her feet at the sight of the covers pulled back and clattered into the kitchen. She was silenced by her ma who pointed out into the garden where Alex sat, eyes closed facing the sun, an empty plate by his side.

'That's the second plate he's eaten, a good sign.' she said, smiling down at Espe.

'Why didn't you wake me?' Espe replied, annoyed.

'Because you needed the sleep yourself.' she replied to Espe's back, as she dashed out the door into the garden.

Sitting silently next to him, she watched his pale face upturned to the sun like a satellite dish. His hair was matted and greasy, and there were stains on his crumpled shirt.

After a few seconds, he opened his eyes and smiled weakly.

'How you feeling?' she asked, knowing she wouldn't get a reply. 'You seriously need a wash and a change of clothes, you're stinking. I'll ask Victor if he's got some spare things you can borrow.'

She found him in the living room, feet up reading a book.

'How's the patient, Nurse Espe?' he joked, placing the open book in his lap.

'Up and sitting outside, I think he's feeling a bit better. I was wondering, do you have some clothes he could borrow because he's totally stinking, it's gross.'

'Of course,' he said jumping to his feet, 'you lead the way, that's it, straight ahead and then to the right.'

She could feel him close behind her and walked a little faster into his bedroom. The thin curtains were drawn so only a soft light etched over the well presented room. Closing the door behind him, Victor stood and looked at Espe for a little too long before saying, 'Right, let's have a look shall we.' Stepping around the neatly made bed to a wide old fashioned wardrobe, he pulled out a couple of polo shirts and placed them on the bed before pulling out some shorts from a drawer. Avoiding his eyes, Espe looked at a large framed photograph of a cyclist in a tight top, arms out in celebration as he crossed a finish line.

'Who's that?' she asked, to break the awkward silence.

'Well, I'm older but I've still got the body.' he laughed. 'Won that race by more than three minutes, beat the record set by Paolo Ocolo in sixty-eight.'

'Right.' Espe replied, picking up the clothes from the bed.

'I've still got that, look,' he chirped, pulling the faded yellow top with 312 on the front from the wardrobe, 'want to see me in it?'

'Err, no thanks, I should get these to Alex.'

'He's a bit old for you isn't he?' Victor scoffed stepping towards her, 'do you prefer older men?'

Opening the door quickly, Espe stepped into the hallway before turning, thanking him for the clothes and running back out to find Alex.

Who knows how long they might have stayed if it weren't for Victor - a river about to burst its banks. It seemed innocent at first, a fatherly hand on the shoulder, 'Let me show you the caged birds in the garden.'

But he was like water on a gradient. Focused on Alex, Espe hadn't noticed Victor's eyes lingering, drinking her in behind dark glasses from a chair in the garden. Julia, of course, had seen it all before and felt crushed by helpless fear.

Still amazed by the luxury of a shower, Espe hadn't heard the click of the door. She hummed a tune to herself, the cool water welcome relief from the heat. She closed her eyes and let it run over her head, wondering what Alex's life was like back where ever he came from. She reached for the soap, the water sounding like rain as it hit the flimsy shower curtain. She slowly washed her body, thinking how much it was changing, it scared her. His back to the closed door, Victor's chest blazed with excitement, his eyes fixed on the shadow behind the curtain; silently he undressed. Pushing her wet hair from her eyes, a frown of confusion spread across Espe's face as she glimpsed movement. Holding the curtains with both hands she poked her head around and let out a yelp of surprise. Victor stood less than an arm's length away, his finger on his lips, penis erect, a formidable look in his eye. Espe froze in terror as he whispered, 'Shhh now, our little secret.'

She retreated behind the curtain, covering herself with her arms as the water lashed down. But Victor stepped into the shower leaving her no escape. She wanted to scream but paralysis filled her. He continued to whisper in gentle tones as if approaching a wild animal.

'No one needs to know.......don't worry, I can teach you.'

He was so close now she could smell his breath and twice his penis brushed against her as he towered above. Still, she froze as if watching the scene from elsewhere.

Then suddenly a knock at the door brought her sharply back to herself.

'Come on Espe, how much longer you going to be?' Carla shouted.

In that second she darted past him, snatching up her towel and racing out the door at a canter, pushing past a confused looking Carla. Puzzled, she stared down at the two sets of clothes on the bathroom floor and then, realisation turning to horror, dashed away to find Espe.

Diego had been right. He'd spied something in their gracious hosts' eyes on their first day, but desperate for some solid ground they'd swept his concerns aside. Well, not entirely. Christina had watched him closely but even she had convinced herself it was nothing, the clean bed and good food so persuasive. Anyway, he was a devout Catholic; she had talked at length with him about their faith.

In the corner of the garden by the bird cages, Carla told Diego and Christina what she had seen, holding Diego back from storming off to confront him.

'We're in his house and it's not as if we can just call the police. He could be dangerous.' she reasoned. 'We'll wait until the moment's right, then we get the hell out of here.'

They sat through an excruciating lunch. Espe didn't look up from her plate, rolling a small piece of bread between her thumb and forefinger nervously as Victor held court, joking and telling them stories of his army days as if nothing had happened.

There was nothing more to be done. When Victor's butterfly eyelashes finally settled (as they always did, wrapped in the blanket of lunchtime wine) they gathered on soft feet. Briefly they paused at the back door clutching bags, eyes locked with Julia who stood motionless at the sink. Christina gestured for her to join them but she didn't move, eyes filling up, wrapped in chains of trepidation.

They said nothing, putting distance between themselves and the house. Finally they stopped, reaching the brow of a hill with views in each direction. There was no plan; they just needed to get away. They stopped by a small row of shops spread out along a wide main road. Some were boarded up, others shrouded in darkness. A couple of cars passed but they didn't see anyone else. Dropping their bags in the dirt, they hugged one another in relief.

Diego shaded his eyes with his hand and looked up and down the road. In one direction the land dropped away to reveal the city, to the east the dwellings thinned, giving way to farmland and dust tracks lined with mature trees. The sun was already high in the sky, and there was so little breeze the street looked like a photograph. Squinting in the direction of the city he fixed his gaze on a group of industrial buildings just down the hill. He glanced at his Ma before slipping into the hardware store they'd stopped in front of, its door hanging precariously from its frame. He returned a minute later with a can of paint and a large brush in his hand.

'Wait here, I'll be back soon.' he said, turning and walking away.

It didn't take him long to find it. He followed a path that cut between the houses at the end of the street and headed across a scrap of land empty but for a lonely flaking goal post anchored in the dust. Vaulting a fence onto another street, he crossed over and could see it down the hill a little to the right, partially hidden by a bank of trees.

Broken glass crunched underfoot as he made his way around the corner of the derelict warehouse. He didn't go inside despite a back door standing open. Instead, he climbed onto the flat roof of what had once been the office and clambered up onto the main roof. The heat was intense but he ignored it, getting to work on the slope that faced the city.

Leaving the paint and brush up there, he eventually climbed down and backed away until the whole roof came into view. It wasn't perfect but it'd have to do, he thought, peeling off his saturated shirt. In blocky letters filling most of the large roof, it read:

DIEGO AND CARLA GONE EAST

Unsure where Diego had gone, the rest of them found shade under a tree laden with lemons and waited.

'Where's Alex?' Espe suddenly said, looking around anxiously.

'He was just here a second ago.' Carla shrugged, 'Probably gone to find more drugs.'

'I'm sure it's not that, and his backpack is here. Maybe he's in one of the shops, let's go look.' Christina coaxed a worried looking Espe, fixing Carla a disapproving stare over her shoulder.

Whilst all eyes were on Diego, Alex had slipped away down the nearest side street. He looked pale and jittery but he was clear in his head where he was going. Finding the path again he upped the pace, his body alive with fury. The more he walked, the more his anger built until he was consumed by it. By the time he clattered through Victor's back door, an irascible buzzing filled his ears, muffling Julia's shriek of surprise as he passed her on his way to the front room. Victor was still asleep in his chair, a peaceful look spread across his face. Alex was helpless as a lifetime of buried emotion rushed to the surface like a burst water main. He threw himself on the sleeping man, landing blow after blow to his face. Like a man in seizure, Victor's legs convulsed, his arms flailing desperately but Alex wasn't finished. Still he struck again and again, long after Victor ceased moving, his face a bloody mess.

Then suddenly he was done, collapsing to the floor on his back and staring up at the ceiling with heaving breaths. He lay there for a while, lost in the swirled patterned ceiling, every part of his body aching. Only when he finally thought of the others wondering where he was, did he drag himself to his feet. In the doorway to the kitchen, Julia stood like a mannequin, one hand covering her mouth, staring past him. He followed her stare to Victor's collapsed face and, horrified, he fled.

'Ah here he is.' Carla said, pointing to Alex as he floundered around the corner kicking up the dust.

Seeing him stagger towards them Espe erupted.

'Fuck you, fuck you!' she screamed through tears, kicking the dirt as she approached him, 'We're out of there for two minutes and you're back on them. You promised!'

Alex dropped to his knees in exhaustion and only then did Espe see his blood soaked hands, still clenched in fists, flesh flapping from the bone.

Eventually Diego returned, pouring with sweat, to find Alex propped up under the shade of a tree, Espe treating his wounds. Once Christina had explained what had happened and he'd helped find some bandages from one of the shops, he took Carla aside.

The others couldn't hear what they said but understood their predicament. Finally they came back to join them, their eyes wet with tears.

'Let's go.' Carla whispered, nodding away from the city.

Picking their way through the tranquil fields was slow going, for a weak and clumsy Alex. On and on they went, without any real purpose. Stomachs aching with hunger, lips dry and parched. They slept in barns or amongst thickets of trees until they finally found the farm.

And there they would have stayed, eating fresh eggs and attempting to grow their own food but Alex found them, in the wooden slatted barn, a short walk from the house, with views down into the wooded valley. The smell hit him first but before he could stop himself he'd flung open the doors. As sunlight streamed through the opening, Alex was struck by how gently they swayed. He stood, mesmerised by those four bare swollen feet, as they gently twisted and turned above the three neatly packed mounds of earth rising from scattered hay, each adorned with a simple wooden cross.

They'd been on the road for a long time after the farm, keeping moving to forget. Life took on a simple rhythm. Walking, finding food and water, always heading east. After a while, they followed a wide, shallow river edged with eucalyptus, that whispered in the breeze. At least they'd always have water they reasoned and there were crops to be found in some of the surrounding fields. They avoided the towns, skirting around them before rejoining the river.

They passed fields of dead cows and sheep. Espe, covering her nose and mouth, tried not to look but the vile stench couldn't be held back. Not long after, they saw a man face down in the ditch by the side of the road, one shoe had slipped off and come to rest at the top of the bank. They didn't need to check if he was dead. Alex stood still in the middle of the road and stared. Christina tried to shepherd Espe and Diego further down the road but the time for protecting them had long passed. There were more bodies along the way and signs warning people away from villages and towns. It's incredible how much the human mind can endure, normalising horror in search of steady ground. But it doesn't come without a price.

Eventually, continuing along the river, they came to a junction where another road swept away to the south. In the shade of a tree on a large flat rock sat a couple leaning back to back. Christina spotted them first and they stopped and watched each other from a distance. They were the first people they'd seen for some time. After a few minutes Carla and Diego went to speak to them, waving the rest of them over not long after. Their names were Helena and Tomas, a couple (that Espe guessed were in their late twenties) who'd fled from a town in the south. Espe liked them at once.

'Where are you heading?' Helena asked, passing around a packet of biscuits Diego had been trying hard not to stare at.

'East. That's all we've got.' Carla admitted feeling foolish. 'You?'

'To the sea.' Espe added through a mouth full of biscuit.

'As good a plan as any. We gave up having any plan months ago. Staying alive, that's got to be about it now hasn't it?' Helena said looking to Tomas.

They walked on together, sharing stories of what they'd found along the way. Tomas and Helena told an animated story of a medium sized town they'd passed called Atonia where someone had opened all the enclosures of the local zoo before turning out the lights. Finishing each others' sentences, they retold how on arriving at the place they'd watched astonished as a giraffe casually strolled across an empty supermarket car park. Helena, wide eyed and expressive, told of zebras grazing in the parks and a rhino in the high street. Like children the group was drawn in by the light hearted energy of the couple, lapping up the story that, however briefly, took them away from themselves.

That night they camped together down by the waters edge a short walk from the road. As the sun began its descent, Helena pulled a fishing line from her pack and settled at the bank. Keen to see how it was done, Diego sat by her side as she hooked the bait and cast the line. She talked him through it, letting him try himself.

'What's with your friend here?' Tomas asked Carla, nodding towards Alex who'd taken himself off to sit alone on the edge of the clearing.

'He doesn't speak, well not since we've known him.' she replied matter of factly.

'He saved my life.' Espe chipped in defensively. 'We couldn't just leave him in the city; his name's Alex.'

Carla rolled her eyes but didn't make further comment.

'We met him at the hotel before we left.' Espe added, ignoring Carla.

'The hotel?'

Swatting away the mosquitoes, as the colour washed out of the sky, Espe told him the story of their escape. Tomas listened attentively, building a fire as she spoke. By the time she'd finished, Diego had returned beaming, holding up four good sized oval fish. They lit a fire and balanced the catch on large rocks placed in it's centre. Passing around the fish, Christina frowned as Espe waved her share away but she was too weary to have the argument again.

'What about you two, what was it like where you came from?' Carla asked.

'We lived in a town, down south, called Foreza,' Helena began, looking up through the smoke to the clear night sky, 'no one's ever heard of it. It was a nice place, half an hour from the sea, nice community. At first not a lot changed after the crash, people were scared but we had food from the surrounding farms, even some power from the solar. I think we all thought if we sat it out things would go back to normal. I worked as a nurse in the hospital, which was tough, but we had a decent stock of drugs and they used generators to have electricity for a few hours a day. People died who needed major surgery because we couldn't send them to the bigger hospital at Jicaral like we normally would. But after a few months, an armed group attacked the hospital.' Helena fell silent and looked into the fire in a way that put a stop to further questions.

From her backpack, Espe pulled a can of sliced pineapple she'd found at the back of a cupboard of the abandoned house they'd checked over that morning. She scooped out a ring and pushed it into her mouth, juice dripping onto her trousers. Tomas wiped his fingers on the grass and continued. 'The radio broadcasts stopped a bit before we left, but the last we heard the government was all but gone and there was violence in most cities. The news said plenty died in the violence but my guess is more died from disease. We passed a couple of places on the way here where a lot were dead....we just didn't know what we had.'

The night was cool so they kept the fire going to shut out the dark as much as anything. Helena (who it turned out could more than hold a tune) sang a couple of songs, her voice wrapping its arms around them in the darkness. They sat mesmerised, as the reflection of the hungry flames danced in the dark pools of their eyes. Espe noticed that for the whole time she sang, Tomas didn't take his eyes off his wife. He perched on a fallen log, the glow of the fire illuminating his knowing smile. When the clapping had been replaced by the gramophone crackle of the fire Espe asked, 'How long have you been together?'

Christina frowned at her daughter's question but Tomas didn't seem to mind.

'We met when we were eighteen through a mutual friend,' he replied, throwing another branch on the fire, 'Helena was in a play we'd gone to watch. The next day we went to the beach all together and we've never really been apart since.'

He glanced her way and they both smiled.

'Was it love at first sight?' Espe asked Tomas, thinking they had to be the most in love people she'd ever met.

'Well, I don't think that really exists, just in stories. But sometimes I look at Helena and it hits me that we're not the same person and if that's not being in love I'm not sure what is.' he chuckled holding out his hand for her to take.

The couple stayed with them after that. They were easy going and pulled their weight so no one had any complaints. On they went, one sore foot in front of the other, limbs aching and hearts heavy in the oppressive heat. Days dissolved into weeks, fugitives of the human condition, grieving hearts splintered, all the way to the sea.

You understand now why they didn't unpack when they arrived at the tall house on the beach. Hope, a fragile luxury of a different time, belonged to men on outlandish boats, who drank foreign wine from polished glasses. Children who slept in clean sheets and thought hardship to be having less than their peers, or simply those who had never known violence, uncertainty, death.

In the morning light, Diego sits next to his Ma watching her, eyes closed in the sun, the sea breeze gently rocking them back and forth. They listen to the seabirds and a distant rumble of the surf. He studies her wiry frame rising and falling, and feels grateful she is still here. She'd lost so much weight it troubled him how much of her skeleton he could see through her cotton blouse. She's eating more now but in the beginning it had just been mashed foods that he'd mixed with a little water and fed her with a spoon. He often thought about the morning he found her.

Waking early, high, thin cloud veiling the sun, he'd gone for a walk along the meandering river. Feeling sticky he'd stripped off his clothes and jumped off a smooth boulder into the deep, inky water. He dove to the bottom and opened his eyes to nothing but black. He stayed there as long as he could, shutting out the world above. Eventually surfacing, breathing rapidly, he dressed and continued to walk along the bank, amongst the young trees, looking for something to eat. When he'd returned with a pockets full of wild mushrooms, he saw the rest were up. Espe smiled and waved, balanced on a thick branch that hung over the water. Alex was nowhere to be seen but his pack was still where he'd slept. Helena and Tomas sat cross legged opposite each other deep in conversation and didn't notice him return. Seeing his Ma still laid out under the trees where they'd slept he walked over to find her motionless on her side, vacant eyes open. Her mouth was twisted slightly and only when she made a soft groan did he realise she wasn't gone. He'd played that morning over in his mind obsessively as if at some point he would be permitted to rewrite the detail.

The stroke stole a lot of her speech and reduced her movement on her right side. Diego is sure she wouldn't have made it without Helena.

'I think it's an ischemic stroke,' she'd announced crouching by Carla's side, 'I can't be sure without a scan but the majority are.'

She turned to Diego. 'If it's a bleed to the brain there is nothing we can do. If, as I suspect, it's ischemic we'll need some sort of anticoagulant drugs to protect against another stroke. But you need to know that if I'm wrong the anticoagulant could make her worse. What do you want to do? It's up to you.'

All eyes fell on Diego.

'Where could we get those drugs?' he finally asked.

'We passed a sign for a town back on the main road not long ago, we could try there.' Tomas suggested.

'I'm going.' Espe almost shouted, grabbing her pack.

'It's best if you stay here and help Diego.' Tomas said gently.

Seeing Diego's panicked face Helena pulled him into a hug, 'She'll be ok, we'll be back in a few hours. You sure about this?'

Diego nodded silently.

As the couple turned to go Alex stepped beside them.

'You coming too?' Helena asked, squinting into the sun.

He didn't answer but followed as they walked away through the trees towards the road.

It took them just over an hour to reach the edge of the small town. The road was barricaded and 'Keep Out' signs warned of disease. They left the road and climbed up onto a small rise of scrubland, where they could look down on the scattering of sorry buildings. Tomas peered through a small pair of binoculars he'd borrowed from a shop back in his home town.

'Anything?' Helena asked.

'Looks quiet.' Tomas said, scanning the main street. 'This place isn't very big, we going to get what we need here?'

'I don't know, maybe. Let's head in, stay together, we'll look for a pharmacy; if there isn't one we'll have to check the houses. No time wasting, we get in and out.' Helena commanded, unsure how much she could trust Alex.

In single file they followed a narrow dust path, that cut

through the bushes down the hill to the first few simple stone houses. There wasn't a sound other than the wind amongst the trees and a weathervane that squeaked as it turned pointlessly on the corrugated iron roof of a house to the left. They crept across overgrown plots of land between the houses heading for the main street. Passing a grubby window at the side of a house, Alex jumped to see a healthy looking cat, sat upright, staring contently at him from the other side of the glass. A bit further along the path they passed two houses opposite each other, their front doors missing.

'Is it worth a look?' Tomas asked, nodding to the house on the right.

Helena peered through the doorway, 'Make it quick, Alex you take that one, I'll go ahead a little and check things out. Meet back here in five minutes.'

The front door led straight into a good sized living room, where faded ripped blinds that the sun was slowly bleaching green to blue were pulled down over the windows. Paint flaked from the ceiling like the open pages of a book, scattering snow across the cracked tiles. Alex stepped into the middle of the room, accidentally standing on a bent metal fork. He glanced around, feeling uneasy. Next to the window a caramel sofa scowled at the favourite armchair, a greying cushion still propped in its lap. Behind a stand up lamp, strips of wallpaper clung to the wall, curling like pencil sharpenings. He rifled through a dresser's drawers but found only official looking letters, a collection of keyrings and a split bag of dog treats. By the armchair was a cheap Formica table with rusted metal legs. Through an arch was a cramped kitchenette, its drawers scattered on the floor amongst broken plates and glasses. Seeing nothing of use he stepped into the hall, pausing to straighten a poorly painted picture of a stone bridge over a wide river, before shaking his head at himself and going to inspect the other rooms. In the bedroom a part of the ceiling had collapsed on to a grubby double mattress, showering it with plaster. There was little else in there except a wardrobe of moth eaten ladies clothes and a faded plastic plant that sat on the bedside table. The bathroom was the only other room but Alex didn't stay long, unable to stomach the stench. Covering his mouth he tried not to look at the overflowing toilet and quickly searched through the bathroom cabinet, it's cracked mirror reflecting white tiles, green and black with mould. Everything of use had long been taken so he turned on his heels and marched back out into the air.

He was the first back and stood awkwardly on the path waiting for them to return. Helena was next.

'Anything?' she asked looking through the door of the other house for Tomas.

Alex shook his head, wiping sweat from his forehead.

Tomas appeared a minute later, 'Not much there, I found a belt, this one's seen better days.'

Helena rolled her eyes and began walking towards the town, 'The main street is just up here, come on.'

They navigated a few side streets of simple stone houses until they came to an alleyway that led to the main street. Opposite them, a dirty, ripped awning drooped down onto faded plastic chairs and tables outside a boarded up cafe. A bit further down *DIOS ESTÁ MUERTO* was sprayed in red across a shop front. Plants grew everywhere, from the pavement, dangling from window ledges and guttering. It was difficult to tell what some of the shops had been, their signs were torn down, the glass absent from the windows. They buried their fear and left the alleyway heading for the main square, side stepping broken glass in the shadow of the buildings. Tomas saw it first, pointing animatedly at a green cross sign that protruded from a building on the near side of the square. Hurrying forward, they passed a burnt out car on its side in the middle of the street. They reached the pharmacy only to find a metal shutter covered the entrance.

'Around the back?' Helena whispered as she scanned the square.

Just past the pharmacy they headed left down a narrow street of older buildings with red tiled roofs, looking for a way in. Alex turned the handle of an arched wooden door but it was locked. A bit further up, Helena waved them over to a broken down doorway that lead into a small courtyard overrun by tropical plants. A couple of birds flapped away as they stepped inside, making them freeze and glance at each other in relief. A simple, round table stood in a sunny corner, two chairs tucked underneath. An espresso cup sat neatly on its saucer in the centre next to a pair of rusting scissors. On the other side of the courtyard a gate took them to a thin alley that ran around the back of the pharmacy. The back door was locked but Tomas climbed up on a flat roof and smashed the glass of the upstairs window, beckoning them to follow. Alex, who'd clambered in last, waited for his eyes to adapt to the darkness. Joining Tomas and Helena on the other side of the room, he peered in the half-light to see what they were looking at. A scattering of bones lay on top of the sagging single bed. Unable to stop himself glancing at the hollow skull, he tried to focus on a battered bible that lay by her side instead.

Helena pulled them out into the dingy corridor, took a torch out of her bag and led them down the stairs.

'I'll find what we need, grab anything else useful.' she instructed without waiting for a reply.

'Here.' Tomas said, passing Alex a spare torch.

The place was just as it has been left, everything neatly on the shelves under a layer of dust. Opening his pack, Alex chucked in boxes of plasters, soap and toothbrushes, until it was full. He walked around behind the counter and found some carrier bags and began filling those. Seeing the light from Helena's torch swinging across the room behind the till, he stepped behind to join her. Every wall was covered in slanting shelves filled with boxes of medicines.

'Any anticoagulant: Warfarin, Heparin, Clopidogrel; get

looking.' Helena instructed, sounding stressed.

Alex took the other end of the room and worked methodically across each shelf. On the third one down he stopped dead as the light caught something familiar. Boxes and boxes of Adderall stared back up at him like an old friend. He picked one up and slipped it into his pocket.

'Any luck?' Tomas asked, startling Alex as he appeared next to him.

'Not yet, take that shelf.' Helena said, shining her torch on the shelf by the door.

His hand already on another box of Adderall, Alex hesitated. Espe's face back in Victor's garden flashed into his mind. The mottled sun illuminating her freckles, her eyes strong and concerned. Feeling guilty, he dropped both boxes back onto the shelf and continued the search.

'Ah yes!' Helena exclaimed, pulling a box down from the top shelf on tiptoes. Once Tomas had helped her remove three more boxes, they headed back out the way they'd come. Wasting no time, they cut back across the square retracing their steps.

'That's far enough.' a grey haired woman said, stepping out from an alley with a battered shotgun pointed in their direction.

Another woman of similar age appeared next to her. They both wore jeans and serious expressions on their weathered faces.

'Those things don't belong to you.' the woman with

the gun stated, waving it towards Alex's carrier bags.

'We're really sorry,' Helena said raising her hands in apology, 'we didn't realise anyone was still living here. It's just we've got a woman in our group who's had a stroke and we need medicines.'

'Looks like you took a fair bit more than that.' she continued, without taking her eyes off them.

'Alright Monica, take it easy, they seem harmless.' the other lady said, placing a wrinkled hand on her old friend's arm, 'but we'll need those things back. We've got a few sick of our own.'

'Of course,' Tomas said placing his bag on the floor, 'but would you be willing to let us have the Warfarin? It could save Carla's life.'

'Nothing's for free any more. You want the drugs, you give something in return.' Monica replied, expressionless, flicking a fly away from the leathery skin of her bare arms.

'Ok, sure,' Tomas said, rifling through his pack, 'how about these binoculars, or this torch, or Helena has a decent penknife?'

'We have all those things.' she said coldly. 'Leave all the bags and go.'

'You said you have some sick of your own?' Helena asked, 'I'm a nurse. Perhaps I could help in return for the medicines?'

Monica lowered the shotgun and glanced at her friend, who nodded.

'Ok. Follow Yun, bring the bags.'

They took them across the square, back the way they'd come, cutting through narrow side streets of old looking houses to an unremarkable door in a tall shabby wall. Yun knocked loudly and spoke briefly to a muffled voice on the other side before the door swung open and they were ushered inside. They found themselves in a small bare courtyard of red brick paving.

'Who are these?' A grubby man asked, who stood blocking the open door.

'Found them raiding the pharmacy. This one here's a nurse, going to trade a little.' Monica stated matter of factly.

'And how do you know she's a nurse, she could be full of shit.' he replied, picking something from his rotting teeth. 'Might as well tell the whole world about the place, Jesus Monica.'

'Why don't you shut your whiny mouth and go back to doing what you're best at Nico, standing by a door.' she spat, pointing a finger in his face.

'Don't mind them, this way.' Yun smiled, leading them through a narrow passageway that led to another courtyard.

'This place is a maze.' Tomas said, running a slender hand over the old stone walls.

'That's the idea,' Yun replied leading them through a door, 'the old part of the town got attacked so much back in the day they built it so no one but the locals would find their way around. Mind your head here.'

Finally, they found themselves in a much larger

courtyard surrounded on all sides by well presented three story houses. Washing hung from lines that stretched from house to house, window boxes were packed with herbs and flowers. In the centre, a compact makeshift border was filled with healthy looking tomato, pepper and aubergine plants. Three squatting young children, who were poking a stick at a beetle, quickly stood up and stared at the strangers.

'Wow, look at this place.' Helena said in wonder, 'It reminds me of how things were before.'

'Well, don't get too used to it, you're not staying long.' Monica asserted as she accepted a hug from one of the children.

'We're all that's left of the town, some fled early on, most died.' Yun said leading them to the other side of the courtyard.

'How many are you?' Tomas asked.

'At the beginning, we were thirty-six. Now we're twenty-three.' she said sadly. 'Some of us are a fair old age for dying, it's the kids I can't bear.'

A huddle of people had appeared in doorways to stare at the newcomers.

'What the hell is he doing here?' a squat man in a tattered t-shirt asked, pushing his way forward and pointing at Alex, 'You bring a fucking gringo in here?!'

Alex looked awkwardly at his shoes.

'Alright, that's enough Rafa, he's with this group and Helena here's a nurse who's going to have a look at Teo and the others.'

344

'Teo would be just fine if it weren't for the gringos. They brought us all to our knees with their greedy companies taking everything we had and then leaving us for dead.'

'Change the record Rafa,' said a young woman in dungarees, with fair hair that dropped in front of her eyes, 'if they can help what's it matter if they've got a gringo with them?

Ignoring them Rafa stepped close to Alex and began speaking to him, softly poking a stubby finger into his chest. 'Weren't happy with fucking up your own lot, you had to mess with ours didn't you. What you really doing here hey? Come to steal what's left?'

Alex stumbled backwards, tripping over a plant pot and losing his footing. Before he could get up, Rafa pushed a boot into his chest, pinning him to the ground.

'I was about to get married, my life was finally going right and you had to fuck it up, didn't you?' He kicked Alex hard in the ribs. He curled into a ball but Rafa lashed out again, catching him in the face. Alex tasted blood, opening his eyes to see Rafa frothing at the mouth, unleashing a tirade of hate. Clamping them shut again he braced for the next impact but it never came. Monica brought the wooden stock of the gun down hard on Rafa's head and he collapsed like a push puppet.

Eventually, things calmed down. The woman in dungarees, whose name Alex discovered later was Lucia, returned with a clean rag and gently pressed at Alex's bleeding nose and lip. Tomas and Monica kept a close eye on the woozy Rafa while Yun lead Helena into one of the houses.

'They're up here.' she said over her shoulder, heading up a flight of steep stairs. Helena followed her into a large bright room, sun spilling through three tall windows. Pushed against the walls, ten single beds lay at regular intervals on the cleanly swept, tiled floor.

'It's always the same, fevers that get better when we give them antibiotics. Then as soon as the course is done the symptoms return. We are running perilously low on antibiotics now. We've been sending runners out to search for more in nearby towns but it's getting harder and harder.'

'How many have you lost?' Helena asked, smiling at a mother who watched her inquisitively from her son's bedside.

'We lost Mena last week. She was the ninth. Please if there's anything you can do, I don't know if I can go through that again.'

'I'll try, but I'm only a nurse, please remember that.'

Yun nodded, 'Where would you like to start?'

Helena cast her eye over the patients who were of varying ages. At the far end an elderly looking woman sat up reading a book, next to her a man was asleep turned away from her.

'Who's been in the longest?' Helena asked, feeling overwhelmed.

'Teo,' Yun replied pointing to a pale boy, his hair matted with sweat.

Helena approached the bed and Yun introduced her to his mother.

'Thank you so much.' she sobbed, hugging Helena.

'I can't promise anything, other than I'll do my best. Tell me everything you can.'

'He's had a fever for nearly three weeks now. We've given him paracetamol, all the usual things you would do but it won't go away. He's hardly eating and getting weaker. We just don't know what else to do.' Yun explained, putting an arm around his mother's shoulder.

'Hi Teo. I'm Helena,' she said sitting gently on the stool by his side, 'I'm going to see if I can help you get better.'

He turned his head away from her and stared out the open window as a warm breeze danced across the room. From her pack, she took out the thermometer and blood pressure monitor that she'd taken from the hospital.

'I'd like to check your temperature if that's ok?' she said softly to the boy, 'I just need to put this under your tongue.'

He didn't resist but refused to meet her eyes.

Helena watched as the figures on the thermometer gradually rose, slowed, then settled on 39.2 degrees.

'His temperature's very high.' she announced to the two worried looking women. 'When was the last time he had paracetamol? Has he had any sickness, diarrhoea?'

'We're running low so we've had to ration doses.' Yun said, lines forming at her forehead, 'You see why we couldn't let you take anything.'

'He hasn't been sick but he's been hardly eating. I wouldn't say it was diarrhoea but not solid either.' The boy's mother added, fiddling nervously with a button on her shirt.

'Have you been keeping them hydrated?' Helena asked Yun, as she attached the blood pressure belt around his arm.

'Yes, that's one thing we have been able to do.'

Helena did every check she could think off. She wasn't a doctor but she tried to use every bit of experience to work through the problem, the way she'd seen doctors do over the years. She spoke to all of them, carefully pencilling the details in a journal. By the time she'd finished, it was late afternoon and a warm light cast over the dishevelled town.

'I just need to get something from Tomas' bag.' she lied to Yun, seeing the expectant look on her face.

Down in the courtyard, she found him sat at a bench chatting casually to a bald, older man with kind eyes. Seeing her, Tomas made his excuses and came over to where she leaned against a wall warmed by the sun.

'You were a long time; what's happening?'

'It's not good, they've got seven ill with fevers and I've got no idea what it might be. I've gone through

348

everything but none of it adds up.'

'That many?' he said, pulling her into a hug.

'That's not half of it. They've already lost nine. You can see the fear in their eyes.'

'Shit. What can I do to help?'

'Just sit with me for a bit.'

For a while they sat in silence, watching the children chase each other across the square. Alex came and sat opposite them, the bleeding had stopped but his lip was swollen.

'We might have to stay the night.' Helena said to them anxiously. 'But I'm worried about Carla. They'll wonder where we are.'

Lucia appeared and asked if they would like something to eat. They gratefully accepted and a few minutes later she returned with a plate of grapes, watermelon and some grilled meat for them to share. She placed them on the table with a pitcher of water and three glasses.

Feeling weary and suddenly very hungry, they shared out the delicious food and ate quickly. Tomas poured them each a glass of water and slid them across the table. Wiping his fingers on his trousers, Alex picked up his glass and put it to his lips. That's when she remembered it. Several years back, a young woman with the same sort of temperatures baffled the doctors for days. All the top doctors came in to try to solve the conundrum. Turns out she had a strain of typhoid in her gut. They thought she got it from drinking water where she went swimming daily, in a polluted river a short walk from her house.

Wide eyed, she knocked the glass from Alex's hand, spilling water down his front and smashing the glass on the stone floor. Jumping to her feet, she shouted over her shoulder at a bewildered Alex, 'Don't drink the water!' and dashed back toward the house.

She met Yun on the stairs.

'I think I know what it is.' she blurted, a little short of breath, 'It's in the water. Tell everyone to stop drinking the water!'

'But we've used the well for generations, it can't be.'

'Where else can you get water nearby?' Helena asked.

'There's a stream just outside the town but it's a twenty minute walk from here.'

'You'll have to use that.'

'But how could it be the water? We were all drinking from that well before everyone got sick.'

'My guess is some pollutant has slowly seeped into the supply from somewhere in the town. Look, I'll happily stay here for as long as it takes but I want you to give Tomas some Warfarin to take back to Carla. We left them hours ago, they'll wonder what happened to us. She has a young son, please.'

'Alright, that's fair, but not all of them. He can take some and return tomorrow.' Yun replied.

That night Tomas and Alex returned late to the camp, startling the others whose hope had faded with the light. Espe jumped to her feet and hugged Alex, fussing over his injuries. They helped Carla to swallow the drugs, water spilling down her chin and followed the instructions left by Helena for her care.

For the next nine days Helena stayed at the town, Tomas walking there daily, resting for a few hours before returning with Carla's medicines. Working tirelessly, Helena stayed in the makeshift ward, monitoring the patients and administering the antibiotics. So she could be close to the patients, she slept for an hour here and there on one of the empty beds.

It wasn't until day three, as she was beginning to doubt herself, that they began to see the change. She woke early to see Teo out of his bed, sat on the windowsill watching the pink glow of the sunrise. Hearing her get to her feet, he turned and smiled, before returning to the view. By the sixth day all seven were on the mend, although some better than others. In her days there Helena and Yun chatted for hours, becoming friends. More than once she asked her to stay with them, offering her and Tomas their own house. It was tempting to stay and abandon life on the road but she was keen to get back and help Carla. What's more, Yun had only said her and Tomas could stay and she felt strange abandoning the others, especially now.

Finally, she left to a hero's farewell, hugging each of the thankful group as they sent her away with small homemade gifts. As she walked away from the dishevelled hamlet, Tomas at her side, she was more thankful than ever for her training. The sun was low in the sky and insects hung over the water by the time she reached the camp by the riverside. It seemed primitive after her time in the town, but she was pleased to see Carla sat up under a blanket on a plastic sun lounger Tomas had hauled back from an abandoned house. They were all keen to hear of her time there but she was weary, and after spending some time assessing Carla, she took to her sleeping bag.

They weren't able to move on for several weeks and even then it was slow going. In the end, driven by hunger, they'd continued along the river. Alex and Tomas took turns to carry Carla on their backs for as long as they could manage. Perhaps the loss of his father and brothers meant he was damned if he was going to lose his mother without a fight, or maybe it was just Diego, but he cared for her tirelessly. No twelve year old should have to strip their mother of her clothes, carefully clean her up before placing a blanket over her so he can go and wash shit stained clothes in the river. But Diego took to her care with the same fierce determination that he took to life. Never one to let his head drop, where there was a problem there was a solution, that was Diego. But when he finally settled her to sleep at night, he couldn't help but wake regularly and under the silvery light of the moon, creep to her side, hold his breath and listen for any sign she was still there.

She opens her eyes and smiles at her devoted son, reaching out and taking his hand.

'You thirsty Ma? I'll get you some water.' Diego asks, already rising from the swing chair.

Carla shakes her head and motions him back next to her. They sit for a time in silence watching the ocean.

'I've been thinking about going out to that ship.' he says eventually. 'There's a small boat up the beach that looks in good condition. Doesn't look that far. I'm sure we'd get out there and back in a morning.'

Carla frowns at him and shakes her head to show her disapproval.

'Don't worry Ma, if we go on a day like today it'll be a breeze. Who knows what's on that thing. There could be enough food on board to feed us for the next ten years. I bet there'll be cans of peaches and boxes of cake and chocolate dessert!'

Rolling her eyes, Carla picks up her book and pen and begins to write a word. She stalls halfway and struggles to find the final letters, tutting at herself. Diego doesn't need to see the word, he knows what it will be.

'Don't worry Ma. It won't be dangerous, we've looked at the thing every day now for weeks and there's clearly no one on board.'

She rests her head on her son's shoulder and gently takes his hand between hers. Looking up she can just make out a bird, high above her, a thin outline against the blue sky. Carla wonders what it must be like to look down on this world from that high. What would you see? She can only imagine.

Since they escaped the city they'd met less and less people. Some told them hideous stories of mob killings and starvation, but most brought no news of the world, instead they laboured to survive in their own small corner and beat back death that waits patiently in the shadows.

Diego turns to see Christina stood by their side, weary eyes turned to the sea. Her long dark hair, streaked with grey, is tied up in a ponytail, that Diego thinks makes her look younger. Noticing him she smiles warmly at a boy whom she loves like her own son.

'Have you seen Espe?' she asks, resting a hand on Carla's shoulder.

'Last time I saw her she was sat with Alex on the beach.' Diego replies, getting to his feet, the chair swinging gently in his absence.

Just as Christina heads towards the beach, Espe appears at the edge of the garden and leans on the remains of a low brick wall. She raises a hand in greeting before stepping, barefooted, down a thin sandy path and slumping next to Carla on the swing chair, pulling her knees up to her chest and resting her head on them.

'You ok sweety?' Christina asks, coming round to sit by her.

Espe doesn't reply, closing her eyes and listening to the breeze moving amongst the wind chimes that hang from the porch.

'He'll be ok.' she eventually says, 'He just needs time.'

Not wanting Espe to see his face, Diego heads into the house, stopping to look at family portraits on the hallway walls. It's a strange feeling living in someone else's house, their clothes still folded neatly in the drawers, matted hair in the upturned hairbrush on the window sill, private letters tied together with ribbon on the desk. Diego studies the black and white image of the lady in front of him and runs a finger through the dust on the glass. She's in her forties, the sun glinting off her angled glasses, her head tipped back laughing. Behind her a kite can just be made out in the sky. In the picture next to it two young children stand stiffly in smart clothes. The girl is taller, with short bobbed hair and piercing eyes that look straight into the camera. The boy, younger with a squat face, appears to be smirking (as if he had just played a joke on what Diego assumes is his sister). Who were these people he wonders, and where did they go?

Standing in a corridor with hideous flower patterned wallpaper, Diego tries to shake off his annoyance at Alex. But however much he tries to talk it out of himself he can't help the irritation in his chest. Every day he watches his Ma battle to let the words escape from the muddled prison of her mind and there he is choosing not to speak, it felt like a betrayal. Many times Diego daydreamed about screaming at Alex, pushing him to the ground and shouting at him until he eventually relents, uttering a tearful apology. He keeps these feelings to himself, knowing how important he is to Espe.

Leaving the hall, Diego strides up to the room he shares with his Ma. The two unmade single beds do a poor job of filling the large room, with its sloping wooden floors and whitewashed walls. In one corner is a sink, a hexagonal frameless mirror hangs above it. There's no running water but Diego keeps a bucket by it, that they fill from the stream nearby. He wears one of the two oversized men's shirts he found in the imposing, wooden wardrobe that looks as old as the house itself.

Annoyed with himself he attempts to smooth over his feelings, after all, they'd been together a long time now. Alex had carried Ma in midday heats, for that he should be grateful. Although he won't admit it to himself, a growing jealousy was unconsciously unfurling. Preoccupied with his Ma, he hadn't the time to spend with Espe like days gone by. Whilst they saw a lot of each other, a distance had seeped between them. Sitting there on the edge of the bed he realises it, finally making sense of his jumbled emotions. He misses her. More precisely he misses Borde; their adventures together, the lightness of their lives, that now seemed utterly absurd.

Squinting, Alex stares down to the far end of the beach.

Rising onto his knees, he continues to watch the figure walking calmly towards him. They hadn't met anyone else in the town, and even before here it had been a while since they'd seen anyone new. Gradually they come into view, silhouetted against the sparkling water. Standing, Alex can see it's a man by his heavy strides that eventually bring him into focus. Despite being clean shaven and wearing a faded Hawaiian style shirt and tatty colourless shorts, Alex recognises him instantly.

'Hello Alex, how are we?' he says, trudging up the sand and flopping down, rubbing his calves. 'Not a bad spot this my friend, very picturesque, bit bloody hot for my liking mind....Oh come on now, don't just stand there towering over me. Be a good fellow and sit the fuck down will ya?'

Alex drops mechanically into the sand, and takes in the pasty face, sweat beading on his brow.

'Well, what a journey hey? Blimey, wasn't sure you were gonna make it at one point but here we are!' Meeth chuckles, slapping Alex hard on the back, 'You know, I quite like that beard on you, gives you a sort of whimsical mystery.' he says grinning, showing badly stained teeth, 'Got yourself into a bit of a quiet spell I see? Well no bother, I'm guessing you've had plenty to be thinking about.'

Out of his shirt top pocket Meeth pulls a pristine looking pack of cigarettes and rips the seal before holding them out in offering. Shrugging his shoulders

357

at Alex's lack of response, he puts one to his lips and lights it, slipping the packet back in his pocket and blowing smoke rings that hang briefly in the air before whipping away on a rising breeze.

'You know, your grandfather was a good fellow, can't have been easy for him back then.' Meeth says finally, shielding his eyes from the sun, 'Lost his wife in childbirth, bringing up a son in those times. I don't know if you know this but you helped him a lot.'

Alex squints at him confused.

'You look surprised, but think about it for a moment. How much do we really understand when we're kids, hmm? Not a whole lot. It's part of what makes it the best time of our lives, drifting along in simplicity like a feather on water. Anyway, that man closed up big time after losing Iris, as you would. Man of twenty-two with a baby boy and just lost his wife after a year of marriage. Had a break down of sorts, built a wall to protect himself from feeling. No one ever told you this I guess but he tried to kill himself twice. Second time your dad found him in the bathroom, wrists emptying. Can you imagine? Hence why your dad was mostly brought up by Iris' sister Elsa, poor man wasn't up to it.'

Alex had long given up being surprised by anything, so sat listening, arms wrapped around his knees, digging his toes in to damp sand.

'Spent years like that keeping busy to forget. Weren't til you came along that cracks began to appear cos in the end there ain't nothing as disarming as a child, nothing that speaks more of pure love.'

For a while they say nothing, watching clouds twisting upwards like mountains forming on the horizon, a warm wind pushing into their faces.

'Well I best be off, people to see and all that.' Meeth says pulling himself to his feet and brushing the sand from his shorts.

'She needs you, you know.' he says after a short pause.

At this Alex flashes his eyes to meet Meeth's, holding his gaze briefly before looking away.

'That girl's as strong as an ox and a fair bit wiser than she should be, but everyone needs a father, ain't no point denying it....and turns out you need her an all, so don't spend too long thinking about it cos if there's anything we learnt recently it's that there ain't no telling what's coming so we all gotta just take it when we can.'

With that, he turns his back and begins to stride away.

'Meeth.' Alex half whispers, his voice dry from lack of use.

Spinning round, Meeth raises one eyebrow and gives a wry smile.

Getting to his feet, Alex reaches into his pocket, pauses briefly, then holds out his hand, 'Here.' he says dropping the coin into Meeth's palm, 'I don't need this anymore.'

For a moment Meeth holds it between index finger and thumb, studying it closely, the sun glinting off Britannia's shield.

'I guess you don't.' he chuckles, dropping it into the top pocket of his shirt, a broad grin across his face, 'Cheerio Alex, best of luck.

Alex steps towards the shoreline and lets the water lap over his toes as he follows Meeth's form shrink from view, until it's just a smudge at the far end of the cove. Out over the ocean seabirds chaotically circle like a handful of thrown confetti, the swelling clouds inching closer, rain sweeping in diagonal lines at the horizon. He turns and faces the house, staring up at its many windows, a lightness spilling through his chest that burns and sends a cold shiver over his skin.

He finds Espe around the front, leaning back on a curved palm trunk, its leaves reaching to touch the faded walls of the house. She doesn't see him at first, her eyes watching the dancing patterns the shadows make on the path. Motionless, Alex watches her kicking at the dust, close to thirty years of bottled emotion rising through his chest like a diver coming up for air. The simplicity of it makes him utter a snort of laughter causing Espe to look up, startled to see him stood there smiling, cheeks wet in the afternoon sunlight.

'Want to go on the supply run now? Looks like rain's coming in soon.' he croaks.

Attempting to mask her surprise, Espe nods, 'Come

on.' she giggles, taking his arm and pulling him along the overgrown pavement. 'I want to check out that group of buildings we saw from the hill yesterday, might be something there that's useful.'

From the second floor, Christina leans on the flaked paint of a window sill. For the first time in a while, she thinks of Jago and wonders where he is. She wonders if maybe he's looking out of a window somewhere in America thinking of her. All her anger has seeped away, replaced by sadness-soaked regret. She watches Espe and Alex, filled with pride at who her daughter has become. So many times on their journey she's been astounded by her stubborn courage, her determination to do what was right. She only wishes Jago could see her now. She can't help but smile when she sees Alex talking to her.

'Well, good for you,' she mutters to herself.

Nose pressed to the glass, the muffled crash of the waves just audible, she watches them deep in conversation as they stroll away from the house. She stays there as they shrink from view, ignoring the storm at their backs.

A message from the author

First, thank you so much for reading my book. Over five year's work went into taking an idea I had on an Egyptian balcony and turning it into the story you have just read. Self-publishing is certainly the tough route up the mountain. I won't pretend it wasn't a long slog, but that you are here reading this makes it all worthwhile. With no big promotion machine behind me, I am reliant on word of mouth and public reviews. If you enjoyed Where Hope Goes please write me an Amazon or Goodreads review (or anywhere else for that matter). It only takes a minute and makes such a big difference. I read every one and they make it all worthwhile. There's no better time than now, so stop reading this and go leave that review!

Thanks

Tim

Acknowledgements

Thanks; to Neeta for your constant encouragement, coaching and friendship, right from the beginning; to my excellent editors, Rachael, Evis, Luna and Christina; to Sima for helping with promotion; to Andy Merrington for the write up; to Evie Goldsmith for being the inspiration for Evie in the book; to Angel for helping to form Espe and for the paperclip orphanage; to The Lost Family for their kind words and love; to my family; my parents, Tash and my girls. Most of all thanks to Laura for gently pushing me along, listening to my endless ideas, being chief editor and for more than twenty years of love.

Tim Cameron Long

Tim was born in Essex and spent his younger years at a stuffy school in Suffolk. He studied Sociology at Brunel University, and stayed in London for over ten years. This time was interspersed with travelling and volunteering in Latin America, India and New Zealand. Meeting people from all over the world and observing considerable disparities of wealth became the germ of Where Hope Goes. When not writing he tutors young people in care. He currently lives in Devon with his wife and two gorgeous daughters.

www.timcameronlong.com

Printed in Great Britain
by Amazon